CW01551662

FAERIE TRIALS

FAE ACADEMY FOR HALFLINGS BOOK 4

BREA VIRAGH

Only the best can make it through the Faerie Trials alive.

Tavi Alderidge went from the frying pan into the fire. Half Fae and half wolf shifter, she thought things would be easier once she won her way into Faerie to escape her bloodthirsty "fated mate," but things have only gone from bad to worse.

Coming up are the Faerie Trials, a series of tests designed to quantify whether Fae students at the Elite Academy possess the Seven High Values. If Tavi doesn't get her grades up and bolster her magic, not only will she be exposed and fail the Trials—she could *die*.

Soon Tavi finds herself doing whatever it takes to get ahead and stay there, even if it means neglecting her friendship with Michael Thornwood, the Crown Prince of Faerie. She has secrets to keep, an ancient society to protect, and a king trying to pin a murder on her. Not to mention someone is killing full-blooded Fae women...women who look a whole lot like Tavi.

Fans of Sarah J. Maas, Bella Forest, and K.F. Breene will find themselves enthralled with this dark paranormal romance full of magic and betrayal.

1

I once more found myself staring at a small, molting Christmas tree that looked like a definite fire hazard... and wondering how I'd gotten to this place.

Except unlike the last one, this tree was alive—well, more like only half dead. It was December again, come all too quickly and bringing the Faerie holiday of Yule along with it.

The little evergreen tree had no pretensions in terms of ornaments or lights or decoration. Someone had magicked the limbs to stay in place and the fake snow to fall in a continual stream from the empty air above the decoration.

Yikes. The snow didn't really help.

"You've had a rough six months, haven't you, Miss Alderidge?"

I jolted at the sound of my guidance counselor's voice, and turned my attention to the Fae woman staring at me from behind a desk carved out of an old tree stump.

Miss Wicks tapped a long, spindly finger against the desk. Sure, she had a beard, but otherwise she seemed a perfectly nice lady. The beard and the spider web-like consistency of her hair went hand in hand, as did the rest of her, which more resembled the bark of a tree than actual human skin. I didn't know what kind of Fae she was and didn't have the nerve to ask her.

"Your classes are getting the better of you and your first full semester nearly did you in. You failed in the Solstice Games…" Wicks trailed off, glancing down at the paper in front of her as though checking to see she hadn't made a mistake about my terrible performance. No mistake. "Yes, absolutely, abysmally failed."

I wanted to shrink into my seat a little further with each word.

Selene thinks I was failed on purpose, I thought bitterly. Somehow, the nosy reporter dogging my every move during the Games became not only an ally but a friend. Did I trust her completely? That would be a hard *no*. Did I think she had a point about me being failed on purpose? I did.

Not that I would tell Wicks about our association. There was enough suspicion swirling around me already.

"Yes, it's been exhausting trying to keep up," I ended up saying to the guidance counselor.

Wicks nodded. "Exhausting is one word for it, certainly."

She and I were in complete agreement then because honestly, it was true. The first semester at the Elite Academy in Faerie *had* nearly killed me. If I had anywhere else in the realm to go, I would have packed up my bags and bolted in seconds, leaving behind the heavy workload, the bullying from the pure-blood Fae, and my forced after-school work in the palace kitchen.

It was just before New Year's Eve and my second semester at the Elite Academy of Faerie was poised to begin. More like it loomed, a giant mushroom cloud on the horizon, and I wanted to hide my face. Ostriches with their heads in the sand may have the right idea there, I thought.

Wicks was still speaking: "…accused of murder, and then

fleeing the realm on a kidnapping claim. Of all the crazy things for you to do, Miss Alderidge! I'd like to think you should have known better, but then again I'm simply not sure." She fixed me with a hard stare. "I suppose no one knows you well enough to make a case for you."

I thought back to the tracking device the King of Faerie had forced me to wear after the whole murder debacle. It had been taken off before the new school semester began, but the humiliation still stung over having had to wear a tracking device. Still stung over how I'd been the prime suspect. Little ol' me accused of harming someone, even a ridiculously dramatic gypsy like Madam Muerte? It was insane.

Odder still was the fact that I could now think about murder without batting an eyelash or breaking a sweat.

What has my life become?

"The kidnapping was real," I insisted. "And I had nothing to do with Madam Muerte's demise."

Miss Wicks gave me a shrewd look. "As you claim. No one here witnessed the alleged kidnapping, or the fight you claim to have overheard the night of the murder."

It had been right after the Solstice Carnival, when the famed gypsy palm reader and tarot card reader had delivered a death blow of a premonition about how I would bring about the end of the world. Me. Destroyer of realms.

Yeah, let that sink in.

And as if that weren't enough, I remembered how Mike had danced with me at the Solstice Ball. How Michael Thornwood, the Crown Prince of Faerie, had whisked me off into the gardens around the palace and kissed me.

Kissed me.

The whole world had slowed down and narrowed around us and there was only the feeling of his lips against mine. And like all good things in my life, the steamy make-out session was cut short by events beyond my control: an argument, a scream, and death.

It was I who discovered the body—I was starting to think it one of my best skills—and unfortunately, the palace guard found me hovering over Madam Muerte's lifeless corpse. He had jumped to his own conclusions about me and the king had followed along with the man's unfounded suspicions. Thus I was the prime suspect in the murder of Madam Muerte.

My stomach sank again at the memory, as it did every time.

No witnesses to the crime, no real suspects, yet they'd frothed at the mouth to put the blame on me because I was new and an interloper, only recently granted citizenship to Faerie and not yet a part of their realm. Not really.

I shook my head and Wicks eyed me strangely, continually tapping her incredibly long fingers. I didn't do the crime, but they also had yet to find out who actually did, so I remained a person of interest and was constantly on my guard.

"I had nothing to do with what happened to Madam Muerte, *honestly*," I insisted yet again. My hands knotted on my lap, wrinkling my newly washed and pressed uniform for the Elite Academy, the black blazer with the royal crest on the right lapel and a crisp white shirt. I shifted my fidgeting fingers to the end of my long red braid, hanging just below my shoulders.

"I'm simply not sure what is going on with you," Wicks said with obvious disappointment.

"It's...been a rough transition. And the whole kidnapping thing didn't help." I thought if I brought up the kidnapping again, maybe she'd take pity and go easy on me.

Apparently not.

"Ah, yes. Of course. You told me you were kidnapped by

someone from your past, who somehow managed to break into Faerie and grab you during the Wild Hunt."

I grimaced. Kendrick Grimaldi, the murderous alpha of the Grimaldi wolf pack—and my betrothed. A shifter who apparently used black magic to keep himself looking young because I knew for a fact he had a half Fae son hiding here, a son in his twenties.

The last time I'd seen Kendrick Grimaldi, he'd tied me to an engine block and had a priest ready to marry us against my will. If it hadn't been for my training at the Fae Academy for Halflings, and my short time at the Elite Academy, I never would have known how to transfigure into a crow and escape before he forced me to say *I do*.

Now I had to wear a special glamour potion my friend Nurse Julie gave me so that Kendrick would not be able to see me even if he somehow found a way to break into Faerie again. Now that he knew where I'd run off to.

I didn't tell Counselor Wicks any of these things. I needed to keep them all to myself. No wonder I couldn't sleep at night! I had so many messed up secrets circling my brain they made any real rest impossible.

"Well, Miss Alderidge, on the bright side, the king seems to think you are worthy of this education." Wicks sighed. I wondered when she'd start to stroke her beard in thought. "He insists we take the necessary steps to keep you here and improve your grades. Not to mention I have heard the prince seems mighty taken with you. You have some powerful allies on your side, which no doubt speaks in your favor."

Yeah, except the king thinks I really did kill Madam Muerte. And Mike... My insides melted at the thought of him, the golden-haired prince who'd first befriended me in the mortal realm when I'd been a stranger in need on the side of the road and he'd stopped to help me.

"Miss Alderidge?"

I barely paid any mind to Counselor Wicks and her concerns. I was consumed with thoughts of Mike.

We hadn't been as close this semester. Honestly, I didn't know where we stood now. Were we still friends? Were we something more than friends, after those flaming kisses we'd shared?

I had no clue.

He'd blown hot and cold since the moment we met. I'd been so busy with classes and work, our relationship hadn't been a priority. The only thing I could do was study with Mike on the occasional free day I had.

Last June, I'd *thought* something was happening between me and Mike, but it fizzled out before it became anything substantial. Not because I didn't still like him and wanted to kiss him, but because we started a new school semester and drifted apart a little. Mike turned into a different person around his friends, those fellow High Fae attending the Elite Academy, and it bothered me.

He hadn't made much of an effort to hang out with me since then.

"Tavi! Are you listening to me?"

I snapped to attention, putting thoughts of Mike out of my head.

Wicks' expression was grim as she said, "I know you arrived in the first few weeks before the summer term began, but your first semester grades are finally in. Aren't you the least bit curious?"

Not really. "Okay. How did I do?" I asked just to satisfy her.

"Well..." Wicks trailed off before sliding a folder toward me. "Dismal, to be honest. You failed most of your classes. I'm not going to try and sugarcoat this for you. You're in trouble."

My numb fingers opened up the folder and I glimpsed the terrible grades written in cursive next to my course descriptions. As amazingly well as I'd done at the Fae Academy for Halflings back in the mortal realm, I'd damn near flunked out after my very first semester at the Elite Academy here in Faerie.

"This isn't really fair," I blurted out, sweat beginning to bead along my hairline. "I'm a second-year student doing fourth-year studies and expected to keep up!"

"I understand," Wicks continued gently, "but it's the situation you're in."

"What am I going to do?"

"This situation may be unusual, but it is not unheard of, Miss Alderidge. I know of a wonderful teacher at the Fae Academy for Halflings sister school here in Faerie, and I've already spoken to her and she is willing to work with you three nights a week to get your progress up to par."

I glanced up at this. "Like a personal tutor?"

"Exactly. Think of her as a tutor who will assist you and support you with your class load." Wicks clucked her tongue. "It is my opinion you need all the help you can get, and this woman was the only one willing to step forward on your behalf."

The only one willing to help me? What kind of crap was that? "I'm already going to school and working," I insisted, leaning forward, hands gripping the edges of the folder. "How do you expect me to find extra time in the day for another commitment? I'm grateful, of course, but this takes time away from other things."

Not to mention my mentoring with Onyx Grimaldi, who happened to be the only son of Kendrick Grimaldi. Onyx was another half Fae, half wolf shifter, who had been working with me several nights a week to help me master my transfiguration magic.

"I have no free time as it is," I finished lamely.

I already knew that nothing I said would make a difference. The matter was decided and out of my hands.

Wicks shook her head, and the four walls of the office closed around me like a stone cage. She didn't care. It wasn't her job to care. She merely carried out the orders of her superiors, and as far as she was concerned her obligation to me terminated at the end of this meeting.

"There is no other option, Tavi. If you don't get your grades up this semester before the Trials begin, you won't just flunk out of Elite and lose your position of favor with King Tywin. You could end up *dead* in the process of trying to compete."

Wicks looked like she hadn't just dropped a bomb on me.

And although it wasn't my first time hearing the warning —probably wouldn't be my last, either—the word echoed through my brain during the entire walk into town once the meeting ended.

2

_____

ead.

It wasn't like I was a stranger to the concept, having seen my fair share of deceased, decapitated, dismembered bodies. A little weird, right? Especially for someone just past her nineteenth birthday. Still, the whole thing about the Trials being so competitive, so dangerous that students had died in the past...that I could die...

But Counselor Wicks had decided a plan of action for me. I shivered, wrapping my arms around my midsection. I needed help and a shoulder to cry on and I knew just where to find them. Well, the shoulder anyway.

Which belonged to my best friend Melia Haversham. Melia rented an apartment in the town of Eahsea, close enough to the castle to keep an eye on me if I needed some guidance—when did I not need guidance?—or if things went south. I didn't have the heart to tell her things were already south. *Way* south. It didn't look like I'd be making a course correction anytime soon, either.

Melia's place downtown was a tiny attic room barely big enough for her bed, a dresser, and a kitchen table. The two of us once discussed getting an apartment together and had even gone so far as to make plans and check on a few available places for rent within the town limits but still in close proximity to my school.

Until King Tywin put his foot down.

He'd refused to let me out of my room in the castle, on the grounds that he'd invited me and the other top students from the Halfling Academy to Faerie—early—and he intended for me to live and work in the palace while I attended school. The surprise nearly had my jaw dropping open in front of the monarch.

Of course I had no choice but to agree and quickly rescind my offer to share with Melia.

I hated being stuck in the palace. While I'd been assigned to the kitchen, which I also hated, for my work–study program, at least I liked my boss Raelynn, so it made the job bearable. The king only wanted me close because of the suspected murder charge. Nothing else. After all, he'd outfitted me with the tracking device, one which sent a signal to him whenever I worked magic of any kind. Thank goodness the tracker had been taken off of me a couple of months ago.

Bundled now against the fierce winter weather—Faerie mirrored the parallel mortal realm insofar as seasons—I climbed the stairs, my footsteps echoing on the rickety wood, and knocked once before pushing inside the apartment. Melia knew I was coming and had left the door unlocked for me. Outside, the world had turned dark, billions of diamond stars alight in the night sky. Many more here than I'd ever seen visible in the mortal world.

The entire land of Faerie was alive. The very earth itself here fed into the powers of the Fae, enabling anyone with fairy blood to use magic. It also meant when things went wrong, the land rebelled. For example, the weeks of thunderstorms that ravaged the town when I first arrived here. I still had no concrete evidence linking the phenomenon to my presence but it made a girl wonder. And worry.

Melia whistled her way around the kitchen, oven mitts covering her hands. Despite the freezing temperatures outside, it was hot in the little attic room, the oven putting off massive amounts of heat.

"What took you so long?" she said, her dusky gold skin covered in a thin sheen of sweat, and her wild brown curls bunched in a messy twist at the top of her head. "I mean, how did your meeting go?"

I shrugged out of my jacket, which had become much too heavy in the nearly oppressive heat. "It wasn't good," I admitted.

"Oh?" She turned around and gestured with a clear indication for me to spill the beans.

I spent the next fifteen minutes telling Melia about my meeting with the guidance counselor and the bad news about the new tutoring I was required to do to stay in the game.

"I've got my first session with the tutor tomorrow." I thanked Melia when she placed a heaping helping of butternut squash casserole in front of me. "Guess they didn't want to waste any time whipping me into shape."

Melia took the seat across from me. If either of us moved too far back, we would run into the kitchen cupboards and the makeshift desk she kept closed against the opposite wall. There wasn't a lot of walking room but the place had a great feeling. Security, warmth. A real homey vibe.

Those were all things Melia possessed in spades. I wasn't sure what kind of universal lottery I'd won by getting her as my mentor when I first arrived at the Fae Academy for Halflings, but it was one of the only good things of my life from the last few years.

"What are you going to do? I mean, you are kinda backed into a corner, girl." She twirled her fork in her fingers before spearing it deep into a cube of steaming squash. "If you don't do the tutoring then you might not make it through your classes and those stupid Trials. Which, can I just say, I'm so happy I didn't have to do because I would have obviously ended up six feet under. But your classes! I mean, *damn*."

I didn't agree with her saying she'd end up dead. Melia had been assigned as my tutor my first semester at the earth-side halfling academy, and not only was she beautiful, she had brains too. She always pushed me to do better, to *be* better. She was the only reason I'd ended up passing with top honors, thanks to her unwavering support and knowledge.

"I'm super nervous!" I said, and groaned when I took a bite of the casserole. So good. "I mean, there are so many hoops to jump through. It's one thing after another. Not to mention, like you said, people have died during the trials. Students! Why would the kingdom allow such a savage spectacle?"

I shook my head as Melia brought a bite to her mouth. She spoke through the food. "Like you said. It's a spectacle. The Fae love nothing more than drama and excitement. It helps break up the monotony of our endlessly boring lives." She rolled her eyes. "There are certainly bad things about living forever, as I'm sure we'll discover."

"Well, I'm going to say this, and don't repeat it, but I wish we were back in the human realm." I rested my chin on my palm. "At least there we were all on the same page. I am way out of my depth here."

"What can I do to help?" she asked immediately. "There has to be something I can do."

"You've done enough. You've helped me a thousand

times over. This is just something I have to get through. I mean, it can't be this hard every semester. Right?" I think we both knew I was trying to convince myself, and nothing I said would do the trick.

"Well...they don't call it the Elite Academy for nothing, Tavi. I'm not sure you should hang your hopes on things getting easier. If anything, they're going to get worse."

I didn't like the way her words settled low in my gut. She was absolutely right, I knew, but I hated hearing it come from anyone. As though saying it out loud made it so much more real, those words stayed there, rock-hard, taking up space instead of the delicious dinner Melia had prepared for us. Nevertheless we spent an enjoyable night together talking and laughing and catching each other up on life. Except I didn't have a life. Not really. Not outside of the constant pressure of school and work.

I made my way out of the small apartment and into the streets a few hours later, drawing in a deep breath of cold air. Wrapping my coat tighter around me, I walked toward the castle, toward the room I'd been forced to keep. It wasn't home to me. I'm not sure it would ever be home no matter what personal touches I added. It was hard to relax with a monarch breathing down my neck.

There were few Fae on the streets this time of year, and especially at night. Mostly it was those who were adept at using magic to manipulate the air temperature around them to keep warm. I'd seen faeries wearing scraps of fabric like we were in the height of summer. I walked past them, keeping my head down to avoid unnecessary conversation or eye contact.

Would I ever get used to living here? Instead of expending energy on a spell, I wore old-fashioned faux fur-lined boots and a thick coat. I would need all of the energy I could hoard for tutoring tomorrow.

Footsteps sounded in front of me as I approached the castle courtyard. The three stories of impressive stone turrets grew taller the closer I came. I didn't glance up at the tinkle of laughter other than to note the couple keeping close to each other, with their breaths mingling in a white mist in front of them.

I did, however, jerk when I recognized the man's voice. I also recognized the man attached to the voice, the same one with his arm around a pretty girl.

The girl I didn't know, but the sight of her walking so cozy next to Mike had me seeing red. Yet there he was, in all his majestic glory. A full-blood High Fae, he embodied the description perfectly, everything about him magical. Golden hair hung down past his pointed ears. Green eyes the color of spring grass narrowed when he laughed again at something witty the girl said.

It took him much longer to realize it was me walking toward him, and although I got a flash of pleasure from seeing the shock in Crown Prince Michael Thornwood's eyes, it was nothing compared to the searing jealousy I felt at seeing him with another girl.

"Tavi," he said quickly. His smile had disappeared when he noticed me and was slow to return. "What are you doing out so late?"

I couldn't speak. I couldn't find the frickin' words to say to him after so many months of distance. So of course when I did, they came out in a ridiculous mishmash.

"I, ah..." I trailed off, biting my lip. Pointed over my shoulder like he would follow my tracks in the snow. "Melia. I had dinner with Melia. Squash casserole," I added inanely.

He shot me a wide smile. "That sounds like a fun night."

"Yeah," I said. And I wanted to smack myself but my heart was racing. Inside, I felt like someone had squeezed me until I cracked. A smashed bag of potato chips with only crumbs left. Of course Mike was entitled to be with other girls. He and I weren't an item. I'd made my stance on dating him clear because I knew it was a bad idea, and yet—

I wanted to strangle him. Then her. Maybe both of them at the same time. And I could do it, too. I had shifter strength neither of them knew about.

"Hey, this is—" He started to introduce the very pretty Fae he still had his arm around.

Nope, I was outta there. Not able to handle any of it. I didn't want to know her name, or how they met, or anything about her. "Sorry, gotta go. Super long day tomorrow. Enjoy your night!"

I raced awkwardly past them, clomping through the snow and trying to pretend I wasn't jealous. And angry. And hurt. No matter how my cheeks turned red and the rest of me felt like I'd swallowed a pin cushion.

Mike and I might not have designs on each other anymore—and most of that was on me—but it sure didn't hurt any less to see him moving on with someone else.

I had a feeling it would always sting.

3

─────────

My head bobbed, threatening to drop right down in the center of the book I was reading as I teetered on the edge of sleep. Too many pages left and not enough hours in the night to get through them.

I had to make it to the next chapter or I'd start the next school term behind. *Fancy that*, my exhausted brain offered up the thought. *Behind before you even begin.* Never in my life had this been the case and yet it was a box I'd stayed stuck inside since coming here.

A tap at the window caught my attention. Insistent, three knocks in a row. I got the message immediately.

Let me in. Let me in.

Rising on stiff legs, I moved to flip the latch and push open the window, letting in a blast of wintry air as I did. A black crow perched on the ledge, beady eyes staring up at me. It clacked its beak once. Squawked. Then hopped down onto my desktop.

"I didn't think anyone was going to show up this late," I told the bird. "Talk about bad timing."

A flash of magic filled the small chamber and when I

recovered from the reflexive blink, a small-boned girl sat on top of the dresser with her legs dangling over the side. With a round face, a splash of freckles across her nose and cheeks, and slightly curling pine bark-colored hair, she was absolutely adorable.

"I know, I'm sorry. But I had to come and get you," Bronwen Minuti told me in a sweet voice. "An emergency meeting's been called."

My stomach dropped and I glanced back at the textbook. "I can't go."

"What do you mean you can't go? It's an *emergency*."

"Whatever it is, I've got classes starting tomorrow and a new tutor to meet. I have too many things to do tonight and then I'd like to get a little sleep if possible."

"Tavi, you made an oath. You *have* to go to the meeting. You have no choice." At least Bronwen sounded sympathetic.

"But—" I broke off with a sigh and knew I'd be running on fumes tomorrow, because she was right. Another choice I didn't have. Arguing would get me nowhere.

I'd definitely made an oath to the Claw & Fang Society the very first night Bronwen showed up to take me to a meeting, stating there were others like me, like us, she wanted me to meet. I thought about the wolf pendant currently nestled between my breasts where no one would see it.

The society met monthly. A silly social club to me, but it did serve a good purpose. It united the half-shifters who had taken refuge in Faerie, those of us who weren't supposed to exist in the first place because Fae and shifters notoriously hated each other thanks to a centuries old prophecy. Contact between the two races was pretty much forbidden, let alone interbreeding. And yet here we were. There were more of us here than I had originally thought.

However, it was kind of nice having a support network nearby.

With a handful of shifter friends and confidants, people like me, I felt less alone.

Bronwen snapped her fingers to get my attention. "Come on, we've got to go. The club is waiting for us," she said.

I shook my head, biting the inside of my lip and trying to order my thoughts. "What on earth could be so important they're dragging everybody out of bed in the middle of the night?"

"Your guess is as good as mine. Selene just sent me to fetch you." Bronwen hopped down off of the dresser and stared at me. "Are you ready to go?"

I slowly closed the book I'd barely been able to read because my eyes were too blurry to make out the words. I sighed. "Yeah, I'm ready."

We had to be careful no one noticed us leaving the castle. Even though the ankle monitor had since been removed, the king still kept a close watch on me after the disaster in the summer regarding not only my kidnapping but the rather mysterious death of the carnival gypsy. If he knew what I could really do with my powers, exile would be paradise compared to what he'd do to me.

Making sure no one outside the window saw us, and with a barrier in place to keep the guards in the hall from feeling the swell of magic, Bronwen and I prepared to transfigure into crows to fly to the meeting site.

I closed my eyes. I stood next to her, away from the open window, and breathed in a deep breath filled with ice and power. The image of the crow filled my mind until I envisioned every detail down to the individual feathers. I had to believe in the change to make it so.

Only half Fae, half shifters were able to manifest the power of transfiguration. According to most sources it was rare and didn't often show up. For me, it had manifested during my last semester at the Halfling Academy during my inherent power test. Right alongside my cognitive manipulation. Which meant I could make people believe anything I wanted them to believe.

Another scary thought.

As it was, I knew of only one other half-shifter here with the same transfiguration power, besides Bronwen. And he happened to be the son of my fated mate.

It really was a small world. Or, well, *two* small and interconnected worlds.

The magic took hold and my body slowly shrank down into a smaller form, my arms folding in and black feathers bursting through my skin. The pain didn't bother me anymore. My receding consciousness didn't bother me anymore.

I knew how to take control of the crow's mind, thanks to Onyx and his teachings, despite the last few months of me being unable to transform. With the king tracking my magic, it was a risk to do anything outside of school besides learn. At least Onyx had taken the setback in stride and switched his lesson plan.

The moment Bronwen and I finished changing, we took off through the open window. The snow-covered ground stretched out around us, the town covered under a blanket of pure crystalline white. We soared high over the buildings in the village, the castle behind us and the Elite Academy in front. The twin buildings flanked either side of the valley, with the school built into the mountainside and the town spread along the swell of land between them.

Instead of heading toward the peaks of the sleeping academy, Bronwen and I banked to the right. Heading for the forest and beyond. The huge meadow beyond the castle melted into a line of darkness, the tree trunks thick and old and rising into the wintry sky. Though no moon showed through the thick clouds, we didn't need one to light our way. I drew on the crow's keen eyesight and animal instincts tonight, drew on the inherent intelligence guiding me toward our destination.

The Claw & Fang met in a secret place high in the mountains outside the king's town. The geography rolled in a way that naturally hid the small clearing of outcropped rocks from view, and unless someone was a serious hiker—with a crazy amount of magic to break down protection wards—they wouldn't be able to reach or see us.

Bronwen and I crested the last hill before we saw the stone circle begin to take shape. Naturally cut from the top of the mountain itself without any magical aid, the boulders speared into the sky like the teeth of some great beast. There in the center gathered my people.

We dropped down next to Selene, the reporter who'd hounded me my first semester at the Elite Academy, now the woman I looked to as leader of this ragtag group. Bronwen transfigured on the way down so that when she landed, she did so in her normal form.

Exhaustion made it impossible for me to do the same. My crow feet clawed against cold stone. A focused thought and a final push of magic had me changing form. Slower than I should have, yeah, but there wasn't a thing I could do about it. I followed Bronwen toward one of the natural stone outcroppings, lichen covering the surface even during winter. The others were already gathered around a small crackling fire, their hands outstretched for warmth, waiting for the two of us to arrive.

These people, though we were few, had opened their doors to me once I arrived in Faerie. They reminded me what it meant to have a community and a group of like-minded people sharing the same kind of messed-up bloodline. I'd had that sense of community once with my wolf pack, under my uncle's rule as alpha, but things hadn't been the same since he'd announced my betrothal to a murderer.

So I'd run away. What choice did I have?

I sat cross-legged next to a fellow member and let out a labored sigh. "How are you tonight, Lisbet?"

She smiled and inclined her head. "As well as can be expected, Tavi. Thank you for asking."

Selene paced beside the flames and greeted me grimly the moment our eyes met. Gone was her normal sly smile and the snarky attitude she affected when she was reporting. She stood several inches taller than me, and more when she donned high heels. Tonight, her chin-length black hair curled beneath her jaw, pointed ears hidden beneath a fluffy red cap. A long black coat hid most of her honey-colored skin from view. Selene gave us precious few seconds to settle in before launching into her speech. The flames reflected off the odd silver hue of her eyes.

"I'm sorry for dragging you all out of bed on such short notice," she stated in an oddly somber tone, "but this was an emergency. It left us little time to prepare and even less time to wait until our regularly scheduled meeting."

The air stilled around us. The tension thickened until it mingled with the wood smoke from the fire. "What's going on?" one of the older shifters finally asked, a grizzled gray-haired man with a long beard.

"Well..." Selene trailed off and for a moment I almost thought she was nervous.

No way. It didn't work with the image of the reporter I always kept in my head. The woman who dogged my every move during the Summer Games, like a shark in the water going after wounded prey. But tonight was definitely different.

At last, she let out a breath. "There's no sense in wasting

more time trying to find a way to put this mildly. A body was found about two hours ago. A pure-blood Fae ripped to pieces by a wild animal." Selene let her words hang for effect before declaring, "This is the third pure-blood found dead this way. *This week.*"

That got the desired effect. As a group, the ten of us leaned forward. Bronwen cried out, "What do you mean the third one? This *week*? Impossible! We would have heard about this."

Selene shook her head. "No, you would not have. The king does not want anyone to know about the discovery. He's been working overtime to keep these deaths a secret because he knows the general populace of Eahsea will be thrown into a panic. Only a select few around him, and now us, know about these deaths."

"This *week*?" Lisbet clarified.

"This week. Sadly, it's true." Selene's expression turned even more grim. "I was there. I saw the last one before the guards rushed the body away."

It didn't seem to surprise anyone how the king was working hard to cover up the murders. I stared around the circle at my fellow half-shifters.

"I'm sure no one wants to hear the gory details," Selene stated, walking around the fire. "However, trust me when I tell you this is cause for concern."

The gray-haired man harrumphed. "If the pure-bloods want to kill each other, then let them have at it. It's no business of ours. Better for us to stay out of the way and let the monarchy chase its own tail."

Selene clearly had more to say, and she silenced the man with a sharp look. "It is most certainly our business, Reginald, as there are those who think it's a half-shifter committing these crimes. And I'm inclined to agree."

4

My intestines tangled themselves into knots and the rest of me froze. At once the exhaustion dropped away and I felt painfully awake. Craning forward, my palms flat on the stones, I stared at Selene as though she held all the answers.

"Wait...you saw the last one?" I asked. And how would she know there was a half-shifter involved?

She avoided making eye contact with me, addressing the group at large, arms loose at her sides. She looked scared. Scared but resolved.

"The three Fae found by the court were mangled, girls roughly between three and six hundred years old. They were all slender, with reddish hued hair. High cheekbones." Selene clapped her hands together and a puff of magic had the condensation in the air gathering until it solidified like a screen hanging above our heads.

And there on the surface were images of the girls. Not as they'd been found at the time of death, thank goodness, because I might have lost my dinner if Selene showed us that.

Bronwen shifted to whisper in my ear: "Tavi, they look like you. Like, weirdly similar to you."

I swallowed hard, shivering. Definitely nauseated and more than a little freaked out. The girls did look like me. It didn't matter that I was nineteen and these Fae were approaching six centuries, because fairies aged differently. Their eyes might have all been different colors but the hair... it was unmistakable. Shades of red too close to mine for me to feel comfortable sleeping tonight.

Damn. Double damn.

My mouth dry, I had a hard time forming my next question. "They were all killed the same way?"

Selene nodded. "Apparently so. The details were not given to me as a reporter but I managed to insert myself into the last crime scene without anyone the wiser. There were tear marks on the body parts they found, deep enough for the authorities to finger a shifter instead of a glamoured Fae claw. The guards do not want anyone to know these details because...well, let's face it. It would incite a mass panic."

Claw marks. Body parts. Terribly, disgustingly similar to the bodies I'd stumbled upon—*literally* stumbled upon—at the Fae Academy for Halflings, and there had definitely been a half-shifter responsible then. I'd stepped through the portal to Faerie, leaving the wolves going wild on the other side.

I drew my knees up to my chest. *Please.* I sent a prayer skyward. *Please don't let the same problems have followed me here.*

Except apparently they had. The last few months had been peaceful in terms of lack of vicious murders, but my luck had just run out.

"I'd like to set up a schedule of patrols around Eahsea. We should help however we can, because although we know the responsible party is not one of us, that does not make us any less responsible." Selene stared around the fire at the ten of us. "As this is a half-shifter crime, presumably, the Claw & Fang should step up to help keep the village and its inhabitants safe."

I found myself nodding. The group certainly valued keeping those with our bloodline as low-key and out of the spotlight as possible. Onyx Grimaldi, my unlikely mentor teaching me how to control my transfiguration power, and I had discussed it at length. Our safety depended on our ability to hide and blend.

I was the only one stupid enough to flaunt myself around the castle. Onyx didn't even want to leave his house.

If the pure-blood law enforcement working under King Tywin found out half-shifters existed in such numbers in Faerie, there was no telling what might happen.

We could all be deported, and for many of us, even those living in other towns, this land was the only home we've ever known. Worse? The king might decide to eradicate the shifter threat completely and have us wiped out.

I wouldn't put it past him.

"I'll be tapping other Claw & Fang members across this world to get them here. Consider it an outreach," Selene said. She bent closer to the flames and balanced on the balls of her feet. "Tavi, Bronwen, I'd like the two of you to start tomorrow. You'll take the first patrol at twenty-one bells."

"We're honored," Bronwen answered immediately for the two of us. And when I glanced over at her, I saw her gaze was hard, eyes shining with zeal. "Twenty-one bells it is."

"Bells" was a Fae term for time, I'd learned. Instead of am or pm, the clock began at midnight and each bell strike signified one hour. I liked to think it was equivalent to fairy naval time, but it didn't make it easier for me to learn and remember.

I have a terrible memory. Have I mentioned that already?

Staring around at the rest of the group, they looked as scared as I felt though many tried to hide it. Lisbet bit her lower lip and Reginald could not stop tapping the top of his knee. The others were in similar states except for Selene. She remained cool and composed. She had an image to maintain and had had plenty of practice keeping her reactions to herself.

I needed to take a page out of her book. *Don't let anyone see you sweat, no matter what troubles you face.*

We stayed around the fire discussing battle plans until well past midnight. By the time Bronwen and I flew back to the castle, I was ready to pass out, and did so the moment my head hit the pillow.

The next morning after my shower I slipped my school blazer over my shoulders and prepared myself for the first day of the new term. The girl in the mirror staring back at me looked pale and beaten down. There were dark circles above her cheekbones and lines around her lips I hadn't seen before. I tried not to think about this latest batch of murders.

I'm a girl on the edge.

On the edge of flunking out of the Elite Academy.

On the edge of not being good enough for the Trials.

On the edge about murders that seemed to follow me from the mortal realm, and how even after the debacle with Madam Muerte, I was somehow involved yet again with more death.

More death. Why did it keep happening? This wasn't what I wanted my life to be.

I stared at my pale reflection a little longer, thought about the physical similarity with the murdered girls. "Can it be true that you are the real target? And if so, what are you going to do about it?" I asked the person I saw. She didn't have any answers for me.

Another hour and classes at the Elite Academy would begin anew. Their semesters worked a little differently than what I was used to at my old schools. Here, we went to class all year round. Except they always punctuated the semesters with something interesting and deadly. Such as the Summer Games I'd narrowly survived and the Elite Trials that Counselor Wicks assumed I would not.

My reflection continued to stare back, brows drawn down and lips pursed in a scowl. Well, I'd certainly do my best to prove Wicks wrong. I was nothing if not resilient, I reminded myself. I was the daughter of an alpha, and had I not run away from my arranged marriage, I would have held the title myself one day.

These people thought I'd give up and walk away with my tail tucked between my legs? Time to do the opposite.

I fixed a fierce look on my face and almost had myself convinced until a sudden knock sounded at the door. My jangled nerves shot adrenaline through my body and my arms flailed about in a protective instinct, knocking bottles of lotion and cosmetics to the floor. Glass shattered and when I glanced up, trying to catch my breath, my reflection had gone pale with surprise.

On edge much?

Onyx would be pissed at me for reacting without thinking. He'd taught me a lot about self-control, muscle memory, and defense.

"I'm coming!" I called out shakily. "Hold on." The broken glass would have to wait until I answered the repeated knocks. I stepped over the mess and crossed to open the door.

My heart stopped.

"Mike! What are you doing here?"

The Crown Prince of Faerie stood in the hallway with his own school uniform conforming to his muscles. Yup, my mouth was dry again. He didn't just look delicious. He looked worried.

"Um, are you okay?" he began. "I thought I heard glass breaking."

I laughed to cover up my nerves and the crazy way everything inside of me rose to a boil when he spoke. Those deep, rich syllables made me quiver. Neither one of us was surprised when my laugh ended on a snort. "Yeah, I'm fine," I insisted. But I kept the door partially closed so he'd have no chance of seeing the shattered glass.

"Okay, I'm glad to hear it."

His smile melted my insides and I turned into a puddle of goo on the floor—luckily not literally. I had to keep a close watch to make sure my magic didn't *respond* to my emotions. Then I remembered him walking with some strange girl last night and my good mood disappeared, anxiety taking its place and my chest aching.

"Are you ready to go?" Mike gestured over his shoulder. "I thought we could walk to the portal for school together. Like old times." He ran a hand through his hair. "I know things got a little weird for us last semester but I thought we might try to get back to how things were. You know."

I did know, yes.

The castle had its own direct route to the academy. Instead of walking through town or using the magic-powered silver bullet train I'd ridden on first arrival, Mike and I used a portal. Being friends with royalty had its perks.

At least, I hoped we were still friends. Part of me really wasn't sure anymore but still managed a small sparkle of hope despite the anxiety.

Would I pass up an opportunity to spend time with Mike now? No way.

"Sure," I agreed quickly. "Let me grab my things. Hold on one second."

I kept the door partially closed to dissuade him from coming inside, then hastily kicked a pile of dirty laundry under the bed. My books were on the desk. I shoved them inside my backpack, dreading what we'd face today and knowing I needed to take advantage of this silver lining.

Once I had everything I needed, I flung the bag over my shoulder and joined Mike in the hall with a wide grin. Cheers to starting fresh and not worrying about him making the moves on anyone else. No matter what my eyes and ears and fears told me was going on. "All right, let's go."

He led the way toward the portal, located next to the throne room on the first floor of the castle. It had taken me months to find my way around the complex three-story monstrosity without any help. And even though I worked in the kitchen after school, as part of my work–study requirement, I still got lost sometimes.

"Hey, I want to talk to you," Mike started as we walked side by side.

I glanced over at him and saw he had his head down. "About what?"

"About last night."

My stomach turned clumsy cartwheels like a cat after a bug. *Oh my God, he knows about the Claw & Fang!* Had Mike somehow seen me transform into a crow and take off? Was he watching me? "I can explain, of course. What you saw—" I stopped abruptly when I realized we'd both been speaking at the same time.

"The girl with me...ah, walking in the village?" Mike clarified. He swallowed hard. "She's just a friend from one of the titled families of Faerie, visiting from a sister school in Khoysas. I was giving her a tour while she and her parents are in town."

"A tour? At twenty bells?" I asked before I thought about just keeping my mouth shut. Then shrugged and tried to act like I wasn't about to freak out. "It's no big deal."

"Twenty bells, yes, because my father insisted on a five-course meal to impress Larissa's family. Her dad is titled but he also owns a gemstone mine, and King Tywin likes to keep an eye on the profits, if you know what I mean. The soonest I could get away was after we ate and Larissa wanted some fresh air. She also has a few anxiety issues around new places. I wanted to make things easier for her."

I waved him away before I heard any more. "You don't have to explain it to me." In all honesty? I was relieved even if it was an excuse. The thought of Mike kissing another woman made me want to puke. Or retaliate. Probably both.

"Larissa and her family will be leaving this afternoon," Mike continued. His shoulder knocked against me playfully. "And with my royal duties at an end, I think you and I might be able to fit in a study session or two. Maybe we can actually get ahead of the curve for this semester and stay ahead before we get too stressed."

"You want to get a head start on studying? Who am I to tell you no?" I joked. Feeling infinitely better without the weight of him with someone else trying to drag me down.

How was it, with him, a single sentence changed my entire mood?

"There's the smile I missed. You looked a little down last night."

I shook my head and tried not to sound strangled. "Oh, I was all right. I wasn't expecting to run into you."

"We haven't really kept up with each other lately, haven't had the time to catch up. I want to know what's going on in your world, Tavi."

"In my world," I repeated as we walked.

Twin guards stood still as statues at the bottom of the

grand staircase. They no longer bothered with me. However, I noted the way their eyes darted in our direction. Making sure the heir to the throne stayed safe with the girl who had killed Madam Muerte.

I hadn't, of course, but I was pretty sure they all still thought it.

"Well, apparently I'm not doing too well in school, based off of my grades from last semester," I said over the echoing clomp of our footsteps. "The school assigned a tutor to help me not only get my grades up but to prepare for...everything we're going to face. She made it sound like I'm going to need a last will and testament in place by the end of this term."

When I glanced over again, Mike was nodding vigorously until hair fell over his face. "I think that's a good idea."

"What?" I blinked at him. "You think I should prepare my will?"

"No, not the will part, the tutor part."

"Yeah?"

"Yeah, it's a great idea," he enthused. "Hey, maybe the tutor will work with me, too."

I laughed, another snort ending the sound like punctuation. "Come on. You don't think I do a good enough job helping you study? I mean, I'm only *failing*. Between the two of us, we should be practically acceptable."

Besides, wasn't Mike the one who'd taken an ancient artifact into the mortal realm to bolster his magic and used it to pass through the Halfling Academy?

I wondered where he'd stashed it and if he'd be willing to lend it to me. Yet I kept my lips zipped as we walked, in case he didn't want anyone knowing about the *Augundae Totalis*. Had he brought it with him through the portal back to Faerie?

"I wouldn't worry about a thing, Tavi. Your tutor is going

to help you out. I enjoy your company, so I still want to hang out whether we're studying or not."

"You do?"

Mike cleared his throat, pausing at the door to the portal with his hand wrapped around the knob. "Say, this weekend?"

Warmth curled beneath my sternum as I turned to stare up at him. "You want to hang out this weekend?" I clarified. Was this the same Mike who had practically ignored me these last few months?

Something strange was going on.

We paused outside of the portal room, the intricately decorated door inlaid with gold and jewels. I'd gotten used to the opulence the same way I'd gotten used to Mike's title. It just took me a bit of time. I didn't exactly come from penury; my uncle was wealthy enough to afford private schools for me when I'd been part of the Alderidge wolf pack.

But that was nothing compared to the castle.

"I do." Mike kept his hand on the door, waiting until he had my answer. "I'm, ah, I'm nervous."

He *what*? "About hanging out with me? No way!"

He grinned but then it faded quickly. "About the Trials." Those spring-green eyes bored into mine and I couldn't look away. He trapped me better than a hypnotist. "The Summer Games look like child's play next to the Trials. I mean, students have died before. Actually *died*. You remember how I told you not to worry during the games because no one was going to let anything happen to me? Those rules go out the window during the Trials." He swallowed hard until his Adam's apple bobbed.

"Wait a minute. You're saying they won't protect the *Crown Prince*? Impossible. The king isn't going to let his only son—"

Suddenly I found it hard to breathe. The pressure on my chest increased because I knew Mike wasn't lying. He was genuinely scared. And if the monarch and the school officials would allow something to happen to *him*, then the rest of us were like chum in shark-infested waters.

I scrambled for options. "Can't we just...I don't know, opt out?"

Mike shook his head with a grimace. "No. It's mandatory. Everyone at Elite is required to participate. Oh, hey, come here. You're breathing funny. It's going to be okay."

Shouldn't I be the one consoling him and his nerves?

I didn't stop him when he reached out and drew me into a hug. "I *feel* weird," I admitted.

His hands massaged large circles on my back. I wanted to purr. "Don't freak yourself out. It's going to be okay. We'll look after each other. I'm not going to let anything happen to you."

"Ditto. Nothing is going to happen to you on my watch."

Because, of course, the other way around. I always worried about Mike. His magic was not what it should be, though I didn't understand why. What if he didn't have the *Totalis* anymore, to help him make it through the Trials?

I could lose him permanently.

We stayed that way for a long moment, our arms wrapped around each other and his scent branding itself in my lungs. I drew in a deep breath until I felt him in my cells. My insides went still. As though everything moved into neutral in his presence.

He's so warm.

Mike pulled back enough to stare down at me.

My lungs hitched. "What...what are you doing?" I asked softly.

His eyes narrowed, head bending lower. His lips parted.

Oh God. He was going to kiss me. I caught myself rising

to meet his lips when I stopped. *Bad idea, Tavi. Really bad idea.*

I pushed away with a small laugh. "We're going to be late."

The moment broke. Mike kept his thoughts to himself, his gaze dropping to the floor. "You're right. Time to focus." He sighed, shaking his hands out. "Are you ready?"

Yeah, right. Focus. It was hard when the whole of me cried out for his touch. When I wanted nothing more than to feel those lips on mine again. What I wouldn't give for his touch.

As the magic of the portal engulfed us, transporting us to the school, I reminded myself that I should not let myself get too close to Mike. Not the way I wanted to be close with him. Because if I gave in to my desire? I could lose *everything.*

5

I barely made it through the first day of school without keeling over. It didn't help when I was forced to keep a smile on my face when dealing with Mike's "friends." They brought new meaning to the term *fake*.

The rest of the afternoon I didn't fare much better and I spent way too much time standing in front of my locker, vision blurry, trying to decide which books to take back to my room. Which ones would I need?

All of them.

Groaning, I let my forehead drop until it landed on the locker door. Tonight would be my first meeting with the tutor and I'd be lying if I said I weren't dreading it with every fiber of my being. I had three major homework assignments due by Friday. Friday! Plus I had to work in the kitchen every day this week, I had transfiguration tutoring with Onyx Wednesday *and* Friday, and my academy tutoring literally every other day for the rest of my life.

Not to mention Bronwen and I started our patrol route this week. Yup. For two hours we walked the streets of Eahsea like we had nothing else to do, pretending we weren't out there looking for a murderer.

No wonder I couldn't think. Couldn't focus. Couldn't concentrate. My mind turned to mush from day one, and although my eyes were open, I didn't see a damn thing. I stood frozen, like my body decided it was done listening to me, done trying to do everything at once. Exhaustion already weighed heavily on my shoulders.

Maybe marrying Kendrick Grimaldi would have been easier than this.

My eyes popped wide at the thought. Had I really just considered a lifetime with a monster as an acceptable alternative? My workload gave a whole new meaning to full plate, true, but still!

How much longer would it be necessary to jump through these hoops? To always do more and always for someone else? Mental fog was no joke. Then I remembered a bright spot and smiled. At least Mike and I were getting along—sort of—but I knew it was a tentative peace.

I had no idea what to expect from any of this. And no idea when things would get better.

"Hey. You. Woo-hoo!"

Fingers snapped next to my face and I shook off my stupor. I knew the voice and disliked the girl it belonged to, one of the snotty upperclassmen who was always up Mike's ass. She sauntered wherever she walked, and stared at me like I was nothing but a bug under her shoe. In desperate need of stomping.

Now she stood too close, invading my personal space. She reminded me of Persephone.

"Yes, you. I'm sure you're busy with your own important thoughts, Tavi, but I have a favor to ask of you." A pause, slightly uncomfortable. "Please."

Coral Ferenze stared down her long, straight, perfect nose at me. Copper-colored hair flowed past her shoulders to curl lightly near her breasts. She filled out her school uniform to perfection, slender and curvy at the same time. Coral magicked her lips a bright red that, instead of looking stupid with her hair color, brought out the rich shades in a way mortal makeup could not.

I blinked at her. She knew my name? I didn't think I'd heard her say it before. "Pardon me?"

Coral cocked her hip, head going in the opposite direction and her hazel eyes wide. "I did say *please*. I need a *favor*."

In other words, *keep up when I'm talking to you*.

I knew the act. The bitch trying to cover up her real personality because she wanted something from me. At least Coral was completely one hundred percent in the open about how she felt about me. And that she wanted something.

She folded her arms across her chest. "I'm having a party this weekend for my birthday and I invited Michael Thornwood to attend. Things simply won't be the same without him there."

That was another thing. I hated how all the people in school called Mike by his full name: Michael Thornwood. The name didn't fit his warm personality the way simple *Mike* did.

"A party? I hadn't heard," I threw back at her, selecting one of the books I needed and putting it in my bag.

"Anyway," Coral continued, her voice sweet and pleasant. All phony baloney. "Michael turned me down because he has plans with *you*. If the prince doesn't come to my party then I'll obviously be the laughingstock of the academy. We can't allow that to happen."

I sighed and selected a second book to take home. Coral wanted me to cancel on Mike? "Aw, too bad. Aren't you already the laughingstock?"

She continued as though I hadn't spoken. "You need to

let him off the hook for your *little plans*." Coral held her fingers up in air quotes. "He has more important things to do with more important people. I'm sure you understand."

"Um, no. I don't understand and I won't cancel on him." Absolutely not. I stood my ground. "But tell you what, Coral. I'll bring him to your party. We'll be there together, stop in for a little bit and make the rounds, then we'll leave. It's the best I can do and a real compromise, if you want my honest opinion."

Coral looked as though I'd suggested she shave her head and donate her hair to needy children. "*Excuse me?*"

I slid my backpack over my shoulder, instantly weighed down from the books. "You heard me," I told her. "I'll bring Mike to the party but we'll be there together and we won't stay long. I would consider it a win if I were you. I don't plan on changing my mind, no matter what kind of party you have in mind." My plans were just as important as hers, birthday or no. I refused to let her bring me down.

I closed my locker and turned to face her, the two of us similar in height. She thought about it, she honestly did. I could practically see the gears turning in her head. Coral was considering her options for one reason alone: she wanted Mike for herself. She knew I wasn't about to back down.

Apparently neither was she.

My expression hardened as I watched her sort through her mental dilemma.

At last she said, "Fine." Short, simple, to the point. She flipped her hair and spoke as if it were her idea. "I'll see him Saturday, then. My place at twenty bells. He knows where it is. Don't be late. It's rude."

I rolled my eyes at her retreating back, pointedly ignoring the sway of her hips although every other person in the hallway was caught like a tractor beam. I was the only one able to look away. Coral was a piece of work, for sure, but I'd stood for what I wanted without compromise. At least I could be proud of something.

Hiking my book bag higher to distribute the weight without crushing my bones, I walked toward the exit. Time for me to meet with my new tutor, to try and get my grades up. Yippee.

Did I seem excited? No. If anything, I looked like I'd stepped in a pile of—well, something unpleasant to say the least.

The sun shone down on the snow and I shielded my eyes against the glare. It was only a short walk to the Fae Academy for Halflings sister school in Faerie, down a long curving stone staircase hugging the hillside. It was the school I'd thought I'd be attending when I crossed through the portal into Faerie for the first time.

Until King Tywin sprang his surprise on me. He claimed it was because I'd shown great promise at my old school. Really, deep down I think he wanted to punish me.

I took the winding lane down from the Elite Academy, no wider than a sidewalk in the mortal realm, although here there were no cars. The hills were blissfully free of any sort of traffic, vehicle or foot. The residents of town used a series of magic-powered trains or portals to get from here to there, not to mention using their natural magical abilities.

I needed the walk. I needed a moment to breathe and gather myself.

Buildings were constructed along the sloping valley walls and every road led down toward the village center and the castle beyond. An ancient forest surrounded us on all sides, with flatland and farms scattered throughout.

Shivering with a strange cold that felt more inside my body than out, I kicked the snow off of my boots the moment I pushed through the wide double doors of the school ten minutes later. Glancing around, I saw that the entrance foyer looked nearly identical to the one at the mortal academy. Until I turned to the right, where the staff offices used to be, and found myself in a classroom. Okay, not so similar.

"Are you lost? You look a little confused."

I turned at the female voice.

"Do you need some help?" the girl continued.

Not used to the kindness, I blinked at her, struggling to catch up. "I'm looking for the school counselor's office. I'm sorry, I don't have a name. I was told to come here to meet my tutor."

The girl walked closer, a smile on her face, and I was surprised to see that instead of white teeth she had little green nubs, like someone had taken pieces of clover and made them thick and solid. "It's fine! I know exactly where you need to go. Come on, follow me. We'll get you set up."

I followed the stranger up the curving staircase toward the second floor, gas lamps lining the corridor and illuminating the way. Why couldn't the students at the Elite Academy be this nice and friendly? It had been nothing but a struggle since I started there.

"By the way, I'm—" The girl let out a low screech followed by several clicks. "I know, it's hard to say. They call me Flora here."

I smiled at the nickname. "Flora I can pronounce."

She smiled over her shoulder. "I know. It's an elf thing. I'm half earth elf, and a lot of our dialect is only spoken in the outer isles of Faerie. Those in the inner villages haven't heard it spoken in years. Flora is a rough translation of my elvish name. It makes it easier to communicate with other students."

"It's a pleasure to meet you. I'm Tavi."

I wondered if people were as cynical toward Flora as

they'd been toward me when I first applied for the mortal academy. Did her being half elf somehow set her apart from her peers the way being half human did for me? Or at least they perceived me as half human. If they knew the truth—that I was really half wolf shifter—I doubted they'd tolerate me at all.

She seemed happy, though, like a person who'd found her place in the world and settled in nicely.

I looked everywhere except at Flora, nerves eating at me as I fought the urge to fidget. Fidgeting would show how nervous I really felt and I didn't want anyone to think me weak even though that's how I really felt. And frustrated. And super confused.

Flora's pace quickened and I did my best to keep up with her. I expected a hush to fall when I passed the other students. I expected them to stare and mutter under their breath about the halfling human in their midst. But that wasn't the case. No matter where we went, up two flights of old stone stairs and along light-drenched corridors, everyone we passed offered me a smile or a kind word. Everyone had something nice to say to Flora and extended the kindness to me.

I couldn't believe it.

The next corner she turned, I knew. This wasn't a mirror image of the school I knew. The flooring on the third floor was a mix of wood and stone, with the walls made up of some kind of luminescent stone that caught the light from outside. Wooden beams were exposed on the ceiling above and massive iron chandeliers hung down at regular intervals. The building pulsed with magic, and the chilly draft I used to feel at the mortal academy in winter did not exist here.

Flora led me directly down a narrow hall leading back toward the professors' offices, then pressed her hand onto the stone to the left and right of the alcove. A pulse of yellow light flashed. Like a welcome. Or a warning.

She cast a final wide grin my way, my gaze focused on those odd green teeth. "Good luck with whatever it is you are doing, Tavi. And don't be a stranger! You are one of us even though you are at the Elite Academy."

"One of you?"

She nodded. "A halfling, yes. I can sense it about you."

"How did you know I came from the Elite Academy?"

"Your jacket." She pointed to the emblem on the breast pocket of my blazer. "It doesn't matter. We are all in this together, yes? Halflings unite! If you need anything, we are here. Come back and see me sometime, new friend."

Then she left and I stood staring after her, fighting the urge to shake my head. Definitely friendly. And I'd gotten so used to the bullying and backstabbing that I found her kindness weird and out of place.

The moment I turned back toward the professors' rooms, another student barreled out of the nearest doorway and damn near ran me over.

Red-faced, looking pissed as all get out, the boy slammed into my shoulder and sent me spinning into the wall.

I hissed when bone came into contact with stone and a flash of pain shot through me. "Watch where you're going, buddy!" I called out after him. "Can you not see there's a person standing here? Flesh and blood and not exactly invisible."

It had been a hot minute since I needed my old potions to hide my shifter nature. Because of the very nature of Faerie, I was able to tap into the magic of the land to cast a glamour to hide my wolf without having to take a nasty potion to mask my essential nature. It also meant I was able to sense other half-shifters with ease.

And the angry red-faced teen? Definitely half wolf.

He whirled around and growled at me, baring straight white teeth. "What are you going to do about it?" he barked out.

Oh, a bully. I hated those. My eyes narrowed as we measured each other. "I'm going to wait until you apologize for nearly running through me."

"I'll rip your arms from their sockets if you get in my way." His threat froze something inside of me before he stalked off. "And you can count on that, little halfling!"

6

The aggressive shifter's words stayed with me for the next few minutes while I paused to take stock. My insides shook. After Flora being super nice and helpful, it seemed like a terribly stark contrast to have someone threaten me like that.

My hands were still trembling as I knocked on the door to the office the angry guy just vacated. What was his deal, anyway? What had happened to him to make him so rude and hostile? The threat had been unnecessary.

I rubbed my hands over my cheeks and told myself to shake it off. The uneasiness, the frustration, *everything*. They had no place in my reality and certainly wouldn't help me make a good first impression today.

"Come in!"

The tutor called me into her office and although my fingers trembled, I held on tight to the doorknob. Okay, time to get this over with and see exactly what I faced.

The inside of the office smelled of lemon balm and lavender. The heady combination went straight to my head. In contrast to the wintry outside world, here it looked and felt like an endless summer. The walls were painted a cheerful yellow to capture the light from the large bay windows, and a fire burned in the hearth though the room didn't feel over-heated. There were no logs in sight to keep the flames going. Hanging baskets of flowers and herbs bobbed in front of the windows.

The air in here...even that was different. Thicker, friendlier, as if the breeze reached out to caress my exposed skin.

A large desk with a comfortable armchair took up most of the space. From behind the desk a Fae woman rose with a smile to match the feel of her office. "Miss Alderidge, I'm going to assume? You're right on time. There's nothing I like more than promptness. It's refreshing."

She held out a hand to shake. The mortal custom took me by surprise and for a second I stood there and stared at her before urging myself forward.

Take her hand, dummy!

Her palm was dry and a little rough—not what I'd expected. "Yes, um, hi. I'm Tavi."

"Wicks told me all about you. I'm Professor Juno Ians. It's a pleasure."

"Pardon me, but you look—"

"Normal?" she interrupted. "I have more control over my external body than most others. My parents are air and sky people. My bones are made of wind and my atoms are clouds. But I also find it makes students uncomfortable to see my true form so I adopt these features. It helps with future interactions." Juno indicated the sharp edge of her sunshine-yellow hair, the heart-shaped face, the brown eyes. A young Reese Witherspoon if I'd ever seen one. She even had the sweet voice.

"Air folk?" I asked her, taking a seat and allowing my heavy bag to drop with a thud.

"Aurae are nymphs of the sky. We control the element of air," Juno said, then shook her head. "I much prefer to mentor. Tutor. Whatever you want to call it. I have always been drawn to teaching and helping to mold young minds. When your school reached out for help with a case—you, as it turned out—I volunteered."

I wasn't sure what to make of Juno Ians, honestly. She might look like America's sweetheart but I wasn't fooled. I'd come across too many strange people in my life. I knew looks could be deceiving.

Juno folded her hands together on her desk and treated me to a smile that did nothing to offset the stern severity of her eyes. "Look, Tavi," she began, "we both know why you are here. And I want you to know I'm going to help you. It's not going to be easy, and I'm sure you'll hate me before our time is done."

"I'm not going to hate you," I objected.

My answer would not have bothered her either way, I knew instinctively. "Many before you have, and there will be many more once you leave this room. I'm used to it. I'm going to push you past the boundaries of your comfort. I want to see you succeed, and in order to do so you are going to have to work."

"I'm no stranger to hard work."

I didn't understand then how right Juno was. Or how hard she'd push me. We dove into the first lesson within minutes of our introduction, moving into an adjacent work-room outfitted with fabric and wards on the walls and a plain wooden floor. The fabric, she explained, was fireproof to keep us safe, and the walls were soundproofed so no one else could listen to our conversations. More for my protection than anyone else's and, I suspected, to protect me from embarrassing myself.

"All right." She stood with her legs slightly splayed and her hands rubbing together. "Show me what you've got.

46

Start with air and run through the rest. Conjure the elements for me."

We went through the basics of the four elements first. I conjured air, fire, water, and earth out of nothing, shaping them into whatever form or fashion Juno wanted while struggling to keep up with her quicksilver demands.

"I read your file. Your potions master, Larch, stated you made a nearly perfect batch of *Eius Repellere* during your final exams. Are you good with potions?" Juno asked.

I wiped sweat off of my forehead before it could burn my eyes. "I guess so." I was good at following recipes, at least.

"I'm not going to drag out a cauldron and ask you to replicate it. We don't have time for that today. Tell me, why use the potion and how many times can you use it?"

"Um...I don't—" This was why I needed *notes*. Except there were no notes. There was only me and Juno, circling each other. Two magic users looking to see who would come out on top. "You use it one time. F-for...I don't remember."

"Think, Tavi!" she demanded.

"It's something about repelling. It, ah, it gets rid of your enemies."

She snapped out her next question before I had time to draw a breath, accompanying it with a flash of magic igniting sparks at my feet for me to extinguish. "And if you do not have your potions handy? What else can you do to repel your enemies from you without causing harm to yourself?"

Shift into wolf form and rip their throats out before they could do the same to me. She'd hate that answer.

One of the sparks caught on my boots and I struggled to tamp it out before it burned me. "I'm sorry, I can't think."

Juno shook her head. "Not good enough. Give me one spell to defend yourself from your enemies."

"Why is it always about enemies?" I asked pathetically.

"Because there may come a day in your long existence when your peace and safety is no longer guaranteed, and you will need your magic as a sword," she said. "Magic is not only for convenience. It is not only to change your hair or eye color, to make your appearance as you wish it to be or to warm your skin on a cold day. Magic hurts *and* heals. It will serve you well to understand the light and dark sides of both."

I wondered if she'd had the same chat with the half-shifter boy who'd run into me earlier, and if that was the source of his bad mood. I understood, because the harder she pushed me, the more frustrated I became.

"I know the light and dark sides of myself."

"But do you know how to use them *both in conjunction* to protect yourself and those you love?" When I failed to answer, she switched tactics. "How would you deal with a Nyad if you're the one in their territory?"

Once again, would it be wrong to say I'd shift into a wolf and kick some ass? I swallowed the answer. "Nyads are from Greek mythology."

"I assure you they are as real as you and I. They preside over brooks, springs, and fountains. Now, what would you do?"

And when Juno had me entirely worn out physically and strained mentally, we retired to her office once again, where she pushed a cup of nettle tea into my hands. My limbs trembled and I almost dropped the cup.

Damn Fae smugness. She didn't even look winded. Was this the difference between us halflings and the full-bloods? Normally I relied on my shifter strength to get me through, and it must have been my exhaustion that kept me low now.

"You're not ready for the Trials," Juno said. Instead of taking the seat across from me, she grabbed a ruby-red throw pillow and tossed it onto the floor near my feet. She

48

folded her body down onto it as though she needed to be closer to the earth, to the ground.

"Yeah, I know," I snapped, and then took a sip of the tea to curb my attitude before I said something I'd regret.

"I'm serious, Tavi. You are going to get yourself killed. And if you get killed then there's no way I can help you improve your grades. You're here to learn, and you were chosen to attend the Elite Academy because the king saw something in you. I'm going to be honest. I don't know what he saw because your skills are mediocre at best." She held up a hand to stop my rebuttal before it began. "They are mediocre compared to the power I see inside of you and the performance I heard about in your old school. You are a well of untapped potential. With the right direction, the right push, you would be a force to be reckoned with. My question is...what is it going to take to let it out?"

The warmth of the nettle tea soothed my insides but did nothing to keep me awake. Despite my anger, my eyes wanted to close, and I would have given anything to take a nap. "I'm not sure what you want me to say."

"There's nothing *to* say. I'm simply talking to you. Over the course of our time together, I'm going to help you bring your skills to the next level. It's the only way you'll make it through the Trials."

I sighed and sank down in the chair. "Can you tell me more about them? Because at this point, all I know is that they are dangerous and people have died in the past. No one will discuss any details with me."

Juno looked up, her expression grave. "The Trials are meant to expose whether the Fae student possesses the Seven High Values: Balance, Bravery, Cleverness, Creativity, Fairness, Justice, Respect."

"And how do they test for those values, exactly?"

"Ah, yes. I happen to have a list of past Trials to look

over. You and I are going to practice every single one over the course of the next three months. We can try one today, if you want. It's a spell to test Bravery." She pushed onto her knees and crawled toward her desk, reaching a hand up to grab a folder filled with papers.

I'd never heard of the Seven High Values before. Not one person had ever mentioned them to me. Was I surprised? No. It seemed the Fae loved to keep their secrets. I was no stranger to secrets, having kept one-half of my bloodline secret my entire life, though it would have been nice to know what I faced before being thrown into it.

"How does one test bravery?" I followed her to a standing position and set the cup of tea down on the desk, trying to hide my wince. Oh yeah, my muscles were screaming.

Juno's expression was mischievous. "You'll see."

The next spell she had me try got me thinking once more about Kendrick Grimaldi. About how I might have, after all, been better off marrying him than putting myself through this bullshit.

I failed the spell miserably and left the office with my arms sore and my legs wooden. Shaken to the core. My time in Faerie was running out. I knew it in my bones. All that remained to be seen was how it came about. Whether I would be revealed as a half-shifter and booted back to the human realm...or killed in the Trials.

7

I shuffled into the castle kitchen after my tutoring with Juno, exhausted yet knowing I still had hours to go before I got to sit again. Exhaustion meant nothing to the kitchen staff and even less to the king who'd ordered me to be there. I was running on fumes and trying my hardest not to let it show.

Maybe dying was a good alternative to living like a zombie.

Raelynn looked up as I walked in, her corkscrew curls covered in something green and gooey-looking. "What on earth is going on with you?" she barked out at once. The strawberry-blond Fae stared at me, her almond-shaped eyes slanted, and her pupils resembling a reptile's.

Despite her rather brash attitude, I liked her. Or at least I liked her most of the time. Today I was too tired to like anyone, even myself.

"I had a rough day," I grumbled, reaching out to exchange my school blazer for an apron. I hadn't even had time to change my clothes. "Sorry."

"Well, get yourself some freesia essence and get to work," she snapped before turning her attention back to her workstation which was covered in some green goop. "His Majesty is entertaining another titled family this evening and needs a *six*-course meal this time. The girls and I are going out of our minds trying to get everything right for him and we only have a few more hours to prepare it. Care to join us and do your job or would you rather stare out the window mooning about nothing?"

Of course the king was entertaining again, and of course the staff were going crazy. Whatever King Tywin was up to, he certainly had a lot of guests in the castle these days and not a lot of free time. I was happy about it on one hand because it left him no room to wonder about my activities. On the other hand, that meant there were many more people for me to try and avoid.

"Here." Raelynn drew a giant blade out of a butcher block and tossed it in the air, catching it by the steel and holding it out handle-first to me.

"I don't trust myself with a knife," I told her, walking up to the countertop. "Especially not right now."

"I don't care what you trust yourself with. I'm going to need these purple carrots diced before you move on to wash the jewelweed. And for God's sake, Tavi, don't crush the blossoms like you did the last time. Her Majesty noticed and she was not pleased."

As it turned out, I definitely crushed the jewelweed today. I also sliced into my fingers a time or two, dropped a bowl of chocolate mousse into the sink by accident, and broke Raelynn's favorite blue-and-yellow piece of crockery and totally forgot the words she'd taught me to fix it. Instead of mending the pieces together, I ended up transforming them into a swarm of crickets that promptly jumped out the open window.

She was not happy with me. My eyes blurred, burning,

and no matter how I tried, I kept thinking about the spell I'd failed. How Juno stared at me with disappointment.

"*You!*"

I jerked up at Raelynn's sharp tone. And when I looked over at the other woman, despite the goo on her nose and in her hair, her scowl made me cringe. She crooked a finger at me to beckon me closer.

"Yes?" The word ended up sounding like a grunt.

"Tavi girl, this is ridiculous," Raelynn said as she pulled me into her office off the kitchen. She closed the door behind us and shut us in together. "It's not like you to mess up this much. I'm going to need some answers because as you are, you are a liability and you are going to hurt yourself or someone else. I can't take a chance on something else going wrong with you around."

I tried to wave a hand and show her I was all right, and could have sworn I did. Until I looked down and realized my hand was still at my side. My muscles didn't want to respond. Uh-oh. "School is wearing me out," I told her plainly. "I'm tired. I haven't even had any time to eat." Or rest. Or do anything normal kids do.

Raelynn nodded knowingly and moved her hands to her hips, adopting her standard akimbo pose. "I understand. I do. *My* schooling felt like it would kill me before it was all said and done. I've been in your shoes, trust me. I think I handled it with a little more aplomb and certainly more grace, but not everyone is blessed with my reflexes."

"What did you do to get through?" I needed to know. I was desperate. Any kind of secrets she had to share, I would take, because at this rate I was going to pass out from exhaustion and not stand again.

Raelynn stared at me for a long moment, her lips pursed, looking rather intimidating for someone who topped out at just under five feet, and then she sighed, blowing out a breath. "Okay, come on. Let me show you something. Something you'd best be keeping to yourself under penalty of sever repercussions from me and my favorite wooden spoon."

Although the lilt of her accent made the words seem joking, I knew better. She'd definitely follow through if I didn't zip my lip.

The pantry to the kitchen remained magically sealed at all times unless you knew the particular spell to open the lock. I did. I also would sneak in there from time to time to steal ingredients I wouldn't be able to get down at the corner store, ingredients for the potion keeping me out of Kendrick's sight. No matter where he went or what kind of black magic he tried to work, he wouldn't be able to find me as long as I kept taking the potion.

Raelynn didn't know I stole from the king's supplies and I needed things to stay that way. She said the spell to the door, and magic twisted around us, the lock clicking open instantly. I stayed a step behind Raelynn with my face schooled into something neutral. Something to show her *I definitely don't come in here when you aren't around.*

She moved to a shelf and reached above her head with a short hop, grabbing a bag filled with fine white powder.

"Ah-ah!" she cautioned as I stepped closer. Not to grab but to see. "Hold your little horses there, girlie. You can't have it all. I'm merely showing you what we've got to work with."

Raelynn took a second smaller bag from the pocket of her apron and poured from the first into the second.

"What is this?" I asked her.

"This," she replied, "is a very special powder made from the root of the Abrichxao plant. It's found only on the north-west steppes of the Dasha plain in Faerie. The plant has to be harvested under the full moon light during the spring flood or else the properties are half the potency needed. Might as well not use it at all." Once she had enough in the second bag, she re-tied the first and placed it back on the shelf.

"I've never heard of it before."

Raelynn tsked. "No, you wouldn't. Your teachers don't want you knowing about this one. It isn't going to be taught in any kind of herbalism or botany class because it can be quite addictive." Memories of her own time in school, apparently, had her chuckling before handing the bag off to me. "This is going to help with your performance and clarity. Think of it as a magical mental boost."

So Faerie steroids, basically. Although a part of me hesitated, wondering about the benefits—and the side effects—of taking something to help my performance, my hand reached out automatically to take the bag from my boss.

"How do I work with this?" I asked.

She held the bag out, then hesitated. "Listen to me carefully, Tavi, because this is important. *Are you listening?*" I nearly expected her to grab my chin. "No more than two teaspoons a week. And you have to spread out those two teaspoons across the seven days. Mix it with food, water, whatever you fancy. You should be good to go as long as you spread it out." She clapped me on the back hard. It was her way. "But you *have* to spread it out and certainly no more than two teaspoons. If you take any more, you run the risk of some serious side effects and chemical dependency."

We left the pantry with her warning echoing in my ears.

"So don't go overboard," she finished. "Got it?"

B ronwen and I took to the streets for our first patrol later that night. We chose to stick to our human forms, feeling it would be less conspicuous despite the snow. Two girls walking along and catching up with school gossip and such would be better than two crows continually circling.

She cast a spell around us to keep the cold from affecting our limbs and I had to say I was grateful for her magic. I wasn't sure I could cast a spell for light at this point, and those were the first things they taught at school.

"Try to keep up," she said with a small chuckle. "You're dragging your feet and leaving a trail."

I did my best to answer her smile for smile, failing miserably.

"I know this seems like the wrong time to say this, but I'm happy we had a chance to reconnect." Bronwen shivered. For show. Her spell definitely kept the worst of the winter wind at bay. "Too many years went by when we couldn't see each other. I wasn't sure we would ever see each other again."

"I know. I'm happy too," I agreed with a nod. It never hurt to have another friend in your corner.

Bronwen and I had met during our childhood when her mother, part of the Alderidge pack, brought her to the park where I used to play. I didn't know then that she was a halfling like me, or that the reason behind her disappearance was anything other than a normal household move. Her mother thought it would be better for Bronwen to be away from the pack and brought up in Faerie.

"What do you think about these murders?" she asked. "I mean, your honest opinion. Scary, right?"

The word fell hard between us and now it was my turn to shiver. "I'm no stranger to murder," I answered carefully, "but it seems like this is too big of a coincidence."

She turned moon-wide eyes at me. "What do you mean?"

"I mean it feels like whatever trouble I had in the mortal realm has followed me here. You remember me telling you about my last semester at school?"

It was better to be honest with her, I decided. She knew what I was, and she had just as much to lose if found out. Well, maybe not just as much, but enough so that I knew I could trust her to keep what I said between us. Selene also knew about the difficult circumstances surrounding my arrival here. I had nothing to fear from the members of the Claw & Fang.

At least, I didn't think so.

"I mean, I understand you being worried about how the murdered Fae share a resemblance to you. But it stops there," Bronwen told me above the crunch of our boots through the snow. "You have nothing to worry about. None of this is your fault."

Did I not have to worry? Somehow, I didn't feel as confident as Bronwen on the matter.

We passed another couple walking the street and fell silent, not wanting anyone else to overhear us. I nodded briefly to them in acknowledgment before we continued on.

"You're saying you don't think this is a terrible but random occurrence?"

"I'm saying I think there's more to this than Selene told us," I stated. "It's clearly a half-shifter doing the dirty deed, I have no doubt about what she said there. It's impossible to mimic or imitate the depth and trajectory of a real wolf paw. And no one else has the power to overthrow a full-blood Fae, unless it was another Fae, but their magicked claws wouldn't be able to do the damage like we saw. Not to mention the sheer viciousness of the attacks."

Bronwen muttered her agreement. "It still doesn't make

sense why a half-shifter would do it, though. Most of us have come here to escape a bad situation. It's no secret that our kind, no matter what half we are, are hunted. We aren't supposed to be alive. Why would someone take the time to make it into Faerie only to throw it away and risk exposure?"

No, it didn't make any sense to me either. Unless someone from Kendrick's pack managed to infiltrate this world—a very big assumption, because the alarms would be raised—then it had to be one of us. The Claw & Fang had members across the land, so there might be a stranger in our midst.

Still, I couldn't figure out a motive.

Not surprising. I was so tired it took me double the time to remember how to tie my shoes. Just raising a fork to my mouth took effort these days.

"Hey." Bronwen caught me by the arm to slow my strides. "Do you smell something?"

I stopped beside her and closed my eyes, drawing in a deep breath and trying to pinpoint what she sensed. My spine went rigid as I sniffed.

Unfortunately, I *did* smell something. The coppery stench of fresh blood. A fresh kill.

Our eyes met. "What are the odds," I said slowly, "that on our first night on patrol we find the very thing we're supposed to be patrolling against?"

She'd gone pale. "I'd say the odds are pretty damn good."

We broke into a jog and followed the scent, bolting around the side of a building and into a back alleyway filled with flowers even in the dead of winter. Their soft blue blooms did nothing to dispel the very obvious aura of death hanging like a black cloud in the air.

Bronwen and I didn't care about our footsteps, visible in the snow. We didn't care about the panicked cries escaping our throats as we approached the dead body. Well, my friend's panicked cries. I hated how unaffected I felt, how numb everything inside of me was despite the Fae woman's red hair spilling around her head. I was more focused on the blood seeping from her empty shoulders. Her arms had been yanked clean out of their sockets.

8

Warning bells pealed in my head at the sight until finally the memory returned full force.

I'll rip your arms from your sockets if you don't get out of my way. And you can count on that, little halfling!

My mind circled back to my run-in with the wolf shifter boy, the one who earlier had threatened to tear me limb from limb in the exact way we found the corpse tonight. I shook my head.

Could *he* have done this?

He'd certainly been angry enough, and all I'd done to him was stand slightly in his way. He had enough unresolved aggression to be a very likely suspect.

My gut swirled. Yup, he'd been angry enough to kill; it was obvious on his face. My eyes did a quick survey of the corpse and I inwardly groaned. The whole of me went hot. It took everything I had not to empty the contents of my stomach right there on the ground. Maybe this was my super power, I tried to reason with myself. Maybe my super power was finding dead bodies. Someone had to do it, right?

Not something I wanted to be known for, though.

I held an arm out on instinct to keep Bronwen in place or else she might contaminate the area. "Stay back. You don't want to step in anything."

I had to give Bronwen credit. She didn't scream. Instead the two of us clustered together staring at blood so bright against the soft white snow.

"Tavi, listen." Bronwen's voice was shaky. "You stand watch over the body, make sure no one else sees it."

My eyes narrowed. "Why? Are you going somewhere?"

"I have to go alert the leading council of the Claw & Fang. They'll want to come immediately before law enforcement gets here, and we—" She broke off, taking a deep breath and keeping her focus over her shoulder. "We have to make sure no one intercepts the communication. It has to be delivered in person."

"You're leaving me alone with a dead body." I wondered if she saw anything wrong with that picture.

"You don't seem too bothered. Besides, you have a stomach of steel." With her back turned to me, she quickly shifted into crow form and darted out into the night before I had a chance to ask her to stay.

I let my head drop back on my shoulders, running my hand through my hair with a groan. I understood why she had to go. To protect ourselves, the members of the society discouraged anything less than direct conversation between members. Electronic communications could be tracked, Selene had told me, even with a spell designed to wipe devices clean. Telepathic communication was also discouraged because those mental waves could be intercepted. So we relied mostly on person to person contact to better ensure our safety.

There I stood, *again*, watching over a dismembered body, with her blood rapidly cooling in the snow, her arms and legs several feet away, wondering how I'd gone from one bad situation to another. Never in my life had I seen as much carnage as I had since running away from my uncle's house.

What was the saying? Out of the frying pan and into the fire? I'd skipped the frying pan to dive head first into an inferno, still trying to convince myself I was okay.

Part of me wondered if this kind of bad luck had something to do with the violence of my parents' deaths. Did the energy of their murders trail me, plaguing me? Would it be this way for the rest of my life, as though I were some kind of herald or harbinger of death?

I avoided looking at the dead woman as much as possible. The smell, on the other hand...no way to escape the smell, not with my sensitive shifter senses. Pressing a hand over my mouth and nose did nothing to dispel the stench.

I hadn't known what to expect when we set out on patrol tonight but it was certainly not another murder. Slowly I turned my attention to the body, the dark red hair draped over the woman's head and blowing in the late December wind.

My knees grew weaker the longer I focused on her hair. The color was flawless. Similar to mine yet richer and deeper.

Bronwen returned shortly with Selene and another one of the leading council members, a slight man named Buzz with two sets of curved horns twisting out of his head, a curling lizard tail, and narrow yellow pupils.

Selene placed her arm around me and drew me close in a hug. "You did well," she whispered. "You held your own."

I didn't want her compliments. I didn't want any of this, although the hug...I'd take the hug.

"The weather made it easy to spot, and easy to keep hidden. There really isn't anyone out at this time of night. Well, except for our killer," I added when I took a step back.

Buzz bent closer to examine the dead woman. His tail

flicked. "We're going to need the rest of the team out here to clean up before the local officials get wind of it," he said in a reed-thin voice. "We don't want the castle guards to find her before we're done. Or find us along with her."

"I'm on it." Bronwen jumped to attention and once more took off in her crow form.

"There's no sign of a struggle," Buzz said, swearing. "She went down easily enough. Probably had the element of surprise on their side, the murderous bastard."

"How could someone in their half form surprise a full-blood Fae?" I asked quietly. "I don't understand." Or the better question: *Why* would anyone do this?

Selene moved to stand at Buzz's side as he cautiously probed the body for clues, her heels sinking in the snow. I focused toward the flowers instead.

"This is someone who does not abide by any code of ethics. It's not for us to figure out why, but rather who is doing the crimes. And to stop them before they do this again."

I dared a glance at Buzz, who was still bent over the prone form on the ground, then looked away again. I gestured for Selene to step closer. Her instincts were razor-sharp, I knew from experience, and she regarded me with narrowed eyes.

"You know something, don't you?" she began straight away.

"Less a *know* and more like something strange happened to me and I'm not sure what to make of it."

I told her about the guy I'd run into, or rather, the guy who had run into me at the halfling academy. Then launched into an explanation about the half-shifter bullies at my old school. The ones who had killed countless people to get to the *Augundae Imperium*.

The same artifact now in the possession of a very nasty doomsday prepping witch.

I cringed at the thick sounds of Buzz maneuvering flesh and bone for clues. I'd hunted animals through the woods during a routine shift before, but this...this level of barely contained violence was something else.

"I'm saying it's a little suspicious," I reasoned. "And a little too strange to write it off as a coincidence. I mean, what are the odds of another half-wolf being at the halfling academy at the same time I was? And running into me?"

Buzz and Selene shared a look.

"You left those half-shifters boys on the other side of the portal, though," Selene clarified. "Yes?"

"That doesn't mean they weren't able to find a way in," Buzz argued. "More and more shifters are crossing the border these days thanks to—"

Selene cut him off with a look.

"The boy I saw yesterday wasn't familiar to me and he didn't have the same smell as the others. *They* were brothers, pack. This one didn't smell like anyone I'd met before, although he had the same bad energy."

Still, Buzz looked grim. His lizard tail flicked behind him again in agitation. "Plenty of half-shifters come through to Faerie by one means or another," he told me. "And not all of them are looking to start a new life. Some of them are tainted, looking to destroy this world as they did their own. For nefarious purposes."

Selene agreed. "I hesitated to tell you this because I didn't want you scared, Tavi, but part of our duty with the Claw & Fang is to find these rogue half-shifters and exterminate them."

"We prefer to say we eliminate the threat," Buzz corrected with a look over his shoulder at the flapping of wings.

Bronwen arriving with the cleanup crew cavalry.

"There's a threat?" I asked.

A shadow flickered in his eyes when he turned to me again. "Tavi, there's *always* a threat. There are also folks like those in the Claw & Fang who have sworn to protect our people rather than sow chaos."

I didn't want to think about it. Even now, having seen more death than most people, I didn't want to think about the boogie man beneath the bed. I'd made an oath to the society, sure...but did the oath cover hunting down rogue halflings?

The two of us were dismissed the moment Selene had the area under control.

"You two are free to go." She gazed between us and flashed a sharp smile. "You did good work tonight."

"How was this good work?" Bronwen countered. "We were too late."

"Your quick thinking and action might give us precious clues to solve this thing before we lose another full-blood, or before the king's guards can sweep this under the rug. Now go home to bed. You've been through enough tonight. Hey." Serene snapped her fingers in Bronwen's face. "Keep your wits about you. Keep your senses sharp. There are terrible things out there, worse than this dead woman. Things prowling the night, ready to devour you. Keep that in mind on your walk home."

The warning was meant more for pale-faced Bronwen than for me. Somehow I got my mouth working again and blurted out, "She's shaken. It's natural. Can you blame her?"

Selene flexed her fingers as though her own claws would soon slip out from beneath her dusky flesh. "Cowardice doesn't suit her, she'll see soon enough."

I wasn't sad to be sent on my way. Honestly, my bed and I had a date I didn't want to miss.

"Was this the first body you'd seen?" I asked Bronwen.

Shadows flickered in her eyes as she nodded. "Yes. I'm afraid I've lived a pretty sheltered life despite the move across worlds."

She stopped then, groaning, and I sensed enough from what she didn't say: she felt sorry for me and everything I'd experienced. She wouldn't want to trade places. Not that I blamed her for it. If I were in her shoes, I would have chosen the sheltered life as well.

On the way back to the castle, I told Bronwen everything I'd said to Selene and Buzz. She needed to be aware in case something like this happened again while I wasn't around.

"I think more than anything, the anger worries me. You remember. We were always taught in the pack to control our emotions because it's the only thing separating us from the beast in our blood. Things get bad when we lose our heads. This kid? He was on the edge."

"It doesn't sound like he was sorry for running into you, either. Do you know what kinds of people they accept into the academy there?"

Realizing she waited for my answer, I shook my head. "I'm not sure. I didn't really do any research on it before crossing the portal myself. I imagine they would have to be bright to make it through the culling. So whoever the boy is, he's intelligent *and* has anger issues."

"A terrible combination."

"I always thought half shifter, half Fae were rare," I told her. "Now it seems as though they are overrunning wherever I am."

"Well, there have been rumors over the years that Dorian Jade is behind the influx of half-shifters in Faerie," she said with a shrug.

I stopped at the name. Literally stopped. "Dorian Jade?"

I'd heard the name many times over and couldn't find a

single speck of information about the man behind the troubles.

"Apparently Jade has taken it upon himself to set up a kind of underground railroad for shifters. That's why there are so many of us here in Faerie. He's responsible."

"The Unseelie King?" I asked sarcastically.

"I understand it's a little much for you to take in at once." She had no idea.

"I mean, yeah. And now having one of our own kind out there slaughtering full-blood Fae as they see fit? It's scary! And if Dorian Jade is responsible for bringing the rogue halfling in, then it creates all kinds of problems—problems you and I aren't equipped to deal with but will feel the effects of nonetheless."

We stalked through the snow with our shoulders occasionally touching and the temperatures freezing my face until Bronwen remembered her magic and set the temperature-altering spell in place. "The rumors are unsubstantiated," she continued without looking at me, "but you know all rumors tend to be rooted in fact. Right?"

9

To say I slept horribly would be the understatement of the century. And despite the burning malice I remembered in the shifter boy's eyes, I woke up the next day to a shining sun and gardens bedecked in banners and flowers. For the courtier family, more than likely. The world continued to turn no matter what kind of bad people were out there.

There was a thin haze of clouds Wednesday morning, and when I threw the window open, I sensed a distinctive wet chill in the air. More than likely we'd have more snow before the day was up and suddenly, from the safety of my warm comforter when I snuggled back under it, I was glad to have a direct portal to the Elite Academy instead of hoofing it to the train station.

Yes, I thought again, being friends with the prince definitely had its perks. And although I hadn't been allowed to move out of the castle and into the apartment with Melia, it was the one aspect of my life that didn't seem too bad right now. The portal, Mike, and our renewed friendship.

After showering and getting dressed, I gathered the books I'd need for classes today and waited outside of my room for my escort. Mike arrived right on time and the two of us walked to the portal together.

Different class schedules kept us apart for the rest of the day. Luckily, I had a free period between lunch and herbalism and used it to infiltrate the academy library with their vast array of resources. It put the library at the mortal halfling academy to shame, and I'd once thought it to be one of the best I'd ever seen.

It was time to do some serious digging on Dorian Jade.

I'd asked Mike about him once but he didn't have much information for me. In fact, the only thing he could tell me was that Jade had set himself up as a sort of monarch to the Unseelie Fae, constructing a magical wall dividing Faerie into two distinct parts. Mike's people, the Seelie Fae, weren't allowed to pass over the wall and into Dorian's territory.

Mike had also told me his father had worked to try and create an image away from the black and white lines of the old Fae court system, no light or dark, until Dorian came in to fan the flames of chaos among the people of this land.

None of this was taught in class. Probably for multiple reasons. I remembered Mike saying Dorian was too powerful for anyone to move against right now, so the professors had more than likely been instructed to keep their mouths shut and their students in the dark as to the conflict.

I grabbed a few books on the history of the old court system and chose a table nearest the windows, where the sunlight felt thin and cold. Good thing the library had multiple fireplaces to keep the room cozy.

Dropping the books on the tabletop, I stared at them, an ache forming between my eyes. How would I focus on the words when I could barely make out the titles? Except this wasn't something I could just let go.

Shaking my head, I grabbed the top one in the stack and

flipped to the first chapter. I made it all the way through the third chapter before I jerked back, half asleep. I wasted precious time before I remembered Raelynn's brain boost powder. Practically burning a hole in my backpack, waiting for me to use.

With a small smile, I unzipped the large pocket and drew out the plastic bag. It looked like normal white powder, like maybe a magnesium supplement, so if anyone asked, that's what I'd say. I glanced around the library and saw no one around.

Better for me.

I had a bottle of water with me and I measured out an entire teaspoon, chugging it down with a wince. It didn't taste terrible but it wasn't exactly candy, either. It left a strange gritty feeling on my tongue and I smacked my lips to try and get rid of the taste.

"You look like you swallowed a lemon."

I wasn't surprised to see Mike walking through the aisles between two bookshelves.

"Close enough," I told him, still trying to get rid of the taste. "Vitamin supplement."

He didn't seem bothered. "You also look like you're reading something you would rather not be and it's giving you a headache."

I set my palm on the book and smiled at him, the sort of tired smile you give when you've been pegged correctly. "I'm transparent, then," I said. And then glanced down at the words that, thankfully, were no longer blurring together. Wow, the brain boost worked quickly! "I'm trying to figure out a little more information on the disintegration and reformation of the fairy court system. Especially since you once told me your family pre-dated the courts."

Mike's lips pursed as he grabbed the chair across from me, pulling it out and turning it around so he could straddle it and lean his arms across the flat back. "Some pretty heavy stuff."

I nodded. The powder made quick work of my brain fog. I already felt my senses sharpening and my focus returning. "Absolutely. Still, I wanted to know more about Dorian Jade," I said.

I wished I could tell him about the murders, but I couldn't, not without revealing the Claw & Fang right along with my shifter nature. Those were the two things I absolutely needed to keep hidden at all costs. Even from Mike. Or maybe especially from Mike.

Kind of a bad situation.

Mike stared at me before slowly shaking his head. He even flashed me an eye roll for good measure. "I know how you get when you're curious about something. You'll research it to death."

I threw a quill at him. "You make it sound like a bad thing."

"Never a bad thing. But there really isn't much information on Dorian Jade and I don't want you spending all of your winter hours holed up in the library." Mike took hold of the quill, the slender stem dwarfed in his large hand, and magicked it back to me with a flick of his wrist and a muttered word. It floated through the air, making designs as it went, before landing smartly next to my arm.

Was it my imagination, or had one of the designs been a heart?

I might have melted right there.

At least we were alone in the library. None of his stuck-up friends were around to see us and ruin the moment. They wouldn't be caught dead in a place like this because they were too concerned about their image. Full-blood Fae didn't need to research or concern themselves with dusty old books. They had enough magic and knowledge and power at their fingertips so that they breezed right through classes, let alone these stupid upcoming Trials.

I leaned closer to Mike and said, "*You* aren't the least bit curious? I mean, he's built a wall cutting your land in half. That's a pretty big cause for concern. Don't you want to know why? Or what's on the other side?"

"Of course I'm curious! But I know my father and I know the grip he and the Elder Council have on the situation." Mike shrugged, and I watched him lick his lips. Remembered how delightfully warm they'd felt against mine. I swallowed. "But if they aren't concerned, then I don't see the need to worry."

I nibbled at my own lips. "Ah, but I didn't say worry. I said curious. There is a big difference between the two."

"Is there?" Mike reached out to tug on one of the loose strands of hair falling down my cheek.

"There is," I told him with mock seriousness, although I felt the way my nerves stood to attention at the light touch. "And if you don't understand the difference then I'm afraid all those extra study sessions will be for nothing."

"Well," he said as he leaned closer and lowered his voice, "I can tell you I have been curious enough to do a little research on the infamous Dorian Jade on my own."

My jaw dropped. "Have you, now?"

"Years ago, before my father decided to send me to the mortal halfling academy, I was scared. Like how you're shivering right now." He slid his hand across the table and I thought I felt the tips of his fingers brush against mine.

"Yes, so scared," I agreed, although I wasn't shivering with fear.

"I did some digging in the castle library but came up with very little for the effort. It wasn't until I cornered one of the imps who hangs around near the swan pond that I received some valuable information."

He was close enough to touch and I found myself leaning closer still, until my skin went hot at his nearness. "What did you find out?"

"I found out you can never trust an imp," Mike murmured. "Tricky little buggers."

I giggled. Our noses bumped together. "The prince should never go unaccompanied to the swan pond. A valuable lesson indeed, sir."

Mike shifted ever so slightly so the side of his nose slid along my own. Had I thought his looks melted me before? His breath on my skin, the slight scent of peppermint, did me in. I could not have moved from the chair if I wanted to. My fingers itched to grab him.

"What will you do about it, Miss Tavi? Will you choose to accompany the prince the next time he gets a wild hair under his crown?" His voice had dropped into growl territory.

"I would be delighted to, Your Majesty," I agreed in a breathy voice. "Whatever impish head you need beaten in or squished, I will come to your aid."

He chuckled, a low rumble in his chest. "One of the many things I appreciate about you."

"My ability to hurt people who would hurt you? Yes, I'm sure it's something you greatly admire." I edged back just far enough to see the way he bit his lower lip. I wanted to bite his lip. Although we were alone, I swore I heard angels singing. "You were awfully mad at me for what I did with the muskie, if you recall."

There were flecks of gold in his eyes, like little lines of sunlight cutting through the green leaves onto the forest floor. "I...may have overreacted," he admitted, and his lips tugged up in a smile. "I was running on adrenaline, upset about nearly cheating, and angry about allowing myself into a situation where some creature got the better of me. Not to mention how you could have been hurt."

I took an uneven breath and stared at him. "You don't have to worry about me."

"How different we are. You are the most unpretentious person I know."

"Ah, not what you meant to say, I'm sure. You meant to say you are the one who has fun all the time and I'm the one who is stuffy and dull," I said.

This time I wasn't imagining it at all. Though our gazes were locked, Mike's index finger definitely trailed a path of pure fire along my own, then the rest of his fingers covered the top of my hand. I felt scorched all the way to my toes.

"You're trying to say I'm an arrogant playboy only after having fun?" he questioned.

"I didn't say anything even remotely similar to that," I protested.

"Well, I know you can't mean it about you being stuffy and dull."

"Maybe I'm just a girl who thinks she can have it all." *And is going out of her mind trying to accomplish it.*

His forehead rested against mine and I closed my eyes, relishing the contact. "It's a wonder we're still friends. You dull, me arrogant, and neither one of us having a clue what to do about it."

Close. He was so close, and I didn't want to think about the distance there really was between us. Not with my lips tingling and his nearing—

Then the giant doors to the room burst open and a flood of laugher from the hallways reached us. The moment broke and Mike slid away, hiding his next words with a cough.

"Anyway," he said, clearing his throat, "I'm not sure you'll find what you're looking for."

My brows drew together. "What?"

He pointed at the open book before me. "There. You aren't going to find anything on Dorian Jade. Not when he wants to remain a mystery and he's willing to go to any lengths necessary to keep it that way."

A hard knot settled beneath my sternum at the approach of two other Elite Academy students. The moment ruined, I could only offer them, and Mike, a small grin. The real world always dashed fantasies. Mike was not mine. Mike could never be mine.

It was better for me to remember that than risk breaking my own heart on nothing but a dream.

10

———

I decided to use my limited free time wisely and search the sister school for more half-shifters. Okay, maybe it *wasn't* so wise and I should have been using my time to practice for the Trials. Yet there I was before my regular meeting with Juno, walking the paths, trailing my hands along the stones and sending my magic senses out in a wide net.

I'd found, through trial and error, I had the ability to use my inherent power—cognitive manipulation—to scan people's energies. To reach out with my magic and touch their minds, to see their energy and, yeah, manipulate them.

I tried not to think about the *manipulate* word. Even though it was my own innate power, it felt unethical somehow. Unethical to cause someone to experience something that wasn't real, merely on my whim alone. But this felt different. If anything, in this case I was doing something good. I was trying to get a baseline energy signature for any other half-shifters in the area, ones even the Claw & Fang might not know about. They hadn't known about that threatening boy when I told Selene and Buzz the story. At least, they acted like they didn't know.

Maybe they did and I was being kept in the dark for a reason.

I didn't want to think about that either.

At any rate, as long as I didn't impose my will, I saw no harm in what I considered reconnaissance. So I sent my power out to search the halls for anyone with the shifter energy signature. We were distinctly different from full-blood Fae or elf or troll. Different from chimeras or griffons or any other creatures we'd learned about in class. I always thought it was because shifters were tied to the moon. We carried a certain something in our blood and energy that other creatures did not. I latched on to those differences now—and found way more than I'd thought I would.

Holy shit. I stopped suddenly, shocked and wishing my senses were betraying me.

Standing outside of Juno's office with my eyes closed, I found the furious boy who'd threatened me, as well as several more shifters scattered throughout the school, presences I hadn't felt before. None of them were familiar to me, and definitely none I'd seen at a Claw & Fang meeting. There were at least five hiding in plain sight! Though I didn't see their faces, I saw their natures, and knew they wouldn't be able to hide from me anymore. Not just wolves, either. I also saw a were-dingo, a were-fox, a were-bird, and something reptilian I didn't really understand.

I shook my head and swiftly drew my energy back to me, half afraid of what else I might discover if I kept at it.

My memory went back to my time at the Fae Academy for Halflings in the mortal realm. The shifter brothers who had been on the search for the Imperium had slaughtered their way to the artifact, and then I'd seen more of them during the graduation ceremony before crossing the portal into Faerie for the first time.

Which led me to question whether the students I sensed

here were working with the ones I'd left behind at the mortal academy. Or were these new shifters, souls who'd found themselves in extraordinary circumstances and went out of their way to hide their shifter natures from the rest of the world?

Was Dorian Jade the puppeteer behind all of this?

I needed to find out, although I had a bad feeling that the more I dug up, the more questions I would find instead of the answers I wanted.

The only thing I knew for certain was this: Dorian Jade was a pure-blood Fae no matter what the rumors said. He considered the royal family and any governing bodies under King Tywin his enemies. It only made sense for him to ally himself with others who saw the royal family the same way.

What if these latest murders were done in his name? And if they were, then I needed to find out how to stop them, to keep the people I cared about safe.

I saw red for a minute thinking about Mike in danger.

"Tavi! I know you're out there." Juno's voice came through the stone walls clearly, as though she stood next to me instead of a room away. "It doesn't matter how you try to delay the inevitable. We have a lesson today and you can't get out of it. Better to come on in and get this over with."

I sighed, rolling my eyes. Of course she would know about my stalling. The woman seemed to have an extra set of eyes in the walls as well as the back of her head.

Time to get this miserable situation over with and maybe, just maybe I'd get into bed before twenty-four bells tonight. Trying to fall asleep at midnight only to wake up at six...an entirely new world for me and one I entirely hated.

I pushed into the office and saw Juno waiting for me, her butter-yellow hair glowing like a candle flame. How did she manage to look this chipper every day? I didn't get it. Even on my best day I would never look as happy or enthusiastic as Professor Ians.

"There you are," she teased with a wagging finger. "Thought you could wait outside the door and waste time?"

I shook my head and took off my school blazer, hooking it on the standing coat rack to my left. "No, definitely not. Just thinking deep thoughts."

"I expect nothing less. Except those thoughts better be about the Trials and not about something trivial. Have you looked over the spell I left with you?"

I thought about my humiliating defeat yesterday and finally told her, "No. I didn't have time. Between work and homework last night, I barely got to sleep."

Her expression went sour and she paused halfway through pouring herself a cup of tea. "Better you make the time now than *die*. All right, then." She finished pouring and then downed the steaming cup in one gulp. "We'll go over a few of the basics before we get started. Consider them a warm-up."

A warm-up. More like the first step down a road to a bleak ending. I didn't have faith in my magic, not really, not when it came down to the wire. We went through a few introductory spells to get my magic bubbling and brewing before Juno went in for the kill.

Her test today? Not one of bravery, like my first day. No, this one would try my resilience. How long would it take me to call down the light from the sun and how long could I hold it between my hands, like I was some god who had control over the stars and the heavens.

How did they expect school-aged people to handle this level of magic? I didn't know. And those kinds of questions wouldn't help me succeed, either.

"Tavi, I'm serious now," Juno called out, sounding far

away. "You need to master this spell. You're only able to call down the barest flicker of light."

I cradled the swirling sphere of yellow–orange that looked like fire but no heat came from it. It had taken me close to twenty minutes to get the wording correct, not to mention pushing my power into an unfamiliar direction. When I finally managed to call down the light, it didn't want to stay and extinguished almost immediately.

My latest attempt I'd been able to hold for about ten minutes but I felt my strength flagging. "I'm trying!" I insisted, shifting from foot to foot. "I'm not sure if it's the words I can't get or—"

"It's your internal fortitude." Juno speared me with a look. "You are doubting yourself and it's not allowing your magic to manifest to its fullest potential. How are you going to be able to hold the heat of the sun for hours like this? You can't!"

"I don't understand why this is important, anyway," I grumbled. Throwing more and more of myself into maintaining the magic connection to the land and coming up short every time. The ball of light in my palm began to flicker.

My energy dipped to a dangerously low level and I gritted my teeth, bearing down. Whoever came up with this stupid test, anyway? And what possible use could there be in calling down the sun? It wasn't like I was actually strong enough—no one was!—to manifest a piece of the *literal* sun. It was just a fancy name for an extremely bright, hot, dense ball of light held on the physical plane.

Yet Juno seemed to think it was life and death.

"What is the point?" I asked, frustration spilling out.

Juno ignored the question. "I need you to put your everything into this because it's really only an exaggerated spell for light. This is something you should have been able to master in the first fifteen minutes, tops. The other students at your level in the academy are doing the same thing. They have to."

"Yes, but they're full-bloods," I argued.

Her brows came together in a hard line. "I refuse to let you use your halfling status as an excuse. I've felt the level of power inside of you. This is not the time for excuses nor is it the time to doubt yourself. You have as much power as any of the students you go to school with, no matter what you think to the contrary. Now *focus*."

Sweat dripped down from my brow line. "I'm trying—"

"You're not trying hard enough!" Juno walked in a circle around me, scrutinizing my every move. Adjusting my posture this way or prodding my muscles that way so I'd shift my stance. When she spoke again, her voice was strained. "It's imperative we work our way through the list of past trials. You'll never be able to get through this year unless you can show some sort of base foundation."

"I was at the top of my class at the mortal halfling academy. I made it to Faerie."

"Then prove yourself," Juno snapped. "I'm done listening to the *oh poor me* refrain."

Was that what she thought I did? Constantly felt sorry for myself? No matter what I said, she would see it as another pathetic attempt at an excuse. No matter what I did, I messed up, and the more time I spent failing these past Trials, the more urgent Juno became for me to succeed. To win.

"Frankly, I'm not sure what the king saw in you."

Her words instantly had a swell of blind panic welling up inside of me. "What do you mean?"

"I mean you would have a hard time making it through *this* school, let alone the Elite Academy," she said plainly. She took a seat behind her desk and in an instant had another pot of scalding hot tea in front of her. She poured out two cups, waiting for me to come and claim mine, though I understood her unspoken demand. She wanted me to drink the tea while maintaining the ball of light.

I shifted my thoughts, trying to balance the two acts. Before I could wallow in another round of self-pity about being tired and tell her to just keep the tea, she shook her head.

"My goodness, Tavi. I see your thoughts clearly. You're not sure you can multitask, and at this point I'd say you are right. I don't understand how you've made it this far, I really don't. Based on what I'm seeing from you now, you should not have survived the first round of culling, let alone made it to Faerie."

I grimaced. "Stop it."

She hesitated for only a moment. "No, I will not stop it. You need to hear this. Whatever barriers you have blocking your power, you need to find the source and surmount them, *yesterday*. Let me make it very clear for you. There is no way for you to get out of participating in these Trials, but when you compete, you will not finish. Do you understand what that means?"

She spoke to me like I was a child, and her gaze sent flashes of burning pain through me. I hated the mirror she held up. What I saw there was everything I wanted to run from. "We're on day two and you cannot divide your attention between holding a spell and taking a drink. It's unacceptable, quite frankly. I'm going to need you to—"

"Stop it," I cried out. "Stop it right now!"

"It's *unacceptable*," she said again, harshly, "and I'm not going to stand for it. Do you want to know the real reason why I am helping you? Because everyone else said no. They didn't think you were worth the trouble."

Desperation and devastation swirled inside of me and

the light I held fizzled to nothing. I needed her to stop talking. I needed her to stop throwing my failures in my face. Did she not see how often I thought the same thing? How many times a day I wondered *why* I was at the Elite Academy when I clearly couldn't hack it?

I scrunched my eyes closed, fists at my sides. "I'm sorry that in your eyes I'm not worthy of being here. I'm doing the best I can but it never seems to be good enough. Every day I get up, and I work hard, and it still isn't enough. I might die during the Trials. I get it. At least I'll go out knowing I did everything I could to get through."

Seconds of silence ticked by until I realized Juno wasn't responding. When I opened my eyes, I saw her staring at me. Her face had gone pale, the blood rushing from her cheeks and her gaze focused on my arms.

"What is it?" I barked out.

It didn't take long for me to understand, for when I looked down I saw how my hands had transformed into claws. I saw lethal talons instead of fingernails, and feathers growing longer by the second.

Oh no.

No!

Whatever internal desperation I'd been struggling with had manifested using my transfiguration power. That I wasn't supposed to have.

And now Juno knew my secret.

11

─────────

I couldn't panic. I would have to keep my tears in check and my wits together, assess the damage and sort it out to the best of my abilities. Then, maybe then I'd figure out what to do with my tutor's look of indisputable terror.

Juno stared at the talons, watching as they slowly retreated into my skin.

"You..." she began. Then stopped, snapping her mouth shut. "Tavi, what did you do?"

I reined in my anxiety. At least the question was better than *what are you*, although I knew she thought it. I knew she wondered what the hell I was, because she understood the difference between illusion and reality. Any Fae with magic had the ability to change their outward form for a small amount of time. But it was just an illusion. It was fake, a mastery over the elements, and completely different from cognitive manipulation.

That wasn't the case with me.

"It's nothing," I insisted, focusing on tamping down the transfiguration until my hands and fingers looked normal again. My senses returned to me slowly, my energy centering, and that's when I felt the pain. Sharp pinpricks of pain beneath my skin like my nerves were mad at me for what I'd done. "It's a stress response."

"Do not lie to me."

"I'm not."

The soft breeze wafting off of Juno, part of her heritage, turned into a gale blowing the hair away from my face with such force I had to close my eyes.

"Start talking, Miss Alderidge. *Now*."

I winced and didn't look down at my hands again. I kept my gaze on Juno, waiting for the condemnation to come. I saw only anger.

My head was so dizzy I feared I might black out, my heart rate too quick, and the rest of me responding to the adrenaline racing through my blood. "It's going to be a long story. A long and stressful story."

"I don't care. We have all the time in the world as long as you are honest with me," Juno stated. She squared her shoulders, losing a bit of the animosity but not enough to make me comfortable. "Take a seat. I'll make some more tea. I seem to have accidentally spilled this pot."

I didn't want tea, even though my mouth was suddenly desert-dry and my stomach had plummeted like an anchor into the ocean. How did I find myself in these messes? Why couldn't I control myself better? I had to learn, no matter how tired, to watch my magic because this kind of mistake was a rookie move. Now I had to trust someone else not to turn me in, someone who didn't know me and didn't have any investment in me.

I deserved this, I thought miserably, plopping into the chair as my trembling knees refused to hold me up any longer. Whatever punishment or harsh words Juno wanted to throw at me, I deserved all of it. Because I couldn't handle myself, couldn't control my own powers. Somehow, I had to make it right.

So I took the leap of faith and came clean with her. About *everything*. From start to finish I told Juno the story of my past, without leaving out any details, and watching for her reactions while she simply stared at me. However the anger was no longer there on her face, and the condemnation never came, though I clearly saw the war waging inside of her.

Juno tapped her fingers on the desktop and the spring breeze around her grew in strength for a moment. I shook at the chill before it settled.

"Look, I know you don't know me," I continued, staring down at my lap, "but please don't turn me in to the king." I spoke louder than was wise. "I've done everything I can to make it here and escape an intolerable home situation. Don't bother telling me I shouldn't be alive. I know, and I..." I wanted to bury my face in my hands but I refused to break eye contact. "I'm trying."

Juno sat back in the chair, her legs tucked under her. "I admit I'm stuck, Tavi. I feel like I'm stuck between a good student in need of help and what I perceive as my duty as a teacher and a member of this community. I would be remiss to not inform the Elite Academy of your heritage."

"No!" I surged forward, gripping the edge of the desk. "Please! I have nowhere else to go."

My terror must have shown on my face because Juno winced.

"What do you expect me to do?" she argued. "You've put me in a terrible position. This is not how I wanted my day to turn out. And I'm sure this isn't the future you had in mind when you escaped to Faerie, either. I...I don't know. Honestly, I'm going to need a little time to think this over and decide on the best course of action."

"Please. I'm *begging* you, Juno. Give me some time to prove my worth. Please don't send me right back into Kendrick Grimaldi's hands. I would rather die a thousand times in the Trials than marry him." My chest tightened to the point of pain.

She stared at me for a long moment, apparently trying to figure out what to say. There were no words. My heart rose into my throat and threatened to choke me. I couldn't draw air into my lungs as I waited for her response. As though everything inside of me hung in the balance waiting on what Juno would say.

At last she sighed, and the air stilled around us. "Tavi... all right, I'll give you some time. I will give you whatever I can. However, you need to make this work. You need to make the effort and master not only these Trials, but work on controlling your secret power of transfiguration, too. If the Trials don't kill you—"

A grim nod. "At this point I'm not even counting on surviving," I admitted. Funny, saying it out loud didn't have nearly as much impact as saying it in my head.

"Well...*huh*. Well. Okay. If the Trials don't kill you, then having your secret come to light just might."

I nodded and barely suppressed a shudder. "I will do whatever it takes. I already have been, haven't I?" My hands curled into fists on my lap and I made sure to leave the cup of tea where I'd set it down. Otherwise I'd break it into dust. "I'm doing the best I can. Okay?"

"I see it. Trust me, I see it, no matter what I said when I tried to push you. I'm simply not sure how long you can keep this up without breaking. But your secret is safe with me. *For now*." Juno held out her hand for me to take and shake.

Half dragging myself from the room, I cut a path toward the castle, picking out details of the town—a certain oddly shaped brick here, or a secret walkway between buildings there. Anything to distract me from what had just happened. I observed more of the town today than I had my entire time here. Maybe that was good, I reasoned. If things went even farther south, if I needed to plan an escape route, then memorizing the town layout might save me.

I was still doing my transfiguration classes with Onyx Grimaldi twice a week, and after that slip-up in front of Juno I had to make an appearance tonight. Although I'd rather sit in a dentist's chair for hours having each of my teeth pulled without anesthesia, I had no choice. I must learn to master all my powers or I would never survive, either in this realm or the mortal one.

Maybe Onyx would have some sage advice on what to do to control myself.

Although I had to work in the kitchen, I cut my time short, doing whatever I could in two hours before taking off to meet Onyx in the forest behind the castle. We had our own secret spot, a place where the trees cleared and the moon shone down brightly. It was the place he'd first taken me when we began meeting and as he'd told me the first night, this was a thin place. I found I had a soft spot for the trees, the boulders, the vibrations. They helped ground me inside my body when nothing else did.

I scanned the forest for Onyx but didn't see him until I tripped over an exposed root and found myself sprawled on the ground on my back.

"You're a graceful one," Onyx said. He was poised on his haunches, one palm pressed flat to the earth. His warm honey-colored eyes stared down an aquiline nose at me. Platinum-white hair, cut short at the sides and longer at the top, fell toward his ears and he sported a goatee and mustache of the same color. Onyx had the looks of an alpha male but the demeanor of a beta. Or so I'd thought when I first met him.

Now I knew the kind of power lurking beneath his skin and the heritage it came from.

He also looked nothing like his father, who used black magic to appear closer to me in years. As a guess I would have put Kendrick Grimaldi solidly in his late twenties or early thirties. In reality, Kendrick's son Onyx was in his mid-twenties and not much older than me.

"When you're right, you're right," I replied with one of my first genuine smiles of the week besides the ones I reserved for Mike and Melia. Although Onyx was pretty damn cute and we got along great, there was no spark. Nothing drawing me to him on the same elemental level as what Mike and I shared.

"Better get yourself together," Onyx answered gruffly. "You're late."

I brushed twigs and ice off of my backside from my time on the frozen ground. "I'm sorry, I had work. I came as soon as I could."

"I thought you told them to let you off early on Wednesdays and Fridays. It doesn't make any sense for us to continue when we have less than our allotted time together."

"I did tell them. That's why I'm here now instead of two hours from now. We have to be happy for small victories." I glanced behind me again to make sure I hadn't been followed. One could never be too careful.

"Are you all right? You look pale." Onyx rose and came toward me, then ran his hands along my cheeks as though he could feel out what was wrong with me.

Onyx could be dead-sexy and gruff sometimes, and mother-hen-like at others. Seemed today we were going with the latter. But this wasn't something as simple as a fever. Pushing his hands away, I said, "Yeah, it's been a pretty shitty week already and it's only just started." I sighed. "Never mind. I'm fine."

"You should always be honest with me," he replied.

I practically snorted. "You don't want to hear me complain."

One eyebrow rose independent of the other. "No, I don't want to hear you complain, because life is too short to fall victim to a bad set of circumstances. I will, however, lend an ear if you want to explain what is making things hard on you and then we can see if I'm able to help in any way. Are you getting enough sleep?"

I rolled my eyes, resigned. "No, I'm not." Shrugging out of my coat, my stretchy pants and black sweater allowing for better mobility, we faced each other. Neither of us was willing to waste any more time. "Along with the rest of my responsibilities, I had to start working with a tutor at the Fae Academy for Halflings school across town."

"That's great."

Onyx leaped into the air and shifted as he went, his bottom legs transforming into eagle talons as he swiped at the space in front of me.

Here with him, I didn't have to hide my powers or my true nature. I didn't have to pretend to be anything other than what I was—or what I wanted to be.

I let my anger do the talking tonight. Everything I'd pushed down and repressed, every terrible feeling causing me to lie awake at night, I used on my mentor. I pushed my body into whatever form it wanted in order to fight off Onyx's physical attacks. Though I bent back to avoid the first blow, his second struck me on the arm, bouncing off impenetrable scales I'd summoned in an instant to protect myself.

I told him about the rest of my troubles as we sparred.

Wow, three days into the week and already things were a tight knot of complications.

"Sounds like you have a lot on your mind," he said. His hair glowed under the light of the moon, a strange white I'd quickly come to accept. This was Faerie. Things that were abnormal in the mortal realm? Perfectly average here.

"Gee, you think?" I snarled when he landed another blow, the spot on my side where he hit already throbbing. Yup, I'd have a few bruises later. "As much as I enjoy our playtimes," I told him, already out of breath when I moved to strike back, "I think I'm going to have to cut back on our hours."

Onyx swung in a circle, a scorpion tail manifesting out his backside and lashing out at me. He transfigured faster than anyone I knew, and although there weren't many of us with that power, Onyx was surely the best I'd come into contact with.

"Are you kidding me?" he said.

"I'm serious. At least until we see if I make it through the Trials. I have to put all of my focus into my studies or else there won't be enough of me left to kick your ass. You understand, right?"

Onyx shook his head, clucking his tongue at the same time. I didn't expect the swoop of a wing to knock me off balance. Not with my attention focused on the sharp stinger at the end of the scorpion tail he still bore.

Not only could he transfigure his shape in a snap, he had mastered the ability to change different parts of his body into different forms and held them all at the same time. I envied him that, not sure whether I would ever reach his level of skill. Maybe with a few hundred years of practice I'd be half as talented.

"You want me to survive, don't you?" I asked softly. Timidly. Because did I really want to know the answer?

This was the son of my *fated mate*, after all. Maybe he really wanted me dead and this preparation was just to make sure I'd be a worthy opponent when we squared off at last.

Onyx glared at me. "Of course I want you to survive and make it through," he growled. "Are you kidding? Why would you even ask such a stupid question?"

He spun around a second time and landed a kick. When I fell on my back, he rose above me and kept me pinned, the sole of his boot pressed to my chest. But he smiled when he looked down at me.

"I understand the need to cut back, Tavi, I do. And I'm not going to be the heartless taskmaster who forces you to do more than you can handle. How about we agree to see each other on Sundays instead? I can spare an hour or two for you then."

"Oh, my hero," I said, my voice dry with sarcasm. Onyx wrinkled his nose at me before holding out a hand.

Was it my imagination, I thought when he helped me rise, or did Onyx look the tiniest bit upset about the change?

12

I clung tightly to the idea of seeing Mike this weekend, to the point where it became the only bright spot in my future. Each day, each hour, became an obstacle to hurdle over in order to spend time with the boy I liked.

The boy I could never be with.

But I scrubbed *that* thought out of my head. Everything standing between us I reproachfully ignored.

The rest of the school week passed in a constant battering of tutoring, schoolwork, and kitchen work. Over and over and over again. I spent all of Friday and most of Saturday trying to catch up on assignments to stay ahead of the game, including some practice Juno sent home with me after tutoring.

Those? Yeah, I failed them too. All of them.

Still at my desk, with my butt going numb from sitting for so long, I glanced over at the bag of powdered brain boost from Raelynn. The brain boost helped, no doubt. It gave me the focus I needed to make it through the studying.

Damn, the bag looked a lot lighter than it had when she'd first given it to me. Had I really taken enough to make a visible difference? No. A couple of teaspoons this week, just as she'd told me, and nothing more because I didn't want to risk becoming addicted. Or risk any of those crazy side effects she'd warned me about.

My brain fog thickened and I shook my head, grabbing the bag and shoving it in the desk drawer. I didn't want to worry about side effects. At least not right now. There was always time later. In fact, that was how I'd gotten through pretty much all of my time in Faerie, by pushing those worries aside for another day.

I grabbed my water and took a long sip before putting the cup down. At least I'd made it through my homework without bending to the temptation. I wondered when it would all come and catch up with me. I had a bad feeling it would be soon. There was only so much I could sweep under the rug until there was no room left.

All of these things tried to come together in my head, and I felt like if I tried hard enough, I could almost grasp them and make them make sense.

I rose and stretched, then went into the bathroom, kicking off my pants and pulling off my shirt to shower. The reflection I glanced at in the mirror offered me a tired smile and didn't even care how strands of red hair stuck out at every angle.

The Fae were supernaturally beautiful. Some of them were unaware, but most knew they had the power to stop traffic. Then there was me. Not bad looking, but nowhere near the ethereal good looks of the other inhabitants of this world. I swiped a hand across the surface of the mirror.

I wanted everything to be *perfect* tonight. Mike and I hadn't gotten a chance to spend quality time with each other for months. My fault, I admitted, because I'd been trying to keep my distance. But he hadn't been trying to bridge the distance either, hadn't put in any effort, and I honestly thought he'd lost all interest in me.

I tried not to think about how terrible we'd both been at keeping our friendship alive this year. Then I tried not to think about the last time he'd almost kissed me, right outside of the portal to the Elite Academy. Or how badly I'd wanted to feel his lips on mine again despite trying to run away.

I undressed and hopped in the shower, set the temperature to scalding.

There was something magical about Mike, I thought as I scrubbed my hair. It had nothing to do with his blood or his title. It came from inside of him, from his good heart and his integrity. He was just a genuinely nice person who wanted the best for everyone around him. He always saw the best in me, at least.

What would he think if he knew how badly I'd botched the spells I'd been assigned to work on? Or the mountains of homework sent back with me? He'd laugh and wonder why he wanted me to tutor him in the first place.

With snow still on the ground, I didn't feel like using the last remains of my energy to maintain the temperature around my body, no matter that the other kids at the party would be doing the same.

Instead I rustled through my dresser for one of my old, favorite outfits. I'd worn it a few times back in the mortal world and always felt like a million bucks. When Mike finally came to my room to get me, I had on a thick burgundy-colored sweater over tight black pants, and boots up to my ankles.

"Hi!" I said to him right away. Feeling sexy, sassy, and more excited than I had a right to be.

He stared at me, his eyes raking me up and down, his face taking on an odd expression so unusual that it took me a minute to realize he was excited.

"This is a good look for you," he commented. "Very comfortable."

My face dropped. Okay, maybe I was wrong about the excitement. Maybe it was embarrassment. "Comfortable is a nice word for *looks like a hobo*," I said.

"No, definitely not." His gaze warmed. "You are about as far from a hobo as one can get. The sweater really brings out your eyes."

And now it probably clashed with my blush. "Well, thanks," I told him. "You don't look so bad yourself."

Putting it mildly, I thought. He always looked amazing no matter what he wore. Tonight, in a black shirt and close-fitting jeans, I could have gobbled him up in one bite, big bad wolf style.

"Are you sure you want to go to Coral's party, Tavi?" Mike shot me a pleading look. "Isn't there anything else we can do instead of socializing?"

"What do you mean? I thought you wanted to go."

He bit the inside of his lip, tapping his fingers against his hips. "I mean, we haven't really seen each other. I kind of thought it would be nice to stay in and have a little time alone. We could watch a movie, eat whatever we wanted. You don't even have to cook," he offered.

Yeah, it sounded amazing. I wanted nothing more than to do everything he said. Still, I had to deal with Coral because I'd given her my word.

I had to wonder why I'd agreed to something so stupid instead of telling her to back off. Definitely must have been temporarily out of my mind. "Let's compromise," I said. Mike didn't need to know how I'd already told Coral we couldn't stay long. "We'll go to the party just for a little bit and then we'll spent the next three quarters of our evening alone. Doing whatever we want."

He looked pretty pleased with the idea, which warmed

my insides further as a smile formed on his lips. Wow. Just *wow*. No matter how hard I tried to stay away from him, he drew me in every single time.

Mike held out an elbow for me to take, and we walked down the hall together talking about classes. Coral didn't live too far away from the castle, he told me as we walked. Her family owned a place a few blocks outside of the main courtyard with a view of the castle at all times. It suited her, honestly, because she'd always given me the impression of being a social climber. And that was putting it nicely.

Coral and her family were among the wealthier citizens of Eahsea. A step below the toadying courtiers who frequented the palace always on the lookout for more. Wealthy enough to have some control but not royal enough to hold an official title.

God, like Coral needed a title to lord over the rest of us.

"The Coldwaters are the same way," Mike was saying.

Ah, he was talking about the leader of his little band of fake friends. Arlyss Coldwater, who thought his friendship with the crown prince put him above others.

"Social climbers?"

He nodded. "Arlyss is the youngest of five boys, all of them having attended the Elite Academy. He and I grew up together, in a way. I remember most of the Coldwaters being present and accounted for during every ball my parents threw. Every dinner, every occasion. They were first in line."

I chided myself for feeling a trifle miffed at the way Mike knew exactly how to get to the Ferenze mansion. I reminded myself that he grew up here. These were his peers, his play-mates. I was the new kid on the block, so to speak. He led the way, chatting merrily about our classmates, and knocking once on the large black door before pushing inside when no one answered. Once the door was open, the sounds of the party assailed us, voices raised in chatter and laughter, and flute music the likes of which I'd never heard before.

The place was full of people, close to a hundred faces and none of them familiar to me. The moment we stepped inside it was a different world, one I wasn't completely prepared for and one I didn't really want to be part of.

Great. We were the last to arrive and everyone noticed Mike instantly. We wouldn't have gathered more attention had a spotlight fallen on us.

"Michael! It's good to see you, buddy." Arlyss the boy wonder separated himself from the crowd, a drink in hand, and clapped Mike on the shoulder. His habitual smarmy smile was in place, his dark hair perfectly styled and the rest of him starched to perfection. When I drew in a breath, I smelled nothing but elderberries.

Classic Arlyss.

I hated it.

"Where have you been? I thought for sure you'd be here when I got here." Arlyss broke off on a laugh before Mike could answer. "You just wanted to make a grand entrance!"

I was ignored entirely. At least it didn't bother me anymore. His initial ridiculing of the "half breed" had slipped into neutral indifference territory, which to me was better than hostility so I was fine with it.

Mike, surrounded by his full-blood social elite friends, seemed to grow broader, stronger. His shoulders puffed out and even his hair seemed a shade darker, like burnished gold. "No matter what time I arrive, I always make a grand entrance," he boasted.

Arlyss laughed. "Took your time about it tonight."

Mike grinned, though it didn't reach his eyes. "I didn't realize anyone was keeping tabs."

Arlyss of the dark wavy hair was a stark contrast to the golden prince at my side. I narrowed my eyes and noted

Lane in the crowd along with several others of the inner circle. The ones who constantly crowded around Mike at school. Good to see he'd fit right in at the party. At least Lane was civil. He spoke to me face to face without anyone having to bribe him. One of the nicer students at the academy but still far from being a real friend. Best of the Fakes wasn't a title to aspire to.

I tried to catch Mike's attention to tell him I was getting a drink. But I couldn't compete with Arlyss without jumping up and down and screeching. So I made my way through the packed hallway and into the heart of the home. The room opened up into a cathedral-like living space with flames roaring in the depths of a fireplace even larger than the king's own. The mantelpiece alone must have weighed a thousand pounds, carved from stone quarried directly out of the surroundings mountains if I had to guess.

I veered right, toward the massive display of faerie and elven delicacies laid out. A fountain of ambrosia trickled down in three layers at the center of the table. Might as well. I mean, I'd take whatever I could get to soothe these nerves. I didn't do well with large crowds and I never had. There must be more people packed into this house than the entirety of the Elite Academy enrollment.

I helped myself to a glass of ambrosia and the first sip warmed everything inside of me. Ten more minutes and I'd grab Mike. Long enough to put in a proper appearance as I'd promised. And then he was all mine...

My mind conjured a picture of the two of us snuggled together—anywhere, it didn't matter—his arms around me. When I turned around, still clasping the glass in my hands, I saw Coral like a bright beacon in the center of the room. So much for me feeling comfortable and appealing tonight. I'd way underestimated the dress code. She'd gone to the extreme and clad her perfect form in a dress the same gold color as Mike's hair.

My face twisted into a scowl. Coincidence? I didn't think so.

The dress left most of her shoulders and chest bare, hugging her curves and trailing down into a pool of fabric on the floor. Even the dress I'd worn to the Solstice Ball paled in comparison to this gown. Real jewels were sewn into the seams and reflected the glittering firelight.

"You don't like her, do you?"

I nearly choked on my ambrosia at the question, but Mike saved me by smacking me on the back. When had he found me? I didn't even notice his approach.

"How did you know?" I croaked, looking up at him through teary eyes.

"You know, intuition," he said with a laugh. "You've hidden it well but I know you. You're the kind of girl who doesn't give the time of day to someone she doesn't find redeemable."

"Actually, I don't think I've hidden my dislike at all. At least I can say it is mutual and Coral knows where we stand with each other."

Mike took a sip of his own ambrosia, keeping eye contact with me. "Which begs the question why you wanted to come here tonight."

"I'm a sucker for punishment?" I suggested saucily.

"Ha! Yes, this I know. How long do you want to stay?"

Was it possible to leave right now? As far as I could tell, Coral hadn't even seen Mike, but in my mind we'd stepped through the door and thus I'd upheld my end of the... bargain? No, not bargain, because I wasn't getting anything out of it and a bargain benefited both parties, right?

"I'm ready to go whenever you say," I told him and took another sip. Like liquid fire. Ambrosia was powerful stuff, much more potent than normal alcohol. I'd have to watch how much I drank or I'd put myself squarely in line for a night of bad decision making.

Then I looked up at Mike and saw his smile. Would a night of bad decision making be such a terrible thing? Suddenly I didn't think so.

"I say we should help ourselves to some food, a little more of this," Mike shook his empty glass, "and then we make a run for it. Those are all the typical date components, anyway."

He thought I didn't register how he'd sidled closer. Trying to be sly. Like I didn't notice. Even if I'd had my eyes closed, my body would have recognized his nearness. Every fiber of me acknowledged his presence. "Is this a date?" I asked coyly.

He also thought I didn't see how his fingers twitched at the word. "It depends on how you feel about the word. And about having one with me."

Ah, the feeling when his voice dropped low, skittering along my nerves in a delicious way. I liked the idea more than I liked the way he looked at me. Which was *a lot*. The two of us on a date...

Yes. A hundred thousand times, yes.

"At the moment I feel pretty good about it." I held my glass up for a toast, delighted when he touched his to mine with a clink.

"You two look pretty cozy over here." Lane joined us at the food table. He flashed me a smile and grabbed a plate to start noshing. "What's up?"

"Nothing for you to concern yourself with," Mike said immediately, straightening his spine. "We're entertaining ourselves in the middle of this free-for-all."

Lane grabbed a bacon-wrapped fig and popped it into

his mouth, speaking around the food. "Oh, come on. It's not that bad."

"I didn't say bad," Mike corrected.

"No, you said free-for-all. Which is equal to or worse than bad. At the very least you're comparing Coral's party with a circus. Which, now that I think about it, you might be right." Lane surveyed the crowd. "Do we even go to school with half of these guys? A lot of unfamiliar faces. They're probably friends of the family or relatives or something."

Mike sighed. "No clue. I only know there are better places to be than stuck here in a room full of...these kinds of people."

I glanced over at him, struck by the odd tone in his voice. *These kinds of people?* I mean, I thought about it constantly, but to hear it come out of Mike's mouth, and in such a cold way? I didn't really like what I heard. Or saw. There was a glint in his eyes, his fingers tapping the side of the glass.

I frowned. Something was up with Mike.

Memory thrust a picture before me of a tall auburn-haired man in an expensive suit in front of a room filled with other men in expensive suits. He'd had the same hard glint in his eyes. The same air of authority that compelled the others to listen to him and accept his opinions as if they were their own. My Uncle William was an excellent defense attorney. Absolutely cutthroat.

"Well, at any rate, I'm going to hit the rest of the buffet and enjoy the spread Coral laid out. She's really outdone herself, in my opinion." Lane shifted farther down the table and when I glanced over again at Mike, I saw him smiling at me once more.

"What was that?" I asked.

He quirked his head to the side. "What do you mean?"

"The quick switch. I didn't realize you were such a talented actor."

He shrugged. "Just giving Lane what he expects."

Mike didn't seem to see anything weird about his haughty behavior, or the way he so easily affected it like putting a coat on and taking it off. But it really freaked me out.

I finished the rest of my ambrosia and he moved to refill for me.

"Now, where were we? Ah, the date discussion," he said when he turned around, his free hand moving to my side and squeezing lightly. "I want to know how you feel about an actual, for-real date. I'm talking we pull out all the stops and we call it what it is."

I accepted the refill with thanks. "Depends on the date, I guess," I replied.

My blood was already singing from the first drink and I knew a second without food in my stomach might not be a good idea. With Mike standing so close to me, what was a little extra fire in comparison? My skin was practically glowing.

"Wherever you want to go, name a place. We'll take off and see what kind of trouble we can get into."

I laughed. "Knowing us, it would be terrible trouble. Except I wasn't talking about a place. I was talking about a *person*. I guess I should say it depends on my date's identity."

The ambrosia definitely helped the final walls come down and unleashed my flirtatious side. I reached out and lightly trailed a finger down his arm. Loving the way a tic developed beneath his left eye. I watched his tongue dart out to wet his lips.

"You are being very mean to me, Tavi. Very mean indeed. Teasing me."

"What will you do about it?" I wanted to know, trailing my finger back up his arm.

And so the flirting began in earnest. Still harmless, though, since we were in a public place with a lot of laughing and drinking and talking going on around us. Nevertheless, with the help of ambrosia—because while they might frown mightily on imbibing hard liquor, apparently Fae elders didn't see the harm in their children drinking copious amounts of ambrosia—Mike and I had a moment.

And then Coral showed up.

Coral didn't need to ask people to move aside. They did it naturally, twisting their bodies out of her way until she stepped forward like she had a spotlight all her own. Her elegant gown dazzled the eye and drew everyone's attention to her. So chic, so sophisticated.

And of course there I was looking *comfortable*.

"Prince Michael," she cooed. Elegantly, of course. She did everything elegantly, even inserting herself elegantly into a private conversation. "It's so wonderful of you to join us. I hadn't realized you'd arrived."

She, like Arlyss, did not acknowledge me. I still didn't care. What bothered me more? The way her gaze fell proprietarily on Mike.

"Coral, thank you for the invitation," Mike said. He reached out for her hand and brought it to his lips very gallantly. Hopefully it was just the custom and nothing more. "It's a lovely party but a little crowded."

"Say the word and I can have everyone go home. Everyone except you, of course. You're welcome to stay as long as you like. I was hoping you'd stop by."

I could have stayed too and fought her for a place at his side. My wolf wanted to. She lurked just beneath the surface of my skin with her teeth bared, prepared to attack, to defend her mate and her territory.

Nope, terrible idea. I needed to get myself out of this situation fast.

I noticed Lane chatting with another boy at the end of

the buffet line and decided it would be better to take myself out of the equation before I did something stupid. It wasn't like I needed provocation.

The ambrosia quickly worked on my system, making my head light and the sweater itchy. I found Lane more than willing to chat. From that vantage point I could keep a close eye on Mike and make sure Coral didn't try to make a move on him.

I knew she'd try at some point. I wanted to be there to intercept it when she did.

Lane was in the middle of a story about last year's Summer Games. I struggled to keep up and laugh when appropriate, express concern when appropriate. Offer up the odd comment here and there, such as wondering why the people here wanted to torture their children.

But the more I drank, and the more I watched Mike with Coral, the angrier I felt. He hadn't looked at me once. He didn't seem to care where I was or what I was doing. She had his complete attention.

I'd nearly had enough when I overhead the juiciest bit of their conversation.

"These are your people, Michael. You should be out there enjoying yourself," Coral was saying. "Instead of turning your focus to less savory outlets."

Me. She meant me.

"You don't trust my judgment?" Mike asked. The haughty persona was back and stronger than ever.

Coral backpedaled a bit. "I trust you to make the right decision in the long run, of course. Except I know how tempting it can be to let yourself be swayed by a pretty face. Where is the halfling, anyway?"

Mike waved his hand. "She's around somewhere. I'll find her soon."

I'd been *dismissed*. The word ricocheted through my mind until I saw red.

The effects of the ambrosia bolstering me, I slammed back the rest of my second round and shoved the glass blindly into Lane's hand, setting off toward Mike with a growl.

"Can I speak to you for a second?" I burst out, grabbing his arm.

"Ah, Tavi. There you are. Wonderful to see you. And looking so...casual," Coral said in greeting. Her smile was fake enough to be made out of plastic as she raked her gaze from my feet to my head. Apparently she found nothing redeeming. "Helping yourself to the refreshments, I see. You might want to go easy on the ambrosia. It can have quite an effect if you aren't used to it."

"Mike, *now*."

I went so far as to take his hand and steer him toward the fireplace where there were fewer people. Less of a chance for us to be overheard in the crowded room. I would have escaped entirely, but for some reason the fuzz in my brain prevented me from finding the door.

"What is it, Tavi? What's this all about?" Mike said, turning his full attention to me.

"You're being two-faced," I told him bluntly.

"*What?*"

Nerves crackled beneath my skin and I found, once I'd started this conversation, I couldn't stop. "You're performing for your shitty friends and it's really getting old. I thought you should know. You act like a completely different person for them than you do when it's just the two of us. I'm not sure why you want to but it's kind of crazy."

This time his gaze turned cold for me. I didn't like it. "Is that what you think I'm doing, Tavi? You think I'm putting on a show?"

"I think you're lowering yourself to their expectations. I'm not sure why you want to, whether you even realize what you're doing, or it's some kind of act you've been trained to put on because of your status. The way you cater to them means…" *Means I can't trust you.* Because I didn't want to be with a guy who switched his personalities on a dime. Did I?

Then again, this was *Mike*. This was the guy I couldn't stop thinking about.

And he wasn't assuring me I was right.

"I think you've had a little too much to drink and you're making a big deal out of nothing," Mike told me slowly. "I've been trying to play nice with them when I clearly don't want to be here. I said as much to you but *you're* the one who wanted to come. *You're* the one who told *me* we were coming here tonight."

I took a deep breath, knowing I'd tossed out too much emotional baggage. Emotions swirled and receded beneath the surface. Could I hold them down? "And now…now I want to leave."

Without hesitation he swept his hand out toward the door. "Go on, then. Maybe I'm not done performing for my shitty friends, as you say. Maybe there are still conversations I'd like to have without you getting angry with me for having them. What's going on with you?"

"Nothing is going on with *me*." I wasn't sure how to suppress these emotions anymore.

"Clearly something is bothering you if you're jumping on me for *this*," he snapped.

"This. Like it's nothing."

"It *is* nothing."

"Okay, fine, no problem. I'm leaving. I can find the door. You stay as long as you like," I said.

I didn't say the words I really wanted to say: *I'm sorry*. I didn't mean to call him out in front of all these people, and odds were good I'd regret having so much ambrosia when the effects wore off.

We'd already made enough of a scene to have our fellow students turned our direction, watching. Waiting for the final performance. To see if I would launch something at Mike's head or break a glass or whatever.

I wouldn't give them the satisfaction.

I turned away from Mike and headed toward the door, clutching my last words close to me.

So much for not letting myself get emotionally attached to Mike. What was he even doing with me? A few measly hours together and I felt like I needed to have all of his attention. And when he adopted that ridiculous cold personality around his friends? It got under my skin and made me cringe. Because that was *not* the Mike I knew and...loved.

Oh God. This was going so wrong on so many levels. Every time I'd convinced myself we could never be together, I'd actually been right. I should learn to trust my instincts more.

He could stay with Coral for all I cared. I had better places to be and apparently better people to be with.

13

I tried to remember that I'd done this to myself when I woke up the next morning wishing I were dead. Mike hadn't been the cruel one. All me. All ridiculous.

The headache, the sour stomach, the terrible taste in my mouth, all because of me and the stupid decisions I'd made the night before.

Rolling over in bed, I dragged the covers up close to my chin and tried not to face the window and the bright streams of sunlight trying to melt my eyes out of my skull. Hungover from ambrosia. I was such a lightweight, I thought with a groan. What kind of fool lets herself over-imbibe a drink she isn't used to?

The same kind of fool who then pitches a public hissy fit with the crown prince. Yeah. That was me.

God, I was *stupid*. Absolutely one hundred percent *stupid*.

I also didn't have a day to take off for a pity party and I should have been remembering my work instead of getting a hot head at Coral's party.

I used the little pot I'd magicked from the kitchen to make myself the biggest cup of coffee I could manage, drinking it straight up and making a face, then went in the shower to let the hot water beat some of the stupid out of me. Surely it would take a lot more than these measures. The shower did nothing for my head, but at least I had a plan when it ended.

Still wrapped in a towel and with my hair dripping down my spine, I went to the desk to measure out some of the brain boost powder for the rest of the week. Then stopped. Paused and stared down at the bag, feeling like the bottom had just been knocked out of me.

What the...?

The bag weighed practically nothing in my hand.

I didn't even have enough for the week, coming up half a teaspoon short. How was that possible? I mean, the bag had looked a little light last night, but to not even have enough for a *week*? Had I accidentally been too rough with it or something and the bag ripped? I checked it over, found nothing. Somewhere along the line I must have spilled some of the powder, or maybe I didn't close it completely and some had leaked out. Accidental. And moot at this point.

I *couldn't* do without the brain boost. Not right now, when it really counted. Juno expected me to be able to get through these past Trials without fail and so far I'd been a huge disappointment to her. I knew the brain boost powder worked because it kept me focused. I needed it to *keep* working.

I didn't really have a choice. If I wanted to make it through this semester, then I'd have to go down to the kitchen pantry to get more of the concoction. But if Raelynn caught me...

The word *murder* came to mind.

She'd specifically told me to be careful with the brain boost powder and would have a hard time forgiving me if I wasted or misused it. She'd been so adamant in her warning, it was a wonder she hadn't come up to my room to measure out my weekly doses herself.

I shivered. I couldn't take the risk of her catching me going for more ingredients. I definitely didn't need to hear another no-nonsense warning about side effects. Like I didn't already know!

Despite feeling like a pile of garbage ready for incineration at the dump, I closed my eyes and let out a breath to call my magic, transfiguring into something small, something with two little handy paws for grabbing.

A mouse. They were pretty smart and easily overlooked. I'd seen a few roaming the halls of the castle.

I held the picture of the rodent in my mind, wanting to cry or puke when my body began to shift. Limbs shortening, hair bursting through every inch of skin. My consciousness shrank and my senses shifted. Pain, a quick zip of agony, and then it was done. Everything settled into place. My whiskers twitched.

It didn't take me long to find my way down to the kitchen on the lowest floor of the castle. At least the mouse didn't feel a lot of the hangover symptoms normal Tavi did. Maybe I should stay a mouse forever. I could live a life of foraging and no responsibility, right? As long as I stayed away from magic traps and cats, I might even be happy. Who knew!

But then I'd never get the chance to see Mike again. Or tell him how sorry I was for acting like an idiot.

So...no mouse. At least not permanently.

I scurried across the kitchen floor, keeping to the areas where I knew Raelynn and the girls wouldn't see me. Wow, we really needed to clean more, no joke. It took little effort to wiggle under the door to the pantry. The ward fell hard on me even as a mouse, like trying to walk through a solid wall of cement. A hum of magic traveled through my tiny body as each nerve ending came alive. A sizzle of heat. The mouse didn't have the right vocal cords to speak the words to get me through the ward.

A stronger push of magic had my ears popping and then —I was through to the other side.

Things looked a *lot* bigger from this point of view.

A simple shift had me returning to normal form. I ignored the exhaustion and the pounding headache, staring at the shelf where Raelynn had gotten the Abrichxao powder. Time to get to work.

I scooped the fine white powder into an empty bag until it was filled. I needed enough to last me for a while, because after this I was ready to buckle down. To get serious, to study and to be ready for the Trials. All of it. Plus I didn't want Raelynn to know I'd been irresponsible. She wasn't too keen to forgive accidents.

And *certainly* no more ridiculous school parties where I drank too much ambrosia and acted like a fool. Shaking my head, I kept the bag close to me, tucking it between the folds of my towel. Luckily, whatever I wore transfigured with me, so no need for my tiny mouse body to lug a full bag of brain boost back to the second floor of the castle.

Talk about suspicious.

I spared a last look at the stocks in the pantry. *Stealing.* Again. I'd never thought it would come to this. At least Raelynn had given me permission to come into the pantry for other things, although she knew nothing about the other ingredients I was forced to pilfer for my concealment potion. She didn't need to know about the extra helping of brain boost powder.

And I needed to keep it that way.

∾

"**W**hat the hell are you doing?"

I squawked, falling out of my chair and landing hard on my tailbone at the sound of Onyx's voice in my room later that night.

When I glanced up, he stood over me with a furious expression, his cheeks red in stark contrast to his nearly white hair like someone had painted rosy dots on his skin.

"What are you doing *here*?" I countered. Anxiety spiked through me. "How did you get in?" I scrambled to get up. Using the desk as leverage, I stood and tried to push my rat's nest of hair away from my eyes. Somewhere along the line I'd fallen asleep, and I hurriedly wiped at the line of drool trailing down my chin.

Onyx tapped his foot in impatience. "How do you think I got in, Tavi? I came in through the damn cracks in the wall as a bug when you didn't show up for our transfiguration lesson."

I hissed, reaching behind me to rub my backside. "What do you mean, I missed our..." I trailed off. It was Sunday. Our new day to meet. "Oh. I'm really sorry." I vaguely recalled us discussing the change in days. "I completely forgot."

After what happened last night, it wasn't a surprise. If my legs weren't attached to me, I would have left those behind too. Especially considering how numb they felt from sitting at my desk all day.

But hey, silver lining. I'd managed to finish my homework assignments for the academy, completed an essay on hedge witches, and even worked through one of the spells Juno sent me home to practice. I felt pretty accomplished, considering the massive headache still lingering. Along with the massive exhaustion.

Too much drama in my life, I thought, staring at Onyx and his hard look. I needed to downsize. Drastically.

"You're sorry?" he repeated.

"Yeah, I am. I've been a little distracted and I really didn't remember we'd changed our day to Sunday."

"I find it hard to believe that you forgot about our practice," Onyx said. He crossed to the bed and sat down, which did not make him any less intimidating. I didn't really like looking at him taking up space on my mattress. "I thought you actually wanted to learn how to use your transfiguration. Especially considering the months where you weren't able to transform thanks to the king's lockdown."

I figured Onyx must take after his father in some respects. Not many, but some. The look on his face was one I'd seen on Kendrick's before. Unyielding. And pissed off. This wasn't a man you would approach on the street. He practically had a sign clearly marked on his forehead warning you away. Except I couldn't go anywhere. He was in *my* room.

"I told you I was sorry," I replied dryly, rubbing my eyes. Wishing I had the power to snap my fingers and send Onyx off somewhere, anywhere as long as it was far away. "I have a lot going on right now."

"Not so much that you need to skip out on our lessons. They're important," he insisted.

There was no good way to make him understand. "Everything is important. I promise you I won't forget the next one. I just had a bad night last night." I stopped and sighed, pinching the bridge of my nose. "Mike and I—"

"Mike!" Onyx interrupted with a scoff. "Michael Thornwood, the Crown Prince? You need to put him right out of your mind. Let him go, Tavi. You can never be together. You have to know that."

A chill shot through me. I didn't care how many times

I'd thought the same thing. Hearing it come out of Onyx's mouth made me furious and a little afraid. My stomach twisted and churned at his words. "Maybe, maybe not." I fixed him with a glare and Onyx threw up his hands.

"There's no *maybe*, Tavi. He's the crown prince and you're a half-wolf shifter. There is no universe where this thing you've got going on becomes a reality. You need to buckle down and focus on staying under the radar. *Staying alive.*"

He spoke to me like I was a child who couldn't understand why cookies for dinner was a bad idea.

"You break into my room just to yell at me?" I snapped.

"No, I was worried about you and had a hard time figuring out why you'd blow off our lesson." Onyx got to his feet, crossing the space in two strides to place his palms on my shoulders, fingers biting down. He was a good foot or so taller, staring down his nose at me, and his gaze pierced me straight through. "It seems I was right to worry. You're not focused. You're losing control.

"I'm doing the best I can."

He shook his head. "Your best isn't good enough right now."

I broke his contact and turned away. "And the last person I need rubbing it in my face is you."

"Why do you say that?"

I didn't turn back around when I spoke to him. Mainly because I didn't want to see his face. And I didn't want him to see mine. "Because we're friends, or so I thought, and I need my friends to have my back, not remind me of how badly I'm doing with my life," I told him. "Come on, Onyx. You weren't really worried about me. You just didn't like that you weren't in control of something."

"You don't think I care about you? You have no idea how

much I care about you. How I think about you when we aren't together."

Warning bells sounded in my head in a sudden alarm. I purposefully shied away from whatever topic he wanted to steer the conversation toward, then physically stepped in the opposite direction to give myself breathing room. *Not now, I can't take any more.* "You shouldn't worry about me."

His voice dropped into something low and soft and soothing. "Tavi, come on. I *am* your friend and I want what's best for you. I also happen to think that what you're doing here, in the castle and at the Elite Academy, isn't in your best interest. Michael Thornwood definitely isn't in your best interest."

I huffed. "Luckily for you, I do take your opinions into consideration. But luckily for me, it is still my life and I get to choose the direction." Kinda. Not really.

"I'm trying to help you," Onyx insisted.

"And I appreciate it. I do. Truly."

When I finally turned around, I watched him run a hand through his hair and muss the strands until it stood out around his face in a halo of white. "I do care about you, more than you know," he said. "More than a friend."

The warning bells reached a new level, blaring at me. "Onyx—"

"You're the first woman in my life who I feel I can truly let my guard down around," he said. "I don't have to pretend with you. And to me, that means something. It means something *special*. You have to understand where I'm coming from."

The look in his eyes...the loneliness...and worse.

The hope. The hope was much worse.

"Don't," I pleaded, shaking my head through a sliver of gut-twisting anxiety. "*Please* don't."

"I can't stop myself. I can't stop feeling this way and

worrying about you and wanting what's best for you. Can you blame me when I feel that the best for you is to be with me?"

"I-I had no idea..."

"I didn't want to scare you off, considering everything you've been through with my...my father." Onyx spat out the word. "I can't keep it to myself anymore, Tavi. Especially not when you're missing our meetings without any word."

This was an area I didn't want to go, not right now. Probably not ever. Onyx was an attractive man, yes, and we were friends. But—

Yeah, but. A big, blond, unsuitable *but*.

My heart was taken and there was no going back.

"I'm sorry, Onyx. Truly sorry. But with everything going on right now, my life is too busy to split into any more pieces. If you aren't okay with what I have going on, and with me missing practices sometimes..." I paused, knowing he would hate this next part. "...then maybe we should just end our relationship for good."

Onyx didn't say anything more after that. There wasn't much left to say, really. I watched him transfigure in the blink of an eye, watched him fly straight out the open window in moth form before I could open my mouth to ask him to wait and let me explain.

I'd either hear from him again or I wouldn't. It made me sick, regardless.

My mentor, the son of my fated mate, had a crush on me. He'd revealed his feelings. And I'd stomped on them.

I could only hope I wouldn't come to regret it.

14

————

January passed in a blur, and between tutoring with Juno, an increased class load, continuing to work in the kitchen, and doing my weekly rounds with the Claw & Fang, I didn't have enough room to breathe. School, work, repeat. Soon my worries took a backseat and eventually Onyx and I came to a tentative truce. We resumed our once a week training sessions.

It wasn't the same. I wasn't sure it would ever be the same, and at first he didn't even want to look me in the eye. No matter what we said to each other, now there was a fissure between us. The easy camaraderie was all but gone. By the end of the month we were barely making small talk with each other.

At least there were no more murders, and the Claw & Fang leaders came to the conclusion that maybe the first three victims were an isolated spree and perhaps our killer had met an untimely end. One could hope. I wasn't sure I believed it but we stopped the rounds and that cleared a bit of space on my packed schedule. I'd take whatever break I could get.

Score one for Tavi.

Halfway through February, I sat at my desk, watching the snow pile higher and wondering how I'd gotten here. Not here physically but here in this wasteland of nonstop work with a decided lack of Mike in my life since our fight. Melia understood, and I found myself using her as a sounding board because she had an insane ability to listen, process, and always offer up the perfect advice.

Unfortunately, in this situation there was nothing she could do in the end besides offer an ear, because although I took her advice to heart, it didn't grant me extra time in the day.

"Don't worry about Mike," she had assured me. "He'll come around. He always does."

It was better to keep my distance from the prince. I tried to assure myself of it repeatedly but nothing I said ever worked. I still missed him.

February rolled into March and spring break finally arrived, giving me a much-needed block of free time where I could lounge in bed for an extra hour without feeling guilty about it. Juno gave me a few days off from tutoring, and Raelynn even let me have the week off from working in the kitchens.

Score *two* for Tavi.

It was a week of pure bliss. Five days where I could do whatever I wanted, whenever I wanted, including reading for fun. Except I found I didn't want to spend my break in my room. Not when there were so many places to roam. And roam I did.

I swallowed a laugh, walking down the hallway toward the hot springs grotto beneath the castle I'd discovered on accident. Although part of me wondered why no one ever told me about the hot springs, I decided to keep them to myself. Maybe they were simply forgotten, and if I inquired about them, that might remind others and they'd become too crowded to enjoy. And if I'd discovered something heretofore unknown, well then, I wouldn't risk giving their location away.

Clutching my book tighter, I walked through the corridors and down the spiraling staircase into the grand hall. Last year at this point, reading for pleasure would have seemed like no big deal. Now I realized I'd taken those lazy days of my past for granted.

I didn't notice the increased number of guards lining the stone walls. I certainly didn't notice King Tywin until he nearly ran over me.

"My, *my*. Tavi Alderidge. Here I thought you'd all but disappeared on us."

I glanced up and up and up until I met his eyes, like twin sapphires pulled from the Arctic Circle. A striking man, Tywin stood much taller than the average person, gray-haired and wearing his power like others did clothing. It crackled around him in a visible aura. Chin pointed, jaw line that could cut glass, his face gave no hint of softness. Everything about him was hard and heavy.

Today the Elder Council surrounded the king on all sides. They stared down at me and there I stood in my bathing suit and cover-up. Heat rushed to my face.

"I've been busy studying, Your Majesty." I kept my head dipped low and spoke softly, feeling absolutely embarrassed. Of all the times for me to run into the king...

"Wonderful. I'm glad to hear it," he replied with a low, unamused chuckle. "You were at the top of your class back in the human realm but at the bottom of your class now. I certainly expected much better from you."

One of the guards behind him joined in the king's laughter, the sound turning into a dry cough. Blood rushed to my head and stayed there until I nearly felt woozy.

"Yes, sir, I am aware. I'm trying my best to get my grades up and keep them up."

What else could I say to him? There was no way for me to defend myself. Not when he was right.

"Good, good. I'm glad to see you aren't allowing the dark stains of the past to influence your efforts in the present. After all, Madam Muerte's murder remains unsolved and the investigation is still ongoing. The strain of this alone would be a burden for anyone to bear."

I glanced up with a start. Did he...? He *did*, I realized when I saw the smugness on the king's face. He still thought I'd murdered the carnival gypsy and somehow gotten away with it. God, I could barely pass my classes. Did he really believe I could get away with murder?

Apparently so.

I kept my mouth shut, unsure how to word whatever I wanted to say to him and deciding silence spoke for itself. It was better not to come across as a smart mouth, as my uncle Will had called me, saying I had a real problem keeping the lips zipped. Well, yeah. Who doesn't when falsely accused?

With my gaze averted and nothing else forthcoming from me, it didn't take long for King Tywin to lose interest and bid me a good day. The Elder Council behind him was silent as they followed.

I didn't trust the monarch as far as I could throw him. Which wasn't far because he was built like an ox. Melia had once told me she didn't trust him either, saying he'd been in power for far too long, longer than any other monarch in recorded history. And I had to admit there was something odd about him. Just thinking it caused a buzzing at the back of my neck I could neither describe nor ignore.

What was his real deal? And what did he want from me?

The king ruled Faerie with an iron fist. Directly beneath him was the Elder Council who handled most of the magical issues and banded together to support the king unreservedly. Beneath the elders were the courtiers with their respective holdings, in charge of their lands and properties and the people beneath them, although ultimately everyone answered to Tywin. There was no democracy here.

Jogging the rest of the way down through the catacombs, I followed the wisps of steam into the grotto. A knot of tension loosened at the sight of the water. Bluer than any in the mortal world and drawing me forward.

Come on, Tavi, let go.

Yes. I planned on letting go.

As if the water called my name, I shucked off my cover-up and tossed it into the corner, holding my book aloft as I stepped into the heated pool. And sighed with contentment. Oh yes, *this* was what I needed. A moment to recuperate, to still the shivering in my insides and let everything slip away.

The unexpected encounter with the king left me feeling ungrounded. Vulnerable. Something about him always felt like it probed my mind for weakness and prepared to stab in whatever tender spots were found.

Like bringing up my failing grades. Talk about a soft spot. He had no idea, of course, what I'd been doing to try and pass the classes in his stupid school.

I *was* improving, slowly, I thought as I flipped to the last page I'd read, keeping the book elevated above the water. Not only would I get to the top of the class again, but I'd do it with style. I'd pass those damn Trials too and come out on top. Then it was only a few more years before graduation and I'd leave this damn city behind for good.

"I'll show him," I muttered.

"Tavi!"

I jerked at the sound of my name, splashing water and nearly dunking my book. Then my mouth went dry and my stomach swooped.

"M-Mike? What are you d-doing here?"

Gah, did I really *stutter*? I gave a little giggle to cover up the nerves, the sound ending on a snort. *Kill me now.* I tossed the book over the edge to keep it safe and dry and sank down until my chin touched the water. Probably red-faced to match my hair, too.

"I didn't realize you knew about this place," he said, walking up slowly.

Mike didn't have a towel with him.

And he was shirtless. *Shirtless.*

He was a golden god. He was sunlight and summer and everything good in the world.

And I was awkward as hell.

My mouth stayed dry and the rest of me began to tingle like I'd walked right into a hornet's nest. Especially when he threw his legs over the edge and let his body slip into the water on the opposite end of the pool.

"I found it by accident," I explained, sounding a bit defensive to my own ears. My mouth slipped too low in the water and some of the words came out as a gurgle. "I wanted a place to relax."

He shot me a tense smile. "It's the perfect place, then. No one really comes here anymore and I think a lot of the palace staff and courtiers have forgotten about it over the years. Mostly my mother and I come down here when we need to get away. And she's been so busy lately. It's good to know someone is making use of the hot springs."

"Yeah."

We stared at each other for a long moment, my gaze searching his. Neither of us had apologized after Coral's party, and I wondered if I would be the one to break first or him. Finally I couldn't take it anymore.

"Have you had—"

"What have you—"

We spoke at the same time and both ended up laughing. "You go," I told him.

"I just wanted to know if you're having a nice spring break," Mike said. His gaze searched my face.

I slipped off the submerged rock ledge I'd been perched on and floated in the center of the pool for a moment, steam rising between us. "It's been necessary," I told him, legs kicking to keep me afloat.

He nodded. "You deserve some time off. I know things have been hectic."

"You have no idea. How about you? Keeping busy?"

This felt awkward. We'd never been good with small talk, not really. Our conversations from the start tended to begin rather shallow but quickly dive deep. Even though there were secrets I could never share with him—like my bloodline—neither one of us was a stranger to the other. We'd always been able to communicate.

Except when we chose to freeze each other out. That we did really well. Seemed he was just as stubborn as I was.

Here in the grotto with the warm water working its magic, I didn't want to shut him out anymore. And it looked like he didn't want that, either.

"Look," Mike said, trailing one large hand over the surface of the water, making ripples, "I'm sorry about what happened at Coral's party. I've been giving it a lot of thought. I...I wasn't sure how to talk to you about it and I ended up staying away because I didn't want to make things worse. I'm sorry."

I straightened. "You are?"

"And you were right."

"I was?" Were my eyes bulging? It sure felt like my eyes were bulging.

He nodded. "Yes. I do change around my friends. I adopt this other persona until I'm a different person because I feel…*lesser* around them." Once the admission was aired, he sent me a nervous glance. "I mean, they always make me feel like I'm not doing enough or I'm not being enough. Which is probably just all in my mind but I don't want to do it anymore. I don't want to hide who I am because I don't feel like I'm someone special."

I couldn't believe my ears. "But you *are* special," I blurted out. Instead of giving myself time to be embarrassed by the admission, I bowled ahead. "You don't need to pretend to be something you're not in order to make people want to be around you. You're a great guy, Mike. People want to be around you because of that and not because of some persona you adopt. The *right* people will be behind you no matter what. You shouldn't have to change to impress the *wrong* people."

He always seemed to have loyal friends around him, I realized, thinking back to our time together at the Fae Academy for Halflings. Take Roman, for example. He'd been so worried about Mike's chances of making it through the culling—although I still didn't understand why, and no one wanted to tell me—that he'd killed to make sure Mike succeeded. Actually killed. As in *murdered*. Why would Mike think he needed to impress people now?

And when was I going to learn the truth about his time at the other school?

His smile loosened at the edges and his eyes lost a little bit of the anxiety darkening them. "Will you help me?"

I froze and every other thought left my brain, probably leaking out through my ears. "Me?"

"Yes, you." He circled closer to me, his arms cutting powerful strokes through the water. "You, Tavi. You've never been afraid to call me on my bullshit. I know I act like a rotten kid sometimes but it's better when you're around. *I'm* better when you're around. And you always stand by my side no matter how rotten I get."

"Come on," I joked. And I couldn't resist splashing him.

Mike's eyes widened. "I'm serious!"

"You want me around because I call you on your crap? That *sounds* like a load of crap."

"I'm going to continue this by saying I'm sorry I haven't been around much after our fight. I was hurting and acting stupid. I'll finish it by saying I would never lie to you, and everything I've said has been the truth. I'm better with you." He swam closer yet and my gaze narrowed onto the beads of water flowing down his collarbone and it shocked me how much I wanted to use my tongue along the same path.

Yikes.

"I'm sorry too, Mike. I'd had too much ambrosia apparently and I let my insecurities do the talking at the party," I told him. "Then I felt too awkward and ashamed to come find you."

"You? Awkward?" Mike shook his head. "No."

I wanted to send up a prayer and thank whoever it was upstairs watching down on me for this time with Mike. I wanted to jump on him and push him back against the walls of the grotto and kiss him senseless. Maybe it was the steam going to my head.

We circled each other, close enough I could touch him if I wanted to. Our legs occasionally knocked each other. The heat of the water was nothing compared to the fire inside of me.

"How do you suggest I help you, then?" I asked him. Surprised when my voice dropped into a low coo.

Easy now. I wasn't flirting, exactly. I genuinely wanted to know.

"I'm not exactly sure. But I'm going to need you to be around. Like, all the time," he replied. "You're the only one I trust. Something else I should have told you sooner. I've made up my mind."

Oh. Ooh boy. "Maybe you shouldn't trust me."

"Why not?" he asked, blinking.

"Because sometimes people are not who they seem to be," I admitted. "Maybe they have things hidden deep down they aren't allowed to share with anyone else."

Mike bit the inside of his lip as he decided what to say. "We all have dark parts of us. And it's up to the people we love to shine a light on those parts without judgment. You know?"

"I'm starting to know. And I want you to know I really am sorry. Sometimes I go too far and say things I shouldn't. You're going to have to watch me. And forgive a lot if...if we're going to be around each other." That sounded like heaven.

"I guess we can both step out of line sometimes," he agreed. "We might have to learn when to stay strong and when to bend."

"Then I think it's a good idea to make it up to each other. Starting now."

The heat definitely went to my head because I was definitely flirting now, and I didn't stop Mike when he pushed a hand against my shoulder, guiding me gently through the water until my rear hit the ledge I'd been sitting on. I didn't stop him when he reversed our positions, sitting down on the ledge and moving me onto his lap with my knees on either side of his hips. His hands were on my waist to keep me in place.

Ooh boy indeed. I knew it was a bad idea. I settled on top of him regardless, my arms rising to loop around his neck.

When his lips found mine in a kiss for the ages, I didn't stop him. I couldn't have even if I wanted to. And I didn't. A rush of feeling went straight to my head and on a groan I pressed against him.

He kissed the last bit of sense right out of my head and I let him. *Gladly.* When his tongue begged for my lips to open and tangled with mine, I swooned. He kept one hand on my waist as the other reached up to grab my hair. Kissing me like his life depended on it. I wanted more. I wanted everything.

This was the happiest I'd felt since coming to Faerie.

Happier than the first moment we kissed outside of the ballroom. Because here, it was only the two of us, with all our shadows in the open. Well, most of our shadows. As the kiss went on and on, his excitement pressing to my core and my body aching, I knew. This could really be something special.

This could be the end for me.

15

Bronwen and I ventured out into the chilly March evening with ice cracking beneath our boots thanks to a late freeze. Although the trees had begun to bloom, ice encased most of the flowers, freezing them in beautiful perfection.

With the world quiet and the murderer MIA, this would be our last late-night rendezvous.

Good. Fine by me. I'd take the extra time every week to study and maybe I'd finally pass one of the past Trials Juno kept throwing at me. She'd be shocked, and seeing the look on her face would honestly make my day.

I told Bronwen as much, surprised when she laughed. Like my academic troubles had become a joke. Still, I couldn't help but smile at her reaction. She didn't mean any harm. In fact, besides Melia, Bronwen was one of the most supportive people I knew, who never failed to cheer me up when my mood plummeted.

With spring around the corner, I was looking forward to the lengthening days, the sun shining much longer than we were used to. But Faerie wasn't like the mortal world. We had seasons here, but they could change on a dime. Whatever the land wanted to do, it did. With or without the permission of its inhabitants.

Except for that one time when I'd first arrived here, I thought with a shake of the head. We'd had terrible storms for days. From what Mike told me, those storms were not natural. Faerie had its fair share of rain and snow days, but nothing like the violent derechos initiated when I came. What can I say? I didn't belong here—and the land itself objected to my presence.

"Are you going to talk to me or stay in your head the whole night?" Bronwen teased. "Come on, girl, you've got to give me a little conversation. I can't be the one to carry the whole thing. That gets boring."

I chuckled, the sound ending on a snort. "Sorry. I've had a long day of overthinking everything. I'm a little tired."

"What's new there?" she joked.

And I was ridiculously head over heels for Mike. No matter how I tried to fight it, it was no use. I positively *glowed*. Surprised when I looked down to see my skin normal instead of lit from the inside. My mind returned again and again to our kiss and I replayed it in my head until it felt more like a dream than a memory.

We'd made out in the grotto for what seemed like hours. The magic properties of the water meant we didn't get prune-like skin no matter how long we spent in it, and with my book forgotten, I focused the whole of my attention on Mike. On his skin, on his taste, on the scent of him, all winding through me until I wasn't sure where he left off and I began.

I could have easily lost myself with him if he hadn't come to his senses first. I'm still not sure how he did it. The moment his lips left mine I felt like my mind had spiraled into the water, gone forever. He'd stopped us before we went too far, and by the time we finally gathered ourselves, we were joking and giggling like we'd *both* had too much ambrosia.

One thing was clear: I'd fought it for too long, the attraction between us. The desire. The pull like a tug through the midsection. I knew falling for him was a terrible idea and something I absolutely, positively should not do. I didn't care.

My expression must have given me away.

"Uh oh. What did you do now?" Bronwen wanted to know. Her elbow dug into my side. "Come on. I want all the details."

I debated telling her about my afternoon but I did not want to spoil it. Then found the words bubbling up anyway.

"I went to read down in the grotto beneath the castle but Mike was there. And we..." I trailed off on another giggle and let my head drop back. "We made up. We made up in the best way!"

"You *made up*?"

Oh. Yeah, I hadn't told her about Coral's party. I dropped my voice as we continued walking. "Well, he and I had gotten into a major fight at a classmate's party neither one of us really wanted to go to. It took us a few very long weeks to get on speaking terms again but he spent the better part of three hours apologizing to me."

The memory brought with it a rush of warmth and I hugged it close to me. Cradled it against my heart like something precious. Because it was precious. Even after everything we'd been through together, I wasn't sure we'd come back from that last fight.

We had, and stronger. After the make-out session we'd talked about everything. Before long we'd missed dinner and had to scramble to sneak something from the kitchen before Raelynn saw us. The two of us laughed and chatted like no time had passed at all as we ate the rest of the food in the library where we knew we wouldn't be interrupted.

I took Bronwen through my day, surprised when she stopped mid-stride and grabbed my hand. Her eyes widened. She didn't look happy.

"Tavi, think about this," she said slowly. "I know you like Mike and all—I mean, he's the crown prince and he's drop dead gorgeous, two things that definitely work in his favor—but you can't be together."

Onyx had said the same thing and I hated it as much now as I had when he'd brought it up. I didn't care. "Whatever problems come up, we've already shown we can get over them," I argued immediately, the smile still on my face no matter how the rest of me threatened to drop. "As long as we talk to each other. Because communication, you know, is key."

But Bronwen didn't appreciate my attempt to deflect her concern and continued to stare at me with her moon-round face and huge brown eyes. Begging me to listen to her, to listen to reason. "I know you don't want to hear me say this, and I'm sure I'm not saying anything you haven't thought of before, but this is a *really bad idea*. He's the heir to the throne of Faerie. He can't be with a half-shifter. *No way*. Even if you somehow did manage to stay together as a couple, you could never be your real self around him." She threw up her hands. "It's a disaster waiting to happen."

Yup, it was Onyx all over again.

"And I'm telling you I can handle it." Wasn't I already adept at keeping my true nature a secret? Hell, I'd been doing it all of my life, practically since birth.

She should know. She'd been part of the same wolf pack, hiding half of her own heritage from our brothers and sisters in fur.

"Girl! There's no way you can justify this."

Too bad for her. I'd already justified it. It didn't matter what she said, or how terrible it made me feel. "He *knows* me."

"He knows what you've *shown* him. How do you think he'd react if he knew the girl he was kissing turned furry under the full moon?"

He'd feel betrayed.

Bronwen started walking again, shaking her head. "Also, what about the king?"

"What *about* the king?" I asked dryly.

"Well, he's already suspicious of you. He thinks you killed Madam Muerte and he's keeping you at the castle so he can watch your every move. What is he going to think when you come out in public as dating his only son and heir to the throne? His baby boy? I'm sure he already suspects something is going on between the two of you. You told me that Mike walks you to the portal every day for school. Or at least he did before your fight, I'm guessing."

I deflated, not so much that Bronwen could see it, but the spark of happiness I'd carried all afternoon began to dim. Little by little, the more she spoke, it dimmed. And I found myself doubtful yet again that it would work out between me and Mike. No matter how confident I'd felt before, she did bring up good points.

Especially concerning the king...

Hadn't Tywin mentioned earlier how he'd expected more from me? He'd even brought up the dead gypsy from the carnival. So he hadn't let it go and he wanted me to know he still considered me a person of interest. He'd have nothing but bad things to say if I began to officially date his son.

Still, I didn't want to give up on Mike. Or the hope that one day we would be together for real, the way I wanted us to be. Connections like we had were rare. You don't throw something so special away. Not without the fight of your life.

"You make valid points," I told her at last.

She knocked against me. "Of course I do. I'm your friend. And I know you've thought of all of this already."

"True."

"What if you find someone else? Someone to talk to who can get your attention away from Mike?" she offered. "You told me once your half-shifter mentor is hot."

I thought back to what Onyx had said to me months ago about his feelings for me and I winced. "No. It wouldn't work out," I said.

"And things with the Prince *will*?"

I didn't answer. I followed Bronwen down the street, raising my gaze to the clear sky and the nearly full moon overhead.

It was nice to be able to walk in the moonlight without worrying about it cancelling out the effects of my potion. In the human world, the disgusting concoction I took would break if I stepped through any kind of moonlight. Now, I used my own magic to keep my shifter side hidden. Although what I wouldn't give to be able to change shape and run on all fours again without fear of discovery.

"Look at us," Bronwen said to break the silence. "Two friends out for a stroll together. Girl talk, camaraderie..."

There hadn't been any more murders for so long we weren't even paying attention to the patrol. It really just gave us a chance to catch up and chit chat.

"I'm not sure if Selene said anything to you, but the council leaders for the Claw & Fang are thinking about disbanding the patrols. I mean, nothing has happened in a few months now."

"Two," I corrected Bronwen. "Two months." Then let my shoulders sag. "It's a good thing."

"A very good thing. Although we won't see as much of each other."

I opened my mouth to answer and quickly snapped it shut. If things went poorly, Bronwen might not see me at all. The Trials began next week and I hadn't made enough of an improvement, according to Juno, to *save my ass*.

Not to mention classes would be getting harder from this point. I had a packed schedule with advanced potions, earth magic, charms, Faerie history...

A pit yawned wide inside of me and I did my best to pay attention to Bronwen afterwards, when all I really wanted to do was bolt off.

"I mean, we did what we could with the patrols. We kept our eyes open. I'm not sure exactly what happened to make the murderer stop doing his or her thing, but I'm grateful," she was saying.

"I am too." Our footsteps fell into rhythm. "Not that I don't enjoy spending time with you. I just have a lot of other things going on and I could use the extra time to practice my incantations." I'd told Bronwen about the Trials and about my piss-poor attempts to work my way through past examples.

She patted me on the head. A stretch for her, considering how short she was. "You'll make it through the semester. I have faith. And you know I'm always here if you need to talk."

We walked closer to the Fae Academy for Halflings sister school, the campus empty and the old stones illuminated by the moon. I thought about how it would feel to take my classes there instead of at Elite. Surely the courses would be easier than the ones I took and not the advanced levels of proficiency expected at Elite. They were training little Fae magic masters at Elite.

It also would have been much nicer to be surrounded by

different people. Like Flora, the half-elf I'd met when I didn't know my way around. She'd been *super* nice. Might have been a good friend if I'd gotten lucky enough to be enrolled with her.

A stupid dream.

Plus, then I'd have to deal with Persephone on a daily basis. Nope. Although if given the choice between Persephone and Coral, well, it was a tough call. Both of them were after my man and thought I was lower than something disgusting found under a rock.

I'd gone to school with my fair share of jerks but at least I'd gotten rid of one of them. "Thanks for the vote of confidence. I wish I felt the same way you did about the whole thing."

"It's kind of crazy how the king feels the need to test students at one particular school for the Seven High Values but not the other. I mean, I get wanting to have a graduating class with integrity, but these Trials kill people. What kind of monarch promotes violence among kids? And clearly shows preferential treatment for one class over the other?"

"You consider the Trials preferential treatment?" I asked her.

Bronwen shrugged, her coat moving with her. "No, I mean, if he's going with the whole violence among kids thing, shouldn't he at least make it equal? Halflings have just as much right to compete as anyone else. Although I think the whole thing is stupid."

We weren't exactly kids anymore; most of us at Elite were between 18 and 22 years of age. But I didn't correct Bronwen. "I take it you don't care much for the Trials themselves."

She shrugged again, obviously hesitant to voice her true opinion. "'I've been here long enough to see a few years of them," she said at last. "And I've heard Selene talking about them. I think it's distasteful and dangerous. It's obscene. Putting kids in danger doesn't show you how valuable they are to society. It's just a ridiculous tradition."

"Some might compare it to our coming of age rank determinations in the pack," I offered. "You might not remember the alpha games we played in the woods."

"Kinda. Sorta. Not really. It seems like the Elder Council in Faerie takes personal delight in making the Trials nearly impossible for normal people to pass. And of course all the school officials are on board." Bronwen held up a fist. "Yeah, great, kill our kids for sport! The ones who make it through will be productive members of society," she said in an affected tone.

"I didn't realize the Council was in charge of putting together the list of Trials." Although it made sense. They'd struck me as the sadistic sort, the kind who might get perverse pleasure out of torturing others.

"I think so, anyway. They have the most knowledge of magic in this world. It makes sense."

It did.

We continued our walk in silence, neither one of us willing to break it to speak again, both of us lost in our own minds. Too bad fate had other ideas.

A bloodcurdling scream ricocheted off the walls surrounding the academy courtyard. The hair on the back of my neck stood on end.

I didn't need to look at Bronwen to see her body tense. Her nose lifted into the air. My wolf stirred for the first time tonight and I bared my teeth. The two of us bolted into action. I was a step behind Bronwen, pumping my arms to move faster, climbing the stairs toward the courtyard with the snow muffling our footsteps.

A second scream ripped through the air.

Oh God, please don't let us be too late.

I wasn't sure what the two of us could do or what we'd face. I only knew we were close enough to do *something*. Walking away would go against everything I believed in. The screeches grew louder the closer we got to the school and when I rounded the corner, I stopped dead.

Big.

The half-shifter was in wolf form and bigger than any I'd seen before. The warrior form between human and wolf was naturally strong; it was the shape most often used for fighting because of its sheer brutality. Black hair stood out at all ends, covering yards of muscle. Between the melding of human and wolf, I couldn't tell who it was. I'd never shifted into half form before and I couldn't help the stark admiration for it.

Until I saw just who was being attacked.

Juno Ians was cornered, flashing in and out of corporeal form in an attempt to get away from the shifter, but it was too fast for her. No matter what magic she threw at it, the power bounced off the creature, disintegrating into nothing.

It rounded on her, jaw dropped and teeth glistening when it roared.

The sound did something to me. It unraveled a piece of me I'd hidden behind a steel cage, and when I moved again, I did so on sheer instinct.

I didn't think. I dove right in, transforming as I went, my human form melting away in a flash of black fur. No matter the consequences.

16

Juno was in trouble.

My heart beat against my ribs as magic surged. My eyesight sharpened, claws lengthened, and I merged with the wolf inside of me under the light of that nearly full moon, letting her have full control for once and hoping Bronwen had my back.

Completing the shift mid-jump, I landed on the other shifter and gnashed out at its neck, teeth tearing into whatever I could reach. Four paws landed instead of two arms and legs.

The shifter roared at my attack and reached behind to slash at and remove me. With my wolf in control, my reflexes were faster than usual, and I twisted my body to avoid the blows, landing on all fours.

I bared my teeth and rounded on the shifter with a growl. Definitely a male, I confirmed with my next inhale. Male and furious. Unfamiliar. Almost as though his scent was masked from me with magic. What pack did he belong to? I didn't know the smell but whoever he was, he had encroached on my territory and threatened one of mine.

It didn't matter *who* he was. I attacked.

My blood thrummed and boiled, gaze fixed on the creature and his enormous shoulders. He glanced once toward Juno and ignored her frightened, keening wails.

I growled, teeth snapping. *You keep your attention on me.*

I didn't take my focus from him although I felt Bronwen creeping behind me, silently moving to situate herself between the creature and Juno. He glanced toward her again and this time I yipped and took a step closer.

Neither of us stopped moving. It didn't matter where I turned, the shifter was a step ahead of me. He breathed in the flow of the fight and after my first initial surprise attack, he never let me get close to him again.

Too bad he didn't realize I had skin in the game. That made me dangerous.

We danced together with skill and precision, him making the first move and me attacking in return. My eyes did not stray from my opponent until Bronwen joined the fray. She threw herself at him the moment he moved to bite me. She was still in human form and in my opinion totally unprepared for the type of creature she faced.

I tried to warn her to be careful. The sound came out as a low whine.

She'd gotten out of the pack much sooner than I did. She didn't know the art of the attack. Maybe she hadn't been around for the bullying, the fights in the woods around our suburban oasis. Maybe she hadn't learned how to scrap, how to play dirty.

The half-shifter slammed the back of his arm into her abdomen and sent her flying before she landed a hit. In the second my gaze left him, he kicked out. The heel of his foot hit my chest dead center.

I landed hard on my side. Each breath felt like swallowing glass. Except now there was blood in my mouth.

His attention focused solely on Bronwen struggling to

her feet as I forced one inhale, then another. One hit and I felt ready to shatter. Great. Time to show him I didn't break easily. When I got behind him again, eyes burning and the rest of me in pain, I lashed out against the shifter, pushed to let him know I was there while attacking with my right paw. My back legs kicked at him in tandem.

He didn't pay any attention to me at first. He advanced on Bronwen with me trailing him. I snarled and whipped around to intercept him, leaping for his face. The shifter gnashed the air in front of my face. I landed a nip before he had me on the ground with his right rear leg. My head knocked into the snow hard enough for me to yelp, vision going blurry.

Too hard, my mind cried. He'd hit too hard.

I didn't know how long I lay there trying to get my wits back. This wasn't like past fights. This time I moved against a male in halfling warrior form. A shape I'd never shifted into before, and one I wasn't sure I could call now. I got to my feet, shaking my head, tongue lolling and pain shooting down my spine. Was there any way to beat him as I was now?

"Stop!"

Juno's cry had me turning to see Bronwen on the ground with the shifter's foot on her windpipe. Crushing. Her hands were on his ankles trying to get him to yield before he killed her.

It was enough to make me detonate.

I whipped around and launched myself at him, dragging my claws against the back of his leg with deep vicious swipes to get him to release her.

Just like we'd done while practicing hunting with the pack. Except this one? He didn't go down. No, he was furious enough to keep going no matter how wounded, no matter how much blood he lost.

He kept approaching Bronwen, his footsteps slow and crimson blood spraying from his wounds. And my friend couldn't get up.

He's going to kill her!

I made sure to keep between them, my gaze on his gaping muzzle with teeth like a bear trap. Worry soured inside of me until it blossomed into full-blown fear. Why did he keep focusing on Bronwen instead of attacking me?

My enraged growl finally got his attention and I dashed at him, ripping at his arm when he swung it in front of him like a shield. He stood a good seven feet tall with beige fur protecting him. Not to mention the claws and teeth.

I had to get through the muscle to get to him.

I charged.

The shifter tipped his head back and let out a screech of rage. Then swiped at the air where I'd been. I dodged and launched myself at his back, aiming for the kidneys. My claws swiped fiercely but slid right off of his ribs, basically accomplishing nothing.

Claws trailed over my shoulder but I didn't stop. I turned and nipped at his stomach, expecting to find softness there but there was none.

The shifter had anticipated the move and leaned back to kick at me with both feet and the full force of his strength. I saw the move coming but there was no time for me to get out of the way. I went sprawling when the pads of both feet caught me square across the chest, sending me flying. The world swam when my head knocked against the snow-covered ground yet again. I curled into a ball, fighting for breath.

The shifter came at me with those lethal claws raised and jaws snapping. I didn't move fast, but I moved, and the creature pounded a fist into the ground where I'd been.

At least I had his attention now.

Right. Then left. I dodged in a wide arc and landed a bite to his thigh. He snarled and backhanded me. I managed to stay on all four legs but only just. I had a feeling being hit by a truck would be less painful. I stumbled, blood dripping from my mouth.

He stared at me for a moment, bleeding from half a dozen places but not enough to slow him down.

That was when I knew I wasn't going to win. No matter what I'd learned from Uncle Will and the rest of the pack, I wasn't going to make it through this, not against a much bigger and stronger opponent. With my attention fractured between downed Bronwen and panting Juno, the best I could hope for was to bleed the shifter enough to get him tired. Then one of them would have to take over.

Focus!

At once I heard Uncle Will's voice in my head. The one time he'd dragged me out into the woods alone, just the two of us before the pack began its alpha testing, and forced me to shift without the help and influence of the full moon. I remembered how he'd tried to guide me to fight on even when I felt it was no use, to keep fighting even when my muscles refused to cooperate, my energy sapped, my spirit broken.

You are never going to win unless you pull out all the stops. You think you can come out on top with a fair fight? No, Tavi, you can't. They got your father because they took him by surprise. Ambushed. Nothing honorable about it. So it comes down to one simple choice. Do you want to fight fair? Or do you want to win?

Because the difference might be life or death.

Funny how the meaning of his words was so clear to me now.

The shifter kicked at me again and I dodged out of the way, transfiguring mid-jump so that my right paw became a hammer instead of a fist. A wolf with a hammer, ha. Bet no one else could do the same thing. I slammed the hammer down in the same place I'd bitten his thigh and watched his eyes go wide as he crumpled to his knees.

My bones screamed from the impact when I landed. But at least I'd gotten him on the injured leg, a vulnerable spot.

He screeched out a roar that I swore shook the bare tree limbs. I wasn't finished. Unless I won this fight, my friends would die. I had to take this guy down and I'd do whatever it took.

He grabbed me while I was distracted and jerked me toward his gaping jaws. Instead of letting him get at my neck, I transfigured again, shrinking my body down just enough to loosen his grip, then I stabbed my fist against his throat. Quick. Accurate.

He gurgled and staggered, hurling me aside.

I expected a return attack. I definitely didn't expect him to run away. Panting, I watched him grow smaller and smaller into the distance. This was my chance. I could follow him and finish him.

Then Juno groaned. I bared my teeth. Maybe he'd realized he couldn't actually beat me. As hurt as I was, I'd still gotten a few good blows in, so I felt like I'd come out on top.

I shifted back into normal form when she cried out. Her eyes focused on me, flashing in the moonlight, between her physical form and air, but still alive. They were both still alive. I grabbed onto Bronwen and stifled a moan when the movement ached. Crap, my chest hurt. My *everything* hurt.

"Bron, come on. Speak to me." I trailed my palm along her cheek. She was cold, but she was breathing.

I touched her neck and found a weak but steady pulse. She slowly opened her eyes. "Did...you win?" she managed to get out.

I gasped with relief. "You know I did."

Helping her to her knees, I checked her all over for

wounds and found a few badly bruised places but nothing serious. Nothing to be worried about. I forced myself upright, head dizzy and the rest of me ready to drop.

"Juno, are you all right?"

I tugged my pain around me like a garment, ignoring the bright spots of blood dotting the snow and praying none of them were mine. It took my mentor a long time to answer me, her butter-yellow hair looking dull. My gaze dropped to the arm she cradled against her and the smoke rising from the wound on her arm.

She stared at me with her mouth halfway open, as though she couldn't find the words. Bronwen limped over and stood next to me.

"What's wrong with her?" Bronwen asked.

I shook my head. "I don't know."

We stood for a moment longer, our breaths combining in a single white mist in front of our faces. It didn't look like Juno was even breathing, but I knew she was an air elemental. Things might be different for her. Then there was the smoke.

"I don't like the look of this. She needs help. Is there any place we can take her? Like a Faerie version of a hospital?"

Bronwen nodded shakily. "There is. Not like we have in the mortal world, but there is a building where the healers gather and tend to the sick. They'll know how to help her," she said.

Okay, think. I had to think even when my mind was in spirals. What happened, and what was the plan?

Juno must have gotten injured before Bronwen and I showed up. If we were able, we should take her to the hospital before anyone came to see about the commotion. We were running on the fumes of luck already.

"Okay," I said to Bronwen, scratching the top of my head and wincing. "You know where this place is? If you're able to get Juno there, I'll stay here and clean up. There's blood everywhere and we don't need the authorities figuring out the types of creatures who were fighting here tonight."

"That's a lot of work. And she doesn't know me. She won't trust me. You take her and I'll stay behind."

"Are you sure that's a good idea? I don't know where I'm going."

"But you'll have a better excuse if someone sees you together, since you know each other. Trust me," Bronwen insisted. Her brown eyes looked like they were on fire. "I can take care of this. I've been maintaining a shield around us anyway."

She had? No wonder we hadn't attracted an audience.

I didn't have a choice. With the next step mapped out, and comprehensive directions on how to get to the Faerie hospital, I looped my arm underneath Juno's uninjured shoulder and gingerly stepped out of the courtyard, supporting her even as my own muscles screamed for rest.

"Come on," I told her. "We need to go. Now."

It was hell walking through the snow with my injured tutor and the secret between us. There was fear in her eyes, her teeth chattering, smoke still rising from the gaping wound in her arm. But no blood.

I had a lot to learn about the different species of Fae.

Each step was pure agony, pain shooting up through my ankles through the rest of my body as I picked my way down the steps from the courtyard. According to Bronwen, the healing center wasn't far off, a few blocks over and down toward the café where Melia often liked to eat, famed for their zucchini blossom appetizer.

Man, when I told Meli what happened tonight...I didn't know whether she'd be pissed at me or applaud.

"Thank you."

Juno's voice came softly and when I glanced at her, her

eyes were watering. "Are you hurt very badly?"

She looked feverish and when she spoke again, her voice shook. "Yes," she said. "I don't know what happened. He...he took me by surprise. I didn't see him out there and by the time I caught the scent on the wind, he was on me."

When I glanced over again, hitching her higher on my shoulder to bear more of her weight, the skin of Juno's face looked stretched too tightly over her features, making her look fragile. Breakable in a way I didn't expect of her. She was always up for anything, pushing me to go harder, farther, faster.

At least she was still able to talk. "Thank you," she repeated, letting her head drop. "For what you did for me tonight."

I struggled to hold her upright, shifting to better accommodate her weight. "I couldn't stand by and do nothing. If we'd gone for help, you would be dead."

"I'm not sure how I can ever repay you."

I knew how. "You can keep my secret."

Juno glanced over at that, swallowing. "What?"

"You know exactly what I'm talking about. I fought for you tonight. You want to repay me? I only ask you to stay silent about what you know," I said. I tightened my hold on her and ignored my own pain. "Please, Miss Ians. *Juno*. Please don't tell anyone about me. I know you've been struggling with it and you haven't made up your mind. Yet. I'm hoping tonight will be a turning point where you...decide to keep helping me."

Her eyes darted back and forth across my face, her skin pale. Her lips were white and dark circles formed beneath her eyes. I saw the moment she relented. The moment when she finally gave in and let her guard drop. "All right, Tavi. I'll keep your secret. I won't tell anyone about your heritage. You have my word."

17

I worried about Juno and Bronwen, with only their word to protect me. Did I trust my future in their hands? One's promise to keep silent and one's promise to clean away the evidence?

I had to. Because I had enough to worry about already.

Someone was out there with enough muscle to *make* me worry, someone who apparently wanted to target the people I cared about. Although Juno didn't look like any of the other women the half-shifter had attacked, he'd gone after her regardless, and it felt personal. His attention on her and on Bronwen felt personal. Was it because of their connection to me?

And if that was the case, then who would be next?

Through the window in my room, I studied the shadows between the bare trees now beginning to bud with green. I stared down at the quiet meadow and found nothing amiss. The moment I'd gotten back to the castle, quietly shifting form so none of the guards would see me enter, I'd shucked my clothing aside. Stared at myself in the full-length mirror and memorized the roadmap of bruises. This wasn't the body Mike had touched earlier. This was someone new.

Someone with battle scars I hoped would heal and internal ones I knew never would.

Mike could never know the extent of it.

I took a long soak in the bath with a few of the herbal remedies I had on hand and a spell or two to promote rapid healing. Between those and the nature of my blood, I knew the bruises would be all but gone by morning. And I didn't have any broken bones.

A small miracle.

Then I was back at the window, watching for...I didn't know what.

The king could never know about the half-shifter terrorizing his domain. As the ruling monarch, he would have to retaliate by launching a massive campaign to clear the land of my kind. We couldn't risk word getting out, but if we didn't find the guilty party soon, it would be too much to keep hidden for long.

The light of the full moon cast the world below in shadows of silver and black. *Stupid*. It was absolutely stupid to watch for the beast's return, to see if he would come for me this time and finish what he started. But nothing moved outside in the courtyard and finally I went to sleep right before the sun rose.

Two days later marked the end of break and the start of the new school week. Although I couldn't say I felt better, I was at least a little refreshed from spring break and ready to deal with the Trials, whatever they may be.

Mike had walked with me through the portal and then found me between homeroom and first period, resting a hand on my locker and casting a warm smile down at me.

"Don't be nervous," he said at once.

It was his standard greeting at the start of any term, as though I might lose it if he didn't say the words. I took small comfort in them nonetheless.

I forced a nonchalant shrug even as every piece of me threatened to burst into flames at his nearness. "I should say the same thing to you. You looked a little green on the trip over here. Something on your mind? Like maybe the Trials?"

The Trials. He didn't want to talk to me about them but from the way he glanced at me, I knew. "What?" Mike scoffed, rolling his eyes. "I'm a seasoned pro at dangerous games, Tavi."

Dangerous, sure, like the one we were playing with each other right now. But I knew that wasn't the kind he meant.

"Oh, I'm sure. Which was why I had to intervene to save your ass during the Summer Games." I lowered my voice to a whisper for the joke. "Seasoned pro. Don't make me laugh."

Mike wagged a finger in my face. "No fair, no fair. You know they brought out the thing I'm most terrified of facing. Then expected me to kick its ass. I had it handled."

"No doubt in my mind."

I'd been so terrified for Mike's safety I'd transfigured into a bird and nearly pecked the eyes out of the muskie he couldn't see or smell thanks to a genetic defect. I'd gotten screamed at for my intervention, feeling like I'd done something wrong by stepping in. I probably should have stopped to think before I acted, but this was Mike, and I lost my head with him.

Still, I had no regrets. I liked him alive and I wanted to keep him that way.

"I need to know *you're* ready for whatever we face. Otherwise I'll worry and it will distract my focus." Mike adjusted his bag over his shoulder and those green eyes practically bored a hole straight through me.

"Well, I haven't been working with a mentor for nothing," I told him. Hopefully with more confidence than I truly felt. "Juno has done everything in her power to get me ready. She and I really developed a plan to deal with the Trials."

I didn't mention how I had yet to make it through and complete a past test or how I'd botched things every single time. Or how I'd gotten my ass kicked two nights ago and still woke up in the middle of the night in a cold sweat, swearing I felt the shifter's fangs at my throat, come to finish the job.

I squared my shoulders to adjust the weight of my backpack with a thousand books stuffed inside. Books I would surely need once they announced the direction of the first Trial. Luckily, they gave us ample time to research and plan our magic accordingly, I believed because they wanted to see the best we could offer.

"What's this? You've had to work with a special tutor, Tavi?" Coral sidled up to the lockers with the rest of the little elite gang in tow behind her, reminding me so much of Persephone, who'd attracted an identical group of little meanions within her first few hours in Faerie.

Lane and Arlyss were ever-present and both flanked Coral. A lot of students found Arlyss to be the most handsome guy in school. He stood over six feet tall with muscles like an ox and the disposition of one too. Sadly, he was one of those students whose big head was helped along by a reputation for being a very powerful Fae. A reputation built on truth. He'd won the Summer Games with ease and since then hadn't let an opportunity to remind us of his superiority pass him by.

He and I had never gotten along and the more I got to see him, the less we liked each other.

"What's this about Miss Perfect needing extra help after class?" Arlyss asked. "I thought since you were good enough to secure a place in this school, you'd need nothing and no one to keep you here. It must be my mistake."

For such a big guy, Arlyss was a worm.

I rubbed at my chest and the knot of pressure there. I knew I shouldn't let him get under my skin. He managed to do it no matter what I told myself. "A little extra help never hurt anyone," I said. "It was a decision the school councilor made."

Shouldn't have said that. It added fuel to the fire.

Even if I'd once been a stupid hopeful fool to think coming to the Elite Academy would somehow make these pure-bloods accept me, now I knew better.

Arlyss eyed me sidelong. "It doesn't hurt anyone when you think you are going to make it through the Trials. These are hard enough that even people like me have a hard time crossing the finish line. What kind of extra work has your tutor been putting in to get you ready, halfling? Do you believe you can keep up with the rest of us?"

"Well, when you spend so much of your time living in luxury and lording your superiority over the rest of us—"

"At least he's fed and comfortable," Mike interrupted, clapping Arlyss on the back. "What more can one ask of in life? Whatever makes you happy."

His voice had gone a little cold but I shook off the observation. He'd promised me...

"We certainly know who's going to make the biggest splash during the Trials." Coral slid closer to Mike and trailed her fingernails along his arm. Shooting a minuscule glance at me as she did. "Crown Prince Michael is never a disappointment. What plans do you have to dazzle us, Your Highness?"

The look she flashed in my direction told me exactly how she thought I fit into the picture. Great, super. Like her opinion mattered to me.

Except it did, and I didn't like the way Mike's eyes narrowed in speculation. I glanced between them, waiting to see what he would say, what he'd do.

"I'm expected to be the best and that's exactly what I plan to do, despite this being my first year competing," Mike boasted. "I'm going to give Arlyss a run for his money. Let's see who comes out on top, shall we?"

"Don't forget about us little guys," Lane joked.

"There always have to be little guys to make the big guys look better."

"And how much better you are, Michael. Better than the company you keep," Coral stated, flipping her hair over her shoulder. "When are you going to learn?"

I held my breath... Nope, there went Mike, slipping automatically into the persona I *really* hated no matter how he told me he'd try to work on it. Though he stood across from me, I reached over, pinching him in the side.

The quick snap of pain did the trick and he jerked. For a split second he looked ashamed, rubbing the back of his neck before saying, "Coral, come on. You're not being very nice. In fact, you're being a real bitch."

Lane sucked in a breath at the statement and the three of us turned to see Coral shifting up to glare at Mike. "What did you say to me?"

He narrowed his eyes and I watched him shrug off the cloak of the haughty persona. "The truth. I don't like it when you insult Tavi, especially when you think no one sees what you're doing. Just because no one has said anything until now doesn't make your behavior proper."

"You have some nerve calling Coral names," Arlyss said, crossing his arms over his chest. "She hasn't done anything wrong."

"I'm only throwing back what she is serving. If she wants to resort to insulting Tavi when she thinks none of us are bright enough to follow along, then it's only fair to call her out on it."

I leaned back. "I appreciate it."

None of *them* appreciated the change in Mike's behavior, though. It was clear to see on their faces. Without saying another word, Coral tossed the rest of her hair over her shoulder and headed in the opposite direction. Knocked down a peg, I liked to think. Then I watched Lane and Arlyss follow closely behind her. Fine, let them go. Things were always better without them around. I mean, Lane seemed like a nice enough guy but I could never tell with the students here.

Mike shook his head until a lock of pure gold fell over his face then shot me a wicked grin. "It's good you caught me. I was starting to slip. And the scary thing? I didn't even realize what I was doing until you pinched me. It seems I'm going to have to keep a really close watch on myself."

"Yes, you will," I said, "because I hate to think I'm going to have to be around you all the time to watch you myself."

"All the time?" His eyes warmed. "I thought we talked about this and you agreed. I believe I spoke to you about it the other night. Do you remember?"

Oh boy. "I remember."

He kept going. "What would we do to keep busy?"

Blood rushed to my cheeks. "I'm sure I could think of a few things. If you want to hear them."

I didn't get a chance to hear his answer. Not when two beefy hands grabbed my elbows from behind and whirled me around. My brain worked furiously to understand what I saw.

Blinking, I stared at the craggy monstrosity with skin like rocks and his—I guessed it was a him—sidekick, tall and willowy with Spanish moss dripping from the tips of her hair. Both of them stared down at me and made sure to block off any escape.

"Miss Alderidge? We're with the Faerie Bureau of Investigation," the rock man stated. "We'd like to ask you a few questions. Come with us, please."

The hallway fell silent around us. The blush on my cheeks turned from anticipation to flat out embarrassment.

"What is this about?" I asked them as my insides went cold.

"Like my partner said. We have a few questions for you and we can't wait for answers. You'll have to make up your class load at a later date. Hopefully this won't take long." The woman with the moss hair raised a hand and beckoned for me to step forward. Her cohort loosened his grip enough to let me breathe and I stepped away from the locker, hiding my shaking hands at my sides.

I cast a glance over my shoulder at Mike. And noticed how Mr. Meat Hands still hadn't let me go completely. His boulder fingers lingered at my wrist, prepared to grab me if I made any sudden moves.

Is this okay? I asked Mike without speaking.

He nodded once. "Go with them, Tavi. It's going to be okay. I'll make sure of it." He took note of the two officers. "Don't worry about anything."

Was it going to be okay? The bureau investigators, which by the way I'd never heard of before, dragged me down the hall without enough time to make excuses with my professors. I listened to the whispers and the snickers behind me.

Great, this would do wonders for my already low image here. Not to mention I'd be put on the shit list with my classes right off the bat.

"Where are you taking me?" I asked them on our way out the front doors. Figuring I at least deserved an answer there.

Rock Man looked down at me with what might have been a sympathetic smile. I couldn't really tell. "Don't worry about it."

Don't *worry* about it? Did he know me? "Sounds like the kind of thing terrorists say before they kidnap someone and they disappear forever."

The moss-haired woman let out a single dry laugh but didn't answer. Neither one of them seemed inclined to do anything except stare ahead with twin stony expressions.

They didn't release their hold until we made it down to the grass-covered train platform, still green even in winter. The train, shaped like a silver bullet with no rails in sight, was powered by magic.

Fear tore me open from the inside and filled the ragged spaces with freezing cold. Colder than the winter air. I didn't want to go inside. Inside meant no room to make a move. It meant having my control taken from me completely.

"Come now, Miss Alderidge," Meat Hands said.

They loaded me into the train without any further conversation. No names, no introductions. No explanations about why they were pulling me from school in the first place. I knew nothing, and the imbalance of power had my stomach rising sickeningly high. The train took off with enough force to send me hurtling into one of the windows.

Neither of the bureau officers moved. They stared straight ahead. Terror tickled the inside of my ribs. Was this about what happened the other night?

It had to be.

And why had I never heard about the Faerie investigative bureau or whatever before? Wasn't this kind of like the king's secret service version of the FBI?

My stomach dropped farther when the train rolled to a stop near the outskirts of the town, somewhere I'd never been before.

"This is us." Rock Man took hold of my arm again with his companion leading the way out. A few steps took us off the platform heading toward a squat one-story building blending in with the landscape like it was shaped right out of the mountainside. Grass grew on its roof, kept growing by a constant stream of magic, and smoke curled from a chimney. To me, it looked like any other Faerie house.

Which meant they'd probably brought me here to kill me. And of course no one would find my body if they didn't want me to be found. I could be officially MIA.

To hell with the questions. The king had decided I was too big of a problem to let live anymore. That must be it.

The woman opened the door with a spell and Rock Man and I followed her inside. I heard the click of a lock behind me and my throat went dry. Great, this was it. This was the end and I never even got to tell Mike how I felt about him. I mean, surely he knew. I thought back to the make-out session in the hot springs grotto with no little regret.

I should have gone for the full experience while I'd had the chance. What would Mike think if I didn't come back?

Glancing behind me at the locked door, I noticed the plaque with the business name in Fae hieroglyphs above the door. Great, perfect. Then I swallowed my shock at seeing the splendid interior of the building. From the outside it was deceptive, a nondescript one-story exterior. But on the inside...

In some ways, the cathedral-like interior reminded me of the great hall of the academy. The walls soared toward a ceiling reflecting the image of the sky outside, with arched doorways and a cold stone floor. We passed a front desk ornately carved of living wood and a chair upholstered in velvet.

I kept my gaze averted, swearing the walls had eyes that watched me.

Rock Man brought me into a small room off a long corridor and closed the door. "Miss Alderidge, please take a seat. Make yourself comfortable."

"I know how this goes," I replied.

And sadly, I did. I'd been interrogated way too many times in my short life to honestly be surprised by the process. Although I would much rather have had Doug Wilson, the werewolf detective, sitting on the other side of the desk. He and I had at least come to an understanding. We each knew how the other worked. He'd been called to the mortal academy many times before and we'd managed to form a tentative mutual respect. I wouldn't go so far as to say relationship.

"We're sure you do."

The woman spoke for the first time since leaving the academy, taking the seat opposite me and obliterating any fantasy I had about Wilson. The small table wasn't enough space for me to feel comfortable.

"Talk to us about what happened with Juno Ians the other night," she began.

I jerked upright in my seat. The cold feeling beneath my heart bit deep and settled into every piece of me. "What do you mean?"

The two of them didn't look at each other but I knew they'd already planned out their interrogation of me. They'd isolated me in here and first one would come with her questions, then the other.

"We know there was an attack on the professor on the grounds of the Fae Academy for Halflings. Eyewitness accounts place a girl of your exact coloring at the scene. We know you are currently under her mentorship. Take us through the events of your intervention."

So much for Bronwen's shield keeping the fight out of

sight. It must have gone down for a bit when she was knocked unconscious.

This was pure hell.

Nothing they found out should have surprised me. Except it did, and I found it hard to catch my breath.

What did the bureau know? How much of their knowledge involved me and what could I possibly say to take the spotlight away?

"Miss Alderidge," Rock Man urged. He scraped out a chair and sat beside his partner, facing me. "Tell us everything. We know you were there. You have no reason to keep the truth from us."

This was a far cry from how I'd felt with Detective Wilson. The werewolf detective didn't exactly put forward his best foot; he had a problem being gruff, but he was pack. He was familiar in a way I knew I could count on. Talking to Wilson had been comfortable, like I could tell him anything. With these two, I didn't know how much they knew or where their loyalties lay.

I wasn't going to be able to get out of this by lying outright. So I had to carefully pick and choose the truths to impart. "I was out for a walk." *True.* "Alone." *Not true.* "I heard screams coming from the courtyard and I went to see what was going on." *True.* I only hoped I could keep from tripping myself up.

"It was a risk for you to run *toward* a scream rather than contacting the proper authorities," Rock Man stated with what might have been a hard look. Still couldn't tell.

"What were you doing out so late? Alone, no less."

"I needed some fresh air," I told them, forcing an appearance of calm. "I've been working hard at my studies and sometimes I go out and take walks. To, you know, clear my head and stuff."

"It's an awfully long way from the castle to the halfling academy campus. You don't go there for classes, either."

"No, but I do go there to meet with Juno. Professors Ians, I mean. I'm comfortable on the campus. It reminds me of my time in the mortal world." My hands knotted on my lap. I didn't regret what I'd done to save her. But this definitely brought the microscope down on me further, and in a way I definitely couldn't afford.

"What did you see that night?" Moss Lady asked.

"I saw a large creature towering over Professor Ians. The darkness made it impossible for me to make out its features but it was tall, powerfully built. It looked like a beast."

"You expect us to believe that a girl of your stature scared away the monster? What weapon did you use?" Rock Man spat. More, I heard what he didn't say yet. Why had I not reported this?

"Nothing. I don't think the creature expected an audience. It was surprised to see anyone and bolted when I called out for Juno. I ran over and saw she wasn't in good shape because of the shock so I took her to the hospital. The, ah, healing center."

"Again, alone," Mossy stated. "You must be awfully strong."

I hoped Bronwen had been able to sweep our tracks clean. "Yes," I agreed without hesitation. "And yes."

"You weren't afraid?"

They stared at me as though the act would get me to spill everything. Except they didn't know what I'd been through, and they didn't know how hard I'd worked to get here. My lips thinned. "I was afraid, yes. But Juno sounded like she needed help. I overcame my fear in order to help her."

"And did you know the creature you came upon is

believed to be the one behind multiple attacks on young full-blood Fae women?"

I knew it so deeply the knowledge would cut me from the inside out. But I didn't tell them anything.

The officers took me through a long series of questions, wanting to know every detail of the encounter from the clothes I wore to what Juno and I said to each other at the hospital.

I saw their faces. They didn't like what I had to say. And I knew if I reached out to their minds, I'd have my answers. Fear kept me rooted in my chair.

"I find it odd, Miss Alderidge, how you've been in Faerie less than a year and you somehow find yourself embroiled in yet another case of extreme violence. Let us not forget what happened to you last summer during the Solstice Carnival."

"I wouldn't exactly call what happened the other night a violent incident," I hedged.

"Still, fascinating. Odd and...fascinating. No matter what is going on you manage to insert yourself into the uproar. Don't you think it's fascinating, Claribel?"

"Oh, infinitely fascinating, Rooker," the woman agreed with a nod.

Finally, names.

It didn't matter if I knew what to call them or not. My nausea continued to beat at me the longer I stayed in the small room, because I knew without a doubt they thought I had something to do with the attack. They thought I knew more about it than I let on. False on one count, true on the other.

I gripped the sides of my chair to hold steady. "Why don't you look at the Halfling Academy students?" I finally blurted out. "Some of them might not be what you think."

The two officers shared a look. "What are you getting at, Tavi?"

"I'm saying people have secrets. Maybe instead of badgering me, you could find the real person responsible."

I thought about the aggressive young half-shifter who'd knocked me into the wall, threatening to dismember me. How was he not a suspect?

Finally, the door to the hall opened and another officer for the bureau, I assumed, called the others away. He didn't look at me, and I didn't like the way he kept his eyes averted.

Claribel finally nodded toward me. "We don't have any further questions for you at this time, Miss Alderidge. However..." She paused. "There are more questions than answers in this case. The details are not adding up. And my gut tells me *you* are the lynchpin."

18

The bureau officers were not done with me. Not by a long shot. They let me go with an order to stay close (or face the consequences) and a promise they would see me again soon.

I believed them on both counts.

"Are you sure you're up for this?" I asked Juno as we squared off in her office. "I don't want to hurt you."

"Don't be silly, Tavi. I'm absolutely fine. I heal fast."

Her face was a bloodless mask and even to me she looked small and tired, her eyes dark. If she were human then what she'd gone through might have warranted a longer stay in the hospital. Although she never got into the details of her wounds, I knew they were bad. The creature had thrown her around and knocked a few things loose.

Luckily, like me, she knitted back together quickly.

I shook my head, remembering the way the shifter loomed over me while I was on my back. Definitely bigger than a bear in his halfling warrior form. One of these days, if I could muster up the courage, I'd talk to Onyx about the form. And how one shifted into it.

My gaze fixed on Juno. "I'm glad you heal fast, but I have

something to ask you." I let my hands hang limp at my sides, unwilling to engage yet, unwilling to do anything except try to stifle the sick feeling in my gut.

"What's the matter?" she asked.

"I was pulled from school by cops today." I'd missed my first two classes thanks to their interrogation. My teachers were not happy with me. "They didn't look like cops, of course. They said they were investigators from the Faerie Bureau of Investigation or something like that. They took me to a building downtown and they really seem to think I had something to do with the attack on you. You wouldn't know anything about that, would you?" I asked. "I've never heard of this bureau before."

Twin butterflies held Juno's hair in place at the sides. One of them fluttered its wings and she didn't bat an eye at the motion, holding up her hand to stop me. "Hold on, wait a minute. *Who* pulled you out of school? You really don't need to be missing classes."

Tell me about it. "Missing classes isn't the point. The point is that we tried hard to keep all evidence of our presence away from the scene and somehow the bureau still knew I was there. They said someone gave them an eyewitness account of a girl with my coloring and build. So someone had to have told them about me." I worked hard to keep the suspicion out of my voice. "You promised me you wouldn't say anything."

Facing Juno today, I wanted to rip into her the way I did with the shifter when I'd saved her ass. She'd given me her word. Made a promise. Did it mean nothing? My old pack mates would say never trust faeries. They were all liars and tricksters, intent on turning your life into hell for their personal enjoyment.

Being half Fae, I'd never agreed with them. And now I hoped the words were wrong.

Juno swallowed and my heart sank. Damn Fae. They made a promise and broke it in seconds. And stupid me, I'd trusted her, I'd gotten involved.

"Tavi, I'm sorry," she said. "Things are different here for pure-bloods."

"You don't get to say that to me." I bit my lower lip to keep it from quivering.

"It isn't an excuse. I'm simply saying it's impossible for pure-bloods to get away with anything under Tywin's watch. Not an excuse," she insisted again. Then sighed, moving around the desk to place her hands on my shoulders, unsurprised when I jerked away. "No matter how we tried to hide what happened, they *knew*. His guards *knew* when they came to question me. They came for me and I had to tell them the truth. At least, shades of the truth."

"You threw me under the bus," I insisted. Wiping at suddenly burning eyes.

She reached for me again, her hands dropping to her sides seconds before they touched mine. "I swear to you, Tavi, I *didn't* tell them. I never said anything about you and your friend being involved. In fact, I told them nothing about you except in general. I said there was a man in the shape of a wolf creature, much larger than me, larger than anyone. I mentioned I was woozy, my head light, and a girl with your description helped me to the hospital. I'm not sure why they think you would have had anything to do with the attack."

Why wouldn't they? I was still suspect number one for Madam Muerte's death.

I closed my eyes for a long moment. "How did they find out it was me?" I asked finally.

"I'm not sure how. But they always do. They always do, honey, but I kept your secret, I swear. They don't know about your blood status, any more than anyone else knows about you."

I saw the looming shape of the halfling shifter in my mind again. Saw those teeth, and his mouth gaping wide. That's who I was, too, underneath the human shape I wore here. Had I really expected Juno to have my back after what he did to terrorize and hurt her?

"Well, they might figure it out after today. They grilled me for hours. I missed classes. I missed everything." I took a deep breath.

"I'm sorry." Juno closed the distance between us and drew me forward into a hug. It felt odd, strange, and awkward, but I didn't resist.

At last, I released the tension I held. I wanted to trust her, I really did, because the alternative meant I needed to watch my back with literally everyone in my life. I thought I could let my guard down at least a little with Juno.

I supposed we'd see going forward. I'd have to make sure I didn't step a toe out of line around her. Slowly my arms moved around her and I squeezed my eyes shut.

"It doesn't seem to matter what I do," I said against her hair. "I always get into trouble. It finds me."

"It certainly seems to."

The more I thought about it, the more I believed Juno hadn't sold me out to the bureau. The king still harbored suspicions about me. If she'd mentioned a girl of any description, no doubt he still would have found a way to pin it on me, or at least make my life very uncomfortable. No matter what he said, he didn't want me to succeed, he didn't want me here. I knew it in my bones.

"Now." Juno released me. "We're going to keep things short today."

"Why's that?"

"Because the commencement ceremony for the Trials

kicks off at sixteen bells and we need you strong. Although I know your strength is not going to be an issue."

Holy crap, the Trials were tonight! I'd actually forgotten. I dropped my hands to my sides and Juno chose that moment to send a blast of tornado-strength wind at me. It knocked me on my ass, sending me skidding along the floor until I hit the wall. Blinking.

"What did you do that for?" I finally managed.

She shot me a small, hard smile. "To remind you to always be on your toes, Tavi. Because the Trials aren't going to go easy on you, and neither will I. Now stand up and let's get to work."

Fanfare kicked off the start of the Trials, with a large gathering held in the amphitheater where the labyrinthine maze from the Spring Games had been held. I remembered the space then with hedges and monsters in place for Elite Academy students to fight their way through.

Tonight, the stands were filled with people, the screaming, stomping masses of Fae and elves and pixies who enjoyed nothing more than to watch a bloodthirsty fight to the death. Especially when it involved young adults.

I even saw a few harpies in the stands, with their wings flattened against their backs and their claws gleaming in the evening light. As though they were anticipating the bloodshed, eager to see how the students tore each other apart.

Climbing toward the top rows of the stadium where Melia and Bronwen waited for me, I'd never felt more lost in my life. I'd always felt in control, planning my next steps carefully because I had to be cautious to protect my secrets. Now I'd finally gotten to one of my end goals: I'd made it to Faerie. And I *hated* it here.

"There you are!" Melia called out when I came into view. She stood up, waving her arms to get my attention. "What took you so long? I thought you said you were on your way."

"Sorry, I ran a little late talking to Juno," I told her, scooting in toward the seat she'd saved for me. "Took me longer than I thought to break away."

"You're fine, girl, you're fine. Although we had a hell of a time keeping this space for you. There were a ton of people looking for a last-minute seat and I had to get a little nasty with some of them." Melia flexed a muscle looking little bigger than a twig. "Show them who is boss."

Bronwen nodded emphatically, her brown hair in twin braids on either side of her face. "Everyone came out tonight to see the show! It's sure to be good."

"Yeah, I noticed." My stomach dropped to somewhere around the bottom row and didn't come back.

It seemed like everyone from town and maybe some of the neighboring cities had turned out for the kickoff of the Trials. It pleased me to see Bronwen and Melia getting along. I'd introduced the two of them several months ago, hoping the three of us would be able to hang out. It seemed like a silver lining.

Tonight, the air above the amphitheater had been magicked to keep the cold at bay and most everyone wore clothes more appropriate for summer. Melia had on a pair of jeans and a tank top while Bronwen looked like she was heading to the beach with shorts and sandals. I'd grabbed whatever was handy on my way out the door, packing it into a bag and changing after meeting with Juno.

It was hard to hear above the roar of the crowd. Especially when King Tywin stepped out from between a pair of stone pillars. He raised an arm for silence to address the stands. A large golden crown sat on top of his head, with precious gemstones gleaming in it. He wore a robe to match in a striking yellow color with white fur trim around the top and sides. It trailed behind him as he strode toward the center of the stage.

As a royal, Mike had to be up on the stage with the rest of his family. He and his mother stood behind King Tywin at a proper distance, their matching blond heads bowed as he prepared to speak.

I sure did miss Mike.

When I glanced over at Bronwen and Melia, their gazes were glued to the stage and the king, unable to look away.

A wave of power pulsed outward and at once the quiet became suffocating. Any move made me uncomfortable, my clothes itchy against my skin. It felt like Tywin had his eyes on me and only me. He'd somehow found me in the stands.

True or not, I felt the pressure of his attention.

King Tywin addressed the crowd with his arms thrown wide and a smile on his face. I held my breath waiting to hear what he would have to say. Wondering if I would like or hate the words ready to pour out of his mouth.

"Welcome, citizens of Eahsea, to the Elite Trials!" the king's voice boomed out, and from the shadows I could make out the hazy outlines of the council waiting in the wings behind him.

The king was not a small man, nor was he a Viking, but with his elaborate crown reaching toward the heavens and his regal robe, he looked like a god tonight. He looked untouchable and all-powerful.

I kept my hands in my lap to keep from fidgeting. Everyone seemed so excited. So ready for this to take place. Were none of them anxious? Nervous about what could happen to people they knew, children and brothers and sisters?

The king continued. "It is my great privilege to welcome you to the first official night of the Elite Trials. The students at the Elite Academy have been graced with magic above and beyond normal. Through these trials, their abilities will be honed, their ingenuity tested, and their true courage revealed." He stopped. Paused for effect and measured the temperament of the crowd. "Not only will they prove themselves to be productive members of our world, they will show their mettle and build character."

I blinked, wondering how bad it would be to start laughing in front of everyone. When would the king get to the part about *dying*? About the young Fae in the past who'd lost their lives because of these ridiculous tests? Probably never, because no one wanted to talk about what would happen if you weren't strong enough or fast enough or brave enough.

"This is an opportunity for us to come together as a community. A chance for our youth to prove themselves, to see how well they measure up to our Seven High Values: Balance, Bravery, Cleverness, Creativity, Fairness, Justice, Respect. These Trials are not for the faint of heart. Some may be hurt."

Wow. He'd come closer to the topic of dying than I'd thought he would.

Tywin clasped his hands together in front of his chest and continued as though he hadn't just casually swept "death" under the rug of "hurt." "We follow in a long line of tradition. The students attending the academy know the risks they are taking in their eagerness to prove themselves. We look forward to watching their progress and know they will make us proud."

Give me a break. I thought the king was full of crap. So full of crap his eyes should have been brown instead of blue. The scary thing? The crowd totally agreed with him. They clapped and cheered and stomped their feet right on cue in every place he expected a reaction.

Even scarier was when I glanced at Bronwen and Melia to find them staring at the king, and not with the twin expressions of horror I thought I'd see on their faces. Instead, they were caught up in it, intrigued. They were watching, listening, as if what King Tywin had to say would make a difference in the sun rising in the morning. They actively wanted to hear what he had to say.

I crossed my arms over my chest. Something inside of me hardened as I turned back to the stage to pretend to listen to the rest of the speech. My attention zeroed in on the king's final proclamation to let the trials begin.

A zip of fire streaked across the stage behind him, followed by a second. Then a third, magic sent out from the council and guards. The tendrils wound their way into the air and exploded overhead in a display of showering fireworks. The mortal realm should be jealous of fae fireworks, I decided on the spot, tilting my face skyward to watch the exhibition.

The colors alone were all shades of the spectrum and some I couldn't put a name to. They curled through clouds, sparks showering down on the earth and the awed crowd.

Faerie magic. There was nothing like it in the mortal world. We watched the swirling colors, the sparks, and the flames, changing direction and shape in the air as if they had minds of their own.

"Wow," Bronwen murmured.

I flashed her a small smile. Sure, *wow*. She was excited for the show, while I focused on what it meant. The start to the Trials. I was forced to participate. She was not.

"*Look!*"

The lone voice cut over the hushed coos of the crowd and it didn't take long for me to see why.

Sparks had somehow gathered and now rained down on a tree near the raised royal dais, alighting the tinder-dry leaves so that the trunk, the limbs, *everything* burst into flame. It shouldn't have happened. Had never happened before, I knew without anyone telling me.

The gasps from the crowd quickly turned into screams as officials and guards surrounding the royal family rushed forward with their hands in the air, sending waves of magic toward the flames.

"Oh shit!" Melia burst out.

"Well," I said as I turned toward Melia and Bronwen, "*that* can't be a good omen."

19

I sat across the library table from Mike and my entire body ached. Deep down. All the way through my cells to my bones. It meant I was still alive, which I might not be able to say in three days. Because why? We'd been given our task for the first Trial, and three days in which to research, practice, and prepare before it would take place on Friday.

All other classes were suspended for the time being. Thank goodness, although I knew a few of the professors were not happy about the pause, my charms teacher in particular. She'd glared around at the class and promised homework the moment we returned.

Mike leaned across the table, silhouetted against the window where the midday sun spilled golden rays over everything. "What do you think?" he asked.

A muscle tensed in his jaw and I knew he was just as nervous as I was. At least I knew that no matter what trouble we got into with this latest test, he would come through with me. He wouldn't let me go alone.

Unlike normal days, the library was packed with students doing their own research. Our first test?

Justice.

For the first trial, every student had to find a way to access the arcane power of the earth and grow a plant. Not just any plant, but a certain species of tree all but wiped out in Faerie thanks to over-harvesting. And we had to find a way to keep the tree alive without being attached to our own life force. Heaven forbid you ask why no one else was accomplishing the task. The school council hadn't had anything to say on the matter during our orientation this morning.

In fact, Headmaster Cyrus remained closed-mouthed on anything besides the barest minimum of information. Find the seed, grow the plant, don't let it die. And don't let it kill you.

Not an easy task by any means. If we managed to grow the tree without first detaching from it, we could expend our own life energy and waste away to nothing.

What a great first start.

I tapped my fingers against the stack of books in front of me. "I think we'd better get to work or else we are going to be sunk before we even begin." I pushed aside the massive brain fog making it impossible to focus.

"We're going to figure out a way to beat this," Mike said firmly.

"They don't want us to find a way." My stomach dropped as I gave voice to my doubt. As though suddenly the whole point of these Trials made sense to me. They made it hard not because they wanted the best of the best to emerge, but because they delighted in our failure. At least I wasn't alone in it this time.

Mike groaned, but I couldn't tell if he agreed or not. "Well, at least they've given us a little bit of time to figure it out. Although this library might not be our best bet."

I shrugged. "Do you have a better idea?"

"I have several ideas, one of which has to do with using the royal library to find a way to beat the Trial."

"Have you ever been involved in the Trials before?" I asked him.

"I've seen a few, yeah. I mean, my father officiates the opening ceremony, so I've had no choice but to be up there with him. They're brutal and bloodthirsty and the people demand more every time. This is my first year actually participating, though."

"You had a hard enough time making it through the cullings," I teased. "How are you going to do now?"

"Well..." Mike winked. "I have a secret weapon."

"Another artifact to boost your power?"

"No, *you*."

I glanced up at the warmth in his voice and watched Mike come around the side of the table toward me. At once, every inch of me lit at his nearness. I remembered the kisses, the hardness of his body against mine. "You had me then, too. Tutoring you. It didn't help much in the long run."

"Ah, true." He scratched his chin, looking thoughtful.

"And I definitely think you're right. If there are going to be books on arcane magic, spells they don't teach us in class, then we aren't going to find them here, especially not with everyone else looking," I murmured.

"At least with two sets of eyes looking it should make the research go faster."

Glancing up at him, I saw him watching me. I wanted to kiss him. Right there in front of everyone I wanted to slide my arms around his neck and never let him go.

God, he was a distraction. I knew that if we kissed, he'd taste familiar. Welcome.

"We'll have to do it off the clock." A small fire kindled in my stomach when he reached out a hand and stroked his thumb over my cheek. "I mean, they aren't going to let us leave school to do outside research."

"I can pull the prince card if you really want me to."

I giggled. "Maybe we should keep the prince card in our back pocket in case we *really* need it," I whispered. "I'll have time tonight after I get off kitchen duty."

Mike moaned softly as he shook his head. "You really don't belong in the kitchen. I'm so sorry about that, Tavi."

"I've almost gotten used to it," I said lightly. Trying not to let him know how very much I agreed. I *hated* working in the kitchen.

"You shouldn't have to get used to it. It's taking your focus away from the really important things."

I grinned. "Like classes?"

"Like...a certain someone who wants to spend time with you," Mike corrected.

Yup, full on blush. I felt the heat creeping up my neck and toward my hairline. I had to get out of there before I did something I'd regret. Something like launch myself at the crown prince and embarrass the both of us in front of our classmates. I was about ten seconds away from doing it anyway.

"I'm going to the restroom. I'll be right back." I broke contact and sent Mike a warm smile.

"Hurry!" he called after me. I heard the librarian shush him.

I bit my lower lip on my way out the door to keep from giggling. Okay, the Trials weren't a joke. They were nothing to laugh at. But the way Mike and I were getting closer...I couldn't believe it. It was a silver lining in the face of chaos.

"Tavi Alderidge?"

I stopped and glanced up at the sound of my name. Two castle guards approached with their weapons at their sides and their faces half shrouded by visors. Immediately my walls went up. I stared at them warily through narrowed eyes. "Yes?"

The library doors had closed behind me. The stomping of boots echoed throughout the hall and the guards halted in front of me. "Miss Alderidge, you need to come with us."

My good mood dropped in an instant. "No, I'm sorry. No time." I pointed over my shoulder. "I have the Trials to research. What's this about?"

They didn't look at each other. They barely looked at me, their eyes hidden. "You're to come with us now," the one on the left insisted.

I dug my heels in. Figuratively, of course. No way was I leaving the school now.

And why was there no one around to see this? "I'm not sure what's going on but I don't have to go with you," I said.

"King's orders." This from the guard on the right.

They strode forward and grabbed my arms, one on either side. "What are you doing?" I managed to get out, locking my knees. But between the two of them, I didn't have the strength to fight, to keep them from taking me.

And if this was on the king's orders, then I knew better than to fight. I stopped myself from putting my foot in my mouth and finally stepped along with the two guards. How glad I felt that Mike wasn't around to see this. He'd been there too many times when his father's bullies came to take me away for questioning. Maybe Mike would be proud of me for showing some restraint.

The guards didn't take me to the throne room, as I expected. They called up a portal but instead of turning left, they went right. Away from the last place I'd gone when the king called for me.

"This is great, guys. Perfect," I finally told them. "Another missed day of school. It's really helping me keep up with the rest of my classmates. The king will be so pleased."

We moved around a corner and they knocked against the nearest door. "Your Majesty?" Leftie called out.

The king's voice sounded from inside telling us to enter. The door swung open on its own. The guards stood to the side and released their hold on me only after they were sure I wouldn't make a run for it.

Tywin's lackies waited while I made my way into the room. An office, I saw from a few furtive glances I dared to take. The walls were done in panels of red silk, with old wooden floors, and in the center a massive desk eight feet long at least.

The inner sanctum of the mad king, I thought. Except the thought didn't make me laugh.

"Miss Alderidge, there you are," Tywin said smoothly. "Please do come in and take a seat. I'd like to have a word with you."

My face void of expression, I shuffled forward on numb feet and sat on one of the ladderback chairs in front of the long, low desk. The king sat behind it, with his fingers steepled in front of him. I zipped my lips. Waiting. Waiting to see what he would say.

This was way, way worse than facing Claribel and Rooker.

"As you can see, I did not ask the rest of the Elder Council to be here for this meeting. I thought it was something you and I needed to discuss privately."

I wasn't sure what chilled me more—the look he speared me with or the fact that he'd wanted the two of us alone.

I inclined my head. "As you wish, Your Majesty." *Keep it respectful, keep it short. Keep it together.*

"As I'm sure you're aware at this point, I have been in

touch with the bureau. I know you were involved in a shifter attack last week."

Tywin looked ready to kill someone. I wanted to die on the spot. "Yes, sir."

Definitely no point in denying it. He already knew.

"I'm not going to ask you what happened. The bureau has already given me the details." Tywin leaned forward, his expression grim. "I wanted to personally tell you that we are reopening our investigation. You are officially our number one suspect in Madam Muerte's death."

"What? Why?" I blurted out. Straining to hold myself in check.

"You were told to keep out of trouble. I'm sure you're aware we do not tolerate shifters in these lands. Abominable creatures on their best day. Bloodthirsty savages on their worst," he said. "I strongly recommend you not leave town, Miss Alderidge. Too many things have happened and too little is adding up to my liking. You must understand this is a concern to me."

Every part of me trembled.

"The way I see it—" His clipped voice snapped against me like a whip. "You have two choices in this situation: Either you maintain your innocence and remain in town as we conduct our investigation, or..." Tywin paused. "You admit your culpability."

"I'm not guilty," I insisted without hesitation.

Tywin continued to stare at me. I focused on the bristles of his closely trimmed goatee. It was better than being frozen by his eyes. "There are fanatics in my land. Fanatics whose only purpose is to sow chaos. And yet even with these issues needing attention, you have been a niggling thorn in my side. Especially considering your odd friendship with my son."

I jerked.

"If we find out you are the culprit," Tywin said, "not only in the unfortunate death of Madam Muerte but behind the recent attacks, you will lose your citizenship in Faerie and find yourself back in the human realm. Forever. Do I make myself clear?"

What could I say? He did not accept my word no matter how many times I'd given it. Despite what the king said about expecting greatness from me, I believed the opposite. He suspected, and with his suspicion, he blamed, despite the truth.

He wanted to find someone guilty. Unfortunately, I'd been in the thick of things too many times.

I nodded slowly. "Yes, sir. Crystal clear."

20

I sat glued to the chair for the longest time, waiting for the king to say something else. *Anything* else. He finally released me without another word and sent me on my way back to school like a good little girl. The guards paid me no mind as I bolted out of the room and down the hall.

I had enough to worry about already, such as not dying during the Trials, to concern myself with the king's crazy, unfounded suspicions. I had to trust that since I didn't murder Madam Muerte, there was no way the investigation would find me guilty. They couldn't find evidence of a crime I didn't commit. Right? The spell that had taken her out was so beyond anything I was able to do. Surely the king must realize that.

So why couldn't they finish with all of this and let me go? What was taking them so long if the king had the investigation reopened?

What a time to be alive.

Tears burned at my eyes. The king wanted a scapegoat. He wanted someone to blame for problems he couldn't seem to control. And there I was, a bright beacon for trouble, perfect for him to focus his ire on.

There was no escape. There was no getting away from the man who ruled these lands. If he knew what Mike and I had done the other day...what would he say then? There would be no investigation there. He'd kill me himself, no matter what I said or what I had going on.

And trust me, I had a lot going on. Too much. Too many things stacked against me. I needed to keep my head down and stay out of trouble or else the king would squash me like a bug.

The next morning felt brutal and cold despite the sun shining. I dressed early, downed a giant cup of coffee, and walked to the royal library. Mike was already there, sitting at a table near the window. I joined him, keeping my head down.

He wanted to know where I'd gone the day before, and why I'd ditched him. I made up whatever excuse I thought he would believe with a promise not to disappear on him again. At least not until we did our fair share of research today.

"I'm here now," I insisted. Determined to focus. "I didn't sleep well last night."

"Well, time for you to wake up. We have a big day ahead of us." Mike pulled a stack of books out of his backpack. "I spoke to Lane last night. He and Arlyss are working together to find their own spell. He didn't want to tell me much and risk giving away what they found, but from what I understand, they feel like they have the first Trial in the bag."

"They're working together?"

My brain was too fuzzy to hold onto a single thought. I needed a little boost if I had any hope of making it through those books. I needed my brain boost powder.

Mike was talking and although I saw his mouth moving,

I couldn't follow the words he said. I held up a finger to interrupt him with another excuse about forgetting something in my room. He didn't seem offended. And I didn't want him to see me taking the powder like some kind of addict.

I wasn't addicted, I said to myself, racing back down the hall the way I'd come. The door to my room closed behind me. Moving to the desk, I reached into the top drawer to grab the bag and portion some of the powder into my water. If I had any chance of getting through this—both the Trials and the whole deal with the dead gypsy and the shifter attacks—then I needed to keep a clear head.

Except the bag was empty.

"What...?" I turned the bag upside down but nothing came out, not even a pinch of brain boost. I checked the drawer but didn't see any loose powder at the bottom. I whirled around in a panic, wondering if someone had come into my room and stolen it. But no, nothing else was out of place.

And I realized this was the second time this had happened, the second time my supply was less than expected. My hands curled into fists.

What was going on?

Thinking back to when I last took a dose, yesterday morning...I couldn't recall mixing it. The space was a big blank, just as it was the day before, and the day before that. The memories around the brain boost became fuzzy inside my head. How...how did I not realize my days were filled with holes? There were blanks spots where there should be memories. Together they added up to trouble.

I leaned against the desktop, taking a deep breath. I'd gone too far. Raelynn had been right when she warned me to be careful. If I'd actually already used up the whole bag—and I had a bad feeling that was exactly what happened—

then it was the first step down a very dark path, one I didn't want to be on. My heart flipped.

Shoving the empty bag back into the drawer, I pulled my hair up into a ponytail, focusing on my breathing. I pushed aside my nerves and the tingle of anxiety. There had to be some kind of reasonable explanation why I didn't remember anything about taking the brain boost in the last couple of weeks. There was something tickling at the edge of my mind just out of reach.

I shook my head. Why couldn't I remember anything?

"It's fine," I told myself. Voice barely above a whisper. "It's absolutely fine. If I stop taking the powder, then things will go back to normal. I just need to find alternate ways to hone my focus."

Yet another problem heaped on the mountain of problems plaguing me.

Mike glanced up at me when I returned to the library, his smile like a ray of sunshine. "Took you long enough. I thought you said you forgot something."

He has no idea. "I was only gone for a little bit," I hedged.

"Did you find what you were looking for?"

"Um, no. I mean yeah. I'm sorry. You know how I am. When I get stressed, I forget everything." Sure, maybe that excuse would work. He'd known me long enough, after all.

He clucked his tongue in admonishment. "I'll forgive you this time, Tavi. But you are going to have to make it up to me if you pull another disappearing act."

I liked the way his eyes warmed when he said it. "I will gladly make it up to you." I set my backpack on the empty seat between us. "As long as we make some headway on a detachment spell today."

"I'm already ten steps ahead of you. Talking to Lane gave me an idea, an avenue to pursue, if you will." Mike held up a finger to get my attention then pointed down at the open book in front of him. "Listen up and let me school you."

$\sim$

I spent too much energy that afternoon cataloguing my missing time and found it added up to much more than I was comfortable with. I had to know the side effects of the potion, considering I'd taken too much. That night in the kitchen, with Raelynn working steadily beside me and singing a song I didn't know, I asked her.

"So, uh, about the brain boost powder... You mentioned side effects. Can you elaborate?" I said with as much casual ease as I could manage.

Which wasn't much, considering the way she turned to me with an eagle-sharp gaze. "Why do you ask?" Seeing right through whatever charade I'd tried to put in place. She reminded me of my old friend Nurse Julie in that respect.

I shrugged with forced nonchalance. Kneading the bread dough with practiced movements, I said, "Just curious. I've been using it to help me get through the Trials, and with the first one coming up this Friday, I realized I might need to know more about those side effects you mentioned. I don't want the Abrichxao powder to, you know, interact negatively with any spell work I do. I'm trying to give myself the best chance possible at passing."

It sounded reasonable enough.

Raelynn studied me for a moment and then went back to dressing the tender cut of beef in front of her. Another one of the king's big dinner parties with the courtiers, she'd told me the moment I walked through the door and grabbed an apron. Everything had to be spot on tonight. Lots of prep, lots of courses. No time to dally.

"Well, the big one is losing time," she said with a sigh.

Glaring at the beef as though it were somehow responsible for the side effect. "That's the one they warn you about first. It can get severe, large chunks of time just gone. Like *poof!*"

Raelynn chuckled at her own joke and the rest of the girls in the kitchen laughed along with her.

She gave me a warning look. "Too much of the powder will literally shut down your brain, Tavi girl, and you'll lose memories from that time. Let me think what else... Oh, there's the dry mouth, but it isn't so terrible. Stomach ache, sore throat—"

I stopped listening after her first sentence. Memory loss. *Literally shut down your brain.* Was that what happened to me?

"Are you listening?"

Snapping to attention, flour flying everywhere, I glanced over at her and nodded. "Of course I'm listening."

"Have you been taking more than two teaspoons a week?" Raelynn was stern. Her eyebrows drew together and somehow I knew she could see down to my soul.

"No way," I told her, lying easily. And feeling terrible about it.

"Good," Raelyn said emphatically. "I'd hate to think you've been overindulging. I refuse to be responsible for any more holes in your sieve-like memory." She rapped me on the side of the head with her knuckles before taking the bread loaf to the oven. "Bad enough you can't remember simple recipes. Have to remind you every bloody week how to make an asparagus casserole."

The girls laughed at her humor a second time. They all understood the pain of having to repeat information to me again and again.

With Raelynn distracted at the oven, I thought back over the past few weeks. There were definitely a few things I couldn't seem to remember. Even a few bits and pieces of my tutoring with Juno—and the whole purpose of taking the powder in the first place was so I could do better with my studies.

I excused myself as early as possible and raced back to my room, grabbing a notebook and a pen, charting out my tutoring sessions over the last week since the attack. Detailing what I'd learned those days and what Juno had me work on. And found I could only remember about half of the days.

My pen dropped with a clatter.

I'd been using the brain boost to help. But what if I'd lost tons of time and memories of tutoring? What if I'd actually gone the opposite way and did more harm than good? Some of the things I'd learned but now forgotten might have been imperative to getting me through the Trials.

What if I'd screwed it all up?

21

Friday was the day of the first Trial.

As the group of students from Elite were ushered into the woods surrounding the town, I stood close to Mike, watching excitement flash across other familiar faces. Coral, of course, spoke to anyone who would listen about her plan for the Trial and how she and her family fully expected her to come in first.

Except the staff didn't want us working together. If we were together then we might be able to help each other with the magic, or share a life force to minimize the effects of the power necessary to work the spell. Whatever spell we chose to use.

I bit my nails down to below the quick and had an upset stomach to show for it.

In the mortal world, normal people looked forward to Fridays. They were the start of the weekend and a time to relax, knowing you'd have two days off to do whatever you wanted, without worrying about work, without thinking of dreaded Monday.

This Friday was worse than all past Mondays added together.

Headmaster Cyrus clapped for attention, his milky eyes sweeping over the crowd. He had little more to say today than he had three days past in terms of what to expect.

Arlyss's eyes blazed. "This is going to be a piece of cake. Lane and I did our research. Do you actually think you can make it through, halfling?"

"Oh, are you talking to me? Sorry, I don't speak idiot," I replied.

"Hey!" Arlyss barked.

"What?" Mike and I said at the same time.

"She's not saying anything worse than what you've said in the past," Mike replied, looking over at me with a warm smile.

Arlyss turned on his heel and walked away toward Coral and Lane, his waiting and no doubt more appreciative audience.

All right. No skin off my nose.

"He thinks he's going to finish first." Mike moved toward me, light on his feet, until our gazes locked. "Let's give him a run for his money and make him eat his words."

"You really have that much confidence in the spell we found?"

Mike's mask of haughty control cracked a little. But only I saw it. "I'm confident we did everything we could to prepare. I just wish we were doing it together."

I reached out to take his hand, squeezing once. "We're going to be fine. Trust me."

Except I didn't trust myself. Not when everything he said sounded tinny and my focus began to scatter in a thousand directions.

No! I refused to give in to the brain fog. Not today, not this time.

"Remember, kids," Cyrus was saying with a wide smile. "Most of this Trial will be deeply personal and not visible to the judges. The goal today is to make it through faster than the rest of your competitors. It does not matter how."

He put enough gravity into the "*how*" to sink the Titanic.

"Don't be scared," Mike whispered to me.

"I'm not." I walked a few steps ahead of him to prove it. Good thing he couldn't see how my stomach jumped and the rest of me shook. I locked my knees to keep myself upright.

He chuckled behind me. "Oh, I don't know, I think I see a few nerves showing."

"You're one to talk. There might be a muskee lurking around the corner prepared to gobble you up."

The joke did not faze him. "Whatever you say, Tavi."

It didn't take long for Cyrus to finish his speech. A shower of sparks accompanied his final statement. And then we were off. I knew that above us were orbs floating, relaying information about the contestants for the viewers watching at home. I'd thought the Summer Games were a big deal? They were nothing compared to the Elite Trials.

People were apparently eager to watch us die.

I crushed that thought and tried to throw it as far away as possible.

Beginning to feel the stress even more keenly, I broke into a run, knowing I didn't have much time to find the right spot to grow the seed. Thinking back to my time with Juno—the time I could remember, at least—I realized we'd focused most of our efforts on air and fire. We should have been practicing earth magic. Juno reckoned that because I was already taking advanced classes on earth magic at Elite Academy, I should focus on other things.

Fat load of good it did me now.

The ghostly echoes of everything I'd tried to cram in my head followed me through the forest, a place I should have been entirely comfortable. I definitely shouldn't feel like I was walking on eggshells.

The forest teemed with life around me and a soft breeze seemed to push me forward. There were deer, and foxes, and squirrels racing from one tree to another. They had no idea their world was about to be turned into a battleground for hundreds of elite Fae students. A battleground where the fastest student won.

I'd be lucky if I made it out of here having completed the test at all, much less in the fastest time.

I sank into the quiet until I found a good spot to stop. I looked up. The clearing stretched in either direction with a clear angle to the sun overhead. Yes, this was good.

I walked over the soft ground, newly thawed after the last few warm days, and eventually decided on a particular place to plant the seed of the tree I was to grow for the Trial. Then I began in earnest to gather all my inherent magic energy. Time to get this show on the road.

Drawing into myself was hard work. Calling my magic took more effort than it should have, and the moment I took hold of it, the moment I felt it growing, my concentration splintered. Repeatedly.

I growled, stomping my feet in an effort to ground myself. "This isn't going to work if you can't focus!" I yelled at myself, unable to resist slapping the side of my head as if that would help.

This was worse than when I'd had to break the Augundae Imperium out of the mortal world. Then, I'd only been forced to unravel a handful of wards the school had placed to protect the priceless artifact. Huh, surprising that the king hadn't said a word to me about the fake Imperium I'd substituted, the fake that exploded the moment it crossed the portal from the mortal world to this one.

Boy, if he only knew...

Cognitive manipulation might be my innate power, but it didn't work on me personally. Nothing helped with the mistakes I'd made. Nothing helped me be better when I kept hurting myself. There was nothing I could do to trick myself into lifting the brain fog. It wouldn't help me get my memories or my lost time back again. Would it?

I dove into my magic to an impossible depth inside of me, clamping my hands over my ears as though that would help me focus. The pressure built until an unnatural breeze ripped the newly opened petals off wildflowers in the clearing. Until there were pieces of bark and twigs catapulting through the air and the world around me faded. And suddenly the world went quiet. It was a deafening quiet.

A flutter...and I caught sight of a pair of wings at my back. My transfiguration power was once again reflexively manifesting due to stress.

I scrambled to return to my normal form. Deep in the woods for the Trial, I wasn't visible to the judges except via the all-seeing orbs. Glancing around for floating orbs, I saw none, but that didn't mean they weren't there just out of my sight. Terror gripped me with icy fingers. If anyone saw what I'd done—

No more mess-ups. I needed to get to work immediately. I knew I wasn't going to win. But I wanted to finish at least. Working to center myself, I called the magic again, focusing it on a smaller and smaller point.

On the seed I drew from my pocket.

"Grow for me," I whispered.

I sent the seed skyward, linking my magic with the life inside of it, with my life. Watched as gravity had it falling back to earth in the spot I'd picked out. Helped it dig deep into the soil of the forest and send out its roots.

I had the magic and I had the determination to get through this. Under my breath I repeated the spell Mike had found. The same kind of spell used to power the Augundae Totalis, the magical artifact designed to bolster and amplify the user's magic. It was the artifact he'd used to get through the mortal school's cullings.

He'd done what I couldn't do, I thought. Mike had found the origin of the ancient artifact. Sneaky little devil.

I crouched down and dug my own fingers into the soil near the embedded seed, grounding myself and tapping into earth magic. The plan was to use the same spell to bolster our own spell but only until the tree took off. Then we'd detach and let the magic of the land boost the tree's growth instead of our own life force.

It sounded simple. And maybe it was actually going to work because after a long moment of fierce concentration that had my limbs quivering with exertion I thought I could see a tiny shoot sprouting through the dirt—

Please don't let me transform again.

That little distraction had me losing the connection to the magic and I worried that the spell had fizzled out before I could complete it.

A string of curses erupted from my mouth and I stomped my feet again in full toddler tantrum fashion. "Rein it in!" I admonished myself out loud. Like the sound of my voice would somehow help me get it together when nothing else had so far.

I fell to my knees and peered at the tiny green shoot that had stopped growing. My lack of concentration had broken the connection, but maybe I could repair the damage.

"Grow, damn it!"

Nothing.

Feeling weary to my bones, I collapsed onto my back and rolled into fetal position on my side. I wasn't giving up. Not yet. But I needed to recharge my energy. Just a few moments of rest...

I noticed a berry bush on the edge of the clearing. It was too early for berries, so what was the flash of gold color I saw through the sparse branches?

My best innate magic was finding bodies, apparently. I was better than a cadaver dog. Tavi Alderidge, cadaver wolf.

I didn't need to investigate to know the sudden ache in my gut was right. The odd premonition, the *knowing* that I was once again in the wrong place at the wrong time.

I approached anyway because I needed to see, to verify. My stomach began to cartwheel and a cold sweat broke out on the back of my neck. The camera orbs would be overhead shortly, surely.

"Breathe, Tavi," I told myself.

There beneath the berry bush was an arm. A leg. The dismembered torso of one of Mike's shitty friends, torn apart.

22

No escape.

No matter what would happen to me for this, I knew it was only a matter of time before the orbs found me and broadcast my grisly discovery anyway.

I uttered the words for the spell to raise the magical alarm and hovered near the body for a second until I was sure the message was out. Too close, my mind said immediately. Although I wasn't sure it would matter now. It was another crime scene where I was the first one there. It meant yet another knife pointed directly at my heart and all eyes on me, determined to rip me down to the bone and examine every piece for answers.

Did I have any choice? No. Now the pure-blood Fae/half-shifter murders were going to be public knowledge, because there was no way for this to be pushed aside. No way for the king and his cronies to keep this private. It was going to be all over the news.

The worst part? I was sure the student had been killed by the same half-shifter. The same one who murdered the other three girls and attacked Juno. It seemed to be his same MO. Both arms had been wrenched from their sockets, with the legs twisted off in different directions, and three deep horizontal slashes—claw marks—across the midsection.

This one, though...she didn't have the red hair. Juno didn't have red hair either, but her connection to me stood out in terms of why she was targeted. This girl on the ground was on the periphery of the group of Mike's shitty friends. I mostly saw her hanging around Lane and Arlyss, hoping for some scrap of their attention. They'd never given it but she'd persisted anyway.

That didn't mean she deserved to die.

The moment I saw someone, *anyone*, arriving on the scene, I took off. Let the cavalry figure things out. They already knew who sounded the alarm and they'd come to talk to me later. I ran as fast as I could through the forest, all the way to the beginning.

I got back to the starting point only to have Mike run over and wrap me in his arms almost violently.

He let out a ragged breath. "I thought it was you." His mouth pressed against the side of my head. "I was terrified when I heard someone was hurt. I didn't know what happened."

News traveled fast in Faerie, no doubt about it. "Not hurt. *Dead*." I shuddered. I returned the hug, drawing strength from him. He had no idea how badly I needed the connection.

"Are you okay?" Mike's hands traced soothing spirals along my shoulders and back.

"Nothing is hurt but my pride. I'm afraid I failed the Trial." I swallowed hard. "Things became a little difficult for me."

"Shh." Mike stroked a hand down my hair and gathered me closer. "It's okay."

Didn't he understand? It wasn't okay at all. I'd failed utterly.

"Extenuating circumstances," Mike insisted. "No one is going to blame you for not finishing when you found...what you found."

I had a feeling the school, and the Council of Elders, wouldn't see it his way.

"How about you? Did you use the spell you found?" I asked him.

He nodded against me before resting his chin on the top of my head. "I did, but the warning buzzer sounded before I could complete the transformation. My seed is still in the ground. Actually, I'm not sure anyone finished."

I scoffed. "I'm sure Arlyss did."

"Don't worry. I'm going to talk to the school and Headmaster Cyrus. No one would expect you to keep going after stumbling on something like you did," Mike continued. "You must be absolutely terrified, Tavi."

I glanced over his shoulder to see Cyrus deep in conversation with the rest of the judges, those chosen professors from Elite in charge of determining the winner of each Trial. They clustered together and none of them looked particularly pleased with this disruption.

"I don't think it will do any good. The rules are pretty explicit." *Compete or else.* I'd barely even begun the spell to make the tree grow. Also, if these were the tests for the Seven High Values, by stopping when I found the body, I'd displayed the exact opposite. Fear. Panic. Definitely *not* Bravery.

"Miss Alderidge?"

I wasn't exactly surprised to glance up from my Mike hug and see Rooker and Claribel from the bureau staring at me. Although Claribel looking at me with a smile like the cat who ate the canary was a bit startling.

Wow, they'd gotten here fast. I hadn't even had time to catch my breath.

"I sincerely hope you are ready to talk about this latest discovery, Tavi," Claribel said. "It's important enough to have the rest of the Trials put on pause until the scene is secured. You must understand this is unprecedented. The king is quite concerned."

Snapping back at her was likely one of the stupidest things I'd done in my life, but I couldn't help myself. "Are you ready to finally catch this killer, or are you going to continue to waste time interrogating me? Because the more time you waste with this baseless suspicion the more the real killer grows in confidence to commit his next crime."

There was a tiny pause before she finally answered. "You're full of fire. Good to see this first Trial hasn't sapped it out of you. You can use some of it to answer our questions."

Mike reached down and took my hand when I made to step back. "I'm coming with you this time," he said.

"I'm afraid not, Prince Michael," Claribel said immediately. "We've been tasked with taking Miss Alderidge in for questioning about the corpse she found today. It wouldn't do to have you subjected to the interrogation too."

"Or having your presence influence her answers," Rooker added with a deep rumble of sound.

So they knew how important Mike was to me. And I to him. I filed that little tidbit of information away for later.

"It's fine," I insisted before Mike could argue. I squeezed his hand. "It won't take long. They need every detail they can get to catch this killer and I'm happy to help in any way possible."

But inside, I was shaking. Let them think I was being cooperative. In truth, they wouldn't get a thing out of me I didn't want them to know.

I definitely didn't want Mike around to witness me weaving more lies.

It took a little convincing but eventually he nodded,

stroking his thumb across the top of my hand once before letting it go. "Find me immediately once you're done."

At least this time the two agents didn't grab me and drag me away like a criminal. They waited for me to approach and then called up a portal to transport us out of the forest. It deposited us right on the doorstep to the same building we'd gone to the first time around.

Bureau headquarters. I might as well get used to being here. I had the sickening sensation I'd be spending a lot more time with the investigators.

Claribel wasted no time. "You sure seem to be around a lot of bodies, don't you, Tavi?" She didn't ask if she could call me by my first name. It would be the only question she didn't ask.

"It must be a gift you have," Rooker added.

The two of them settled behind the table, with Rooker glancing at the empty chair across from him. I knew the look. *Sit.*

I did, realizing I had very little experience to navigate this encounter. My fried brain didn't want to work. My strength was all but completely sapped. Taken all together, it put me on thin ice. Very thin ice indeed.

Proceed with caution.

"A gift? More like a curse," I replied shortly. I was done playing nice. Done pretending like I wasn't absolutely exhausted by these proceedings. Did they not think this was hard on me? Did they think I actually liked all the trouble that kept finding me? The mounting pressure on my shoulders?

Silence reigned for a long moment. "There are five bodies, Tavi," Rooker stated. "Five dismembered bodies of pure-blood Faes, taken down with a sort of ferocity we have not seen in this land for generations. You must understand why we're concerned. Especially considering the issues you seem to be having lately and the fact that you've not only found yourself at this latest crime scene but seem to have in fact personally stopped the attack on Juno Ians. We simply want to understand what you're capable of."

"Tell us about this latest body," Claribel finished for her partner.

I shrugged, trying for innocent nonchalance. "It was ripped apart." But every part of me went numb as I pictured the body in my mind.

"Do you believe this is connected to the attack you interrupted the other day? The one involving Professor Ians?"

I grimaced. "Yes, I absolutely do," I answered. "Now why don't you tell me what you really think?"

More silence. Finally, Claribel sighed. "What we think about what?"

"About my involvement. Because I'm sure you've had the same thought I had. Someone has it out for me, especially considering how I stepped in to *save* my mentor." Let them chew on those words. "I'm exhausted and worried and tired of dead bodies, too."

Claribel tilted her head to the side. "I'm sure you are," she said gently. It was the first spark of sympathy I'd ever seen out of her. "It does seem to happen to you more than the average Faerie citizen. I'd be disappointed if you didn't put the pieces together."

"I didn't even get to complete the first Trial." I stared down at the floor and noticed the dirt on my sneakers, the stray leaves and twigs attached to the soft fabric of my pants. Surely they knew, at this point, all about my issues with classes at the Elite Academy. They couldn't possibly think I'd done this on purpose, brought more attention to myself with everything else going on.

Things had gotten complicated in a hurry.

Both agents took me through a round of questioning to

make Detective Wilson's investigations look like a kid with a school report. They made a big production now of keeping eye contact and going for the sympathy approach rather than the knuckle-down hard way they'd adopted the first time around. They even offered me a glass of water.

I turned it down, thinking it was better not to ingest anything.

I made it through without losing my temper and with as much honesty as possible. Until their final set of questions.

Claribel smiled. "We do appreciate your attention to detail, although I feel obliged to let you know there are a few holes in your story."

I shook my head. "Not surprising. I've been having trouble concentrating with my classes. I believe it's called being overworked."

And let's be honest. I had crappy memory retention at the best of times. My recollections of the crime scenes outside of today were vague at best. I'd already described the beast that attacked Juno, a large and shaggy creature whose face I didn't recognize because, well, *beast*.

"I suppose we can't expect a little halfling to have the memory of a pure-blood Fae, even one attending Elite Academy," Rooker said with more than a touch of sarcasm.

He flipped through a stack of papers, and briefly I caught the flash of a color photograph. One of the same ones Selene had shown us during one of our meetings for the Claw & Fang. I saw a close-up of the second victim. There were pages of notes, probably more interviews than just mine.

"I'm not sure what you want me to say to that."

"One last thing before we let you go," Rooker stated. "We know you're a halfling, of course. An orphan. And we know from your initial citizenship questions that your mother was

Fae. What was her name? And who—or rather what—was your father?"

My insides screamed at me to keep the information to myself. Sitting there, staring at their faces, I knew one way or another they would extract the info from me. Whether I wanted them to or not.

23

Mike must have worked his magic, because when I returned to school the next day, shaken, I was promptly informed by Miss Wicks that I was still eligible to compete in the Trials due to extenuating circumstances.

If one could call a murderer on the loose and finding the latest body an *extenuating circumstance*.

The woman stared down at me with her long neck craned and her thin fingers twitching. "You do know this is outside of the ordinary, Miss Alderidge."

"Is it?" I asked. Every part of me drooped. My school uniform hung limp and wrinkled on my shoulders and I hadn't showered. I was exhausted and numb and my chest felt heavy as if carrying a boulder inside of it.

Miss Wicks shook her head. Her body hunched and I was every second more reminded of a spider when I looked at her.

"It was a lucky roll of the dice for you," she continued.

Lucky. Right. I kept my face void of all expression. It didn't take a genius to know what she was thinking. She thought I was somehow cheating, or I had outside help. She wasn't exactly wrong.

I didn't want to ask for more details. I didn't want to stir the pot of crap any more than it was already swirling.

With a small nod, I thanked Miss Wicks and hurried on to my first class, knowing we'd have an assembly later to announce the results of the first Trial and the preparation for round two. My mind constantly circled back to the conversation with the bureau agents last night.

Your parents' names, Miss Alderidge. Now. Rooker wasn't going to tolerate any more bullshit answers from me. His expression was fierce. I must have spent enough time with him by now to be able to discern the slight changes in his rock-like appearance. The look he wore now I called his *shakedown scowl*.

What would they say if I told them I didn't know my mother's last name? Only her first name.

My parents are both dead. I'd tried to make him understand, even knowing the pleading had no effect.

Then giving us their names won't matter, will it?

I'd hesitantly given over my mother's first name. *Dey.* Claiming truthfully how I didn't know the last name because I'd been so young when she died. Afterward, my uncle did everything in his power to keep her part of my ancestry a secret; we didn't discuss her at all. There were no pictures of her anywhere in the house, let alone any of the three of us together.

Neither of the agents was happy with only her first name. Apparently "Dey" was a common enough Faerie name. They'd demanded to know my "human" father's name as well. I didn't know what difference it would make, so I told them. *Baronne.*

Now they knew as much as I did and that didn't sit well with me. Names held a certain power anywhere you went, but especially in Faerie. Knowing someone's or something's true name gave you knowledge, which also gave you some power and control.

I replayed the interrogation over and over in my head until it became blurred. Everything blurred after a while, a tension headache taking up residence between my eyes and staying there, making it hard to think. Hard to focus.

Fingers snapped in front of my eyes and I blinked, struggling to focus.

"I asked what you think about our plan for the second Trial," Mike said, studying me with clear concern.

Did I look bad enough to warrant his expression? Yeah, probably so.

I blew out a breath, pushing the hair out of my eyes, blinking again until the fuzz cleared. "Um...I think it's a good plan," I told him.

What had we been talking about?

"It's getting late and we need to make sure we know exactly what we'll be doing to beat this one. Cleverness." Mike shook his head and the lines deepened between his eyebrows. "Who thinks up these things?"

"Who thought growing a tree from a seed would somehow exemplify and validate Justice? The same kind of sadists who have planned these Trials in the past. Trust me, I've seen some doozies."

"Oh, yeah. You've been working through some of these with your tutor, haven't you?"

"Yup."

I didn't feel clever at all. And I wasn't sure how we'd handle this problem. The task this time? We had to find a way to cross from the castle to the mountain peaks on the other side of the valley without ever touching the ground, without the use of modern technology—so no ATVs or off-road vehicles—and without using the four elements in any of our spell work. And speed was a huge factor.

Mike and I were trying to find alternative ways to animate an inanimate object to carry us. So far we'd found a few things but even with the two of us combined, we couldn't channel enough power to get the suits of armor in the castle to move ten feet, let alone cross an entire forest.

"So what do you think?" he tried again.

"I'm sorry. Can you go over it one more time? I'm still a little fuzzy on the details."

Mike sighed and leaned back in his chair. "Well, we were talking about breaking out the old *Totalis* to boost our powers to get the spell to work, but you said you didn't want to take any chances of getting caught cheating. I understand where you're coming from, after what happened with the last one."

Had I said that? I pinched the bridge of my nose, my nerves jittery. I hadn't taken the brain boost powder since before the first Trial because I'd terrified myself over memory loss. Now I knew I'd been right to stop because I'd gone too far, and I was having withdrawals. My brain was foggier than usual, and I felt more tired today than I did before I'd started taking the stuff.

I'd needed to stop for a number of reasons, truth be told. Not only had I lost too much memory and time, but the bureau was watching me annoyingly closely, as were the palace guards. The king had not been joking when he said there were eyes on me at all times. I felt them now more than ever.

Glancing up, I noticed the two guards at the entrance of the palace library even now, standing just out of sight and watching Mike and me study like I was some kind of criminal. Even though I'd had nothing to do with the murders of any of the people who had died, outside of simply being in the wrong place at the wrong time.

"We've already been over it a few times. You need to pay attention," Mike said, playfully tweaking my nose.

"I'm *trying*," I snapped and swatted his hand away. And instantly felt bad about it. I softened my tone. "Believe me, I'm trying. And we aren't going to use the *Totalis* for the Trials. There are too many people from the Elder Council around and they'll recognize the signature of its magic."

"Maybe you can use your cognitive manipulation to convince them otherwise." This accompanied by a wink and a smile hotter than the desert.

Ha, if only he knew. My cognitive manipulation hadn't been good enough to get a replica of the *Imperium* across the border into this world.

If the bureau agents knew about *that*...

"I'm still not sure why you needed to cheat to get through the mortal academy, anyway," I said. Partly to take the focus off of me. Partly because I really wanted to know. "I mean, you're a prince! You shouldn't have needed an artifact to make it through the lottery."

That was what they'd called it: a lottery. Like we were somehow supposed to feel lucky for working hard enough to make it to the next semester. Maybe Headmaster Leaves and the rest of the faculty should talk to the council here.

Nah, I didn't want things to be harder for any future halflings.

Mike's expression went stony. "Why I needed the Totalis isn't the point. We're trying to figure out a way to beat this Trial without killing ourselves, Tavi. And we have an ace in the hole with the artifact. It's something no one else has."

Ooh, a little sensitive. He didn't want to answer me. My last comment must have gotten under his skin.

"But you've never said why you need it," I said.

"Because I didn't think it was important!"

"It was important enough that Roman decided he needed to kill for you."

Good going, Tavi, I thought as Mike instantly shut down. I should not have mentioned his friend Roman. Or questioned why Mike had had such a hard time making it through the cullings.

"Low blow. It's not fair of you to say that," Mike said almost in a whisper. He slowly closed the book in front of him. "It makes me feel like you don't trust me."

How could I let him know? At the core, I didn't trust myself, either. I was about to keel over, my brain was fried, and the rest of me on edge from my interviews with the bureau. Not to mention, oh yeah, the half-shifter killer on the loose and the canyonful of secrets I had to keep.

"Mike, it's not about trust. I was just wondering why you had the need to use an artifact to boost your magic in the first place. And I notice you've still never given me a good answer."

He wasn't about to, either. Frowning, he pushed away from the table and took the book we'd been reading for research with him, pressing it to his chest. No longer willing to look at me. "I'm going to go take a walk."

"You're just walking out?" I matched his tone of voice. He didn't like it.

"Get some sleep, okay? We'll talk about this tomorrow."

His footsteps echoed on his way out and the doors to the library swung closed behind him, leaving me alone in the suffocating silence. I let my head drop to the table with a loud *thunk* that did nothing to wake me up.

"Nice going," I muttered to myself.

The guards were probably laughing at me.

Why did I always feel the need to start things? I hadn't even wanted to, but I'd snapped at Mike anyway and on instinct went right for the subject I knew would hurt him the most.

I did need sleep. Maybe a few straight hours would help clear my head and I'd act like less of an idiot. We hadn't really solidified our plan for mobilizing the suits of armor to carry us, but at least we had a solid direction for the Trial tomorrow. And they were allowing me to compete again. I should be happy for small blessings.

Except when I got to my room, the tiny kernel of a good mood shriveled up and disappeared. Bronwen waited for me there. She did not grin when she saw me. I hurried to close the door before any of the guards trailing me in the hallway saw her.

"We have patrol tonight," she said the moment we were alone with a sound barrier spell keeping overeager ears from listening.

I slumped down on the bed with a groan. The little chinks in the wall I'd been building since my interviews with Rooker and Claribel began to crack. "Not again."

"I'm sorry. Selene feels we stopped our watch too early and someone else died. She wants you and me back out there and searching for clues, especially considering our past history with the half-shifter." Bronwen sat next to me and sighed.

I wasn't sure what she did all day to keep busy, and she'd never really told me outside of *working*. I didn't know where she worked or what she did. Funny how I could trust someone so easily without knowing the details of her life.

Maybe that was why I kept getting into trouble.

"I can't, Bronwen. I'm sorry, really, but I just can't. Absolutely, one hundred percent cannot," I told her firmly. "I'm barely making it through the day as it is." I hadn't told her about the newest hurdle or my issues with the bureau, although surely at this point she'd heard about me finding the latest body. It was all over the Faerie news network.

"Talk to me," Bronwen said. She reached out to pat my knee. "I'm here to listen. If you're having issues, then maybe I can help."

I puffed out my cheeks, wondering if I should spill about everything or keep a few things to myself. I ended up going through the story from start to finish, with Bronwen listening wide-eyed without interruption. She knew about Madam Muerte and the magic tracker I'd been forced to wear for months on end. She didn't know about the king pulling me aside to tell me he was reopening the case. I'd even told Bronwen about the brain boost powder and how I'd backslid into some pretty bad withdrawal symptoms. She hadn't judged me.

When I finally finished, rubbing my eyes and close to tears, she put her hand on my arm. "Tavi, you need to run." Her hand bit down into my skin as she squeezed. "It's not safe for you here anymore. I shouldn't even be here! Have you told Selene?"

I shook my head. "I can't run. There are too many things I need to do here."

"Look. The Claw & Fang has sister groups in other villages, other cities in Faerie. We could reach out through the network and find you a safe haven somewhere far away. Somewhere you can hide."

Hiding sounded amazing right now. It also sounded like an easy out. Too easy.

I appreciated what she was trying to do. How she wanted to help and get me clear of this mess. Unfortunately, I knew better. "If I run, then I look guilty. I'm not guilty. And besides, the king would probably tear the kingdom apart to find me. I have to see this through and do my best to keep my chin up."

"I know it's hard for you to be open, Tavi. Especially when you aren't sure who to trust. I appreciate your trust in me and I won't betray it. But you need to rest, so why don't you stay home tonight."

"What?"

"I'll find someone else to patrol with me. You rest tonight and I'll be there to see you at the Trial tomorrow. It'll be fine."

"You really don't have to—"

She patted me on the knee again before pushing off the bed. "I know I don't have to. Consider it done, anyway. You don't need to worry about anything else. Well, at least for tonight. There's not much I can do about the rest of it."

Those tears I'd tried so hard to keep to myself broke free and trailed down my cheeks. "Bron—"

"Oh, hey, no crying now!" Bronwen drew me forward in a hug, wrapping her arms around my shoulders. "It's going to be okay. Also, maybe we should find a new meeting place. I don't want the king to see us together and get more suspicious of you than he already is. No more meeting in your room."

Luckily, none of the questions the bureau had asked me regarding the attack on Juno had mentioned Bronwen or anyone fitting her description. As far as they knew, I had been alone when I stepped in to help Professor Ians. I needed to keep it that way because I didn't want my friend involved.

"All right." I sniffled as I returned the embrace. "We'll think of something."

"We always do." She broke contact and leaned back to smile at me. "Sleep," she insisted. "I'll tell Selene we need someone to cover for you for a little while. You need to be prepared to face whatever happens tomorrow. And when this is all over, you and Melia and I are taking a girls trip."

My face broke into a similar grin. "Where will we go? I can't take time off work, much less school."

"I don't care. Get the time off and we will go to the coast. You haven't had a chance to see anything outside of this town. It's time for you to blow off a little steam. Girls only."

She transformed into her usual crow form and darted out the window. I watched her fly off until she became a speck on the horizon, and I felt lighter than I had all day. Bronwen was a good friend.

Grateful for the reprieve, I wasted no time changing into pajamas and snuggling under the covers. But when I finally fell asleep, it was with the weight of the Faerie world on my shoulders, and I didn't dream.

24

I stood with the rest of the students from the Elite Academy waiting for the buzzer to sound and launch Trial Two. We were gathered outside of the castle on the green space where the Summer Carnival had been set up. My legs were like stone and the rest of me just as hard. Nerves, I knew. But knowing didn't make me feel any better.

A crowd had gathered on the vast green meadow at the edge of the forest to watch the proceedings, with who knew how many waiting at the base of the mountain at our final destination, to see exactly what we would do and how creative we got with our spells. Behind me were people from the palace, as well as school officials, members of the Elder Council, and friends and family cheering us on. Overhead there were orbs floating from the news networks. Real-time coverage for the many viewers who could not be here in person.

I wasn't sure I had a handle on my magic. Not one bit. Glancing around at the rest of the students who'd made it through to round two, I knew I should be worried. They were much better than me. None of them looked like they were ready to bend over and spill their guts.

But I remembered what Juno had said during one of our first tutoring sessions: I had more power than I thought. I simply needed to find a way to release it. Maybe she was right, maybe not. Mike and I had briefly discussed our plans for today but not in any detail after I'd alienated him in the library.

Yeah, good going on that. Idiot.

Anxious energy skittered along my arms until my hair stood on end and I shook my hands to try and get rid of those nerves. This wasn't any way to behave. The others expected me to be a failure. No need for me to act—

Two arms came around my neck and I screamed.

"Girl! It's me. Calm yourself."

Immediately I drew in a breath filled with Melia's familiar scent. Eyes closed, I turned around and grabbed onto her, my head against her collarbone because of our height difference.

"I wanted to come out and support you today, tell you good luck," she said into my hair. "I know you've got this. Just like I know you are probably freaking out and telling yourself you are going to trip over your own two feet."

"I definitely *don't* have this," I replied quickly.

"Of course you do! Remember who taught you? Yes, I'm referring to myself and my absolutely fabulous mentoring skills, showing you the ropes when you had no one else. I know there are a few tricks up your sleeve that none of the other students have going for them. Not to mention you are quick and resourceful. You showed everyone in the mortal world what you were made of." She scoffed. "This? This is nothing compared to what you've been through."

"This could kill me."

"So could Kendrick Grimaldi when he kidnapped you. Yet here you stand, stronger than ever. Have I told you how proud I am of you?"

She had, and it meant the world to me.

I could have held on to Melia forever. But she gently pushed back and our eyes met, my lips quivering a little. "I wish there were a spell to transfer your confidence into me," I told her. "Because I am about to either freak out or puke. Maybe both at the same time."

"Do you remember how nervous you were about the first culling? When you didn't think you would make it through? And what about the lottery?" She held up her fingers for air quotes around the last word. "You thought you were going to panic then but you didn't. What happened to you during the first Trial was nothing but sheer bad luck. It's not going to happen again."

"You're right," I said, more for her benefit than for my own.

Today the school had let us wear whatever we wanted, anything to make us more comfortable for the long trip to the base of the mountains. I'd forgone the usual school blazer and went with a trusty pair of yoga pants and a navy-blue long-sleeved t-shirt against the slight chill in the air. Typical clothing for shifting, although no one knew that.

I had my long hair done in a braid hanging along my spine, and I wore a worried expression. Which was the perfect accessory for today's task.

"I just want this all to be over."

Melia gave me a somewhat stern smile. She meant business. Gold sparked in her eyes and if I didn't know her inside and out, I'd say she might have a little wolf in her blood, too. "And it will be, soon. I'm going to be waiting for you at the finish line with a drink and some chocolate. Know that whatever you choose to do will be the right thing because not a one of these spoiled, pampered buttholes has anything on you, Tavi. Got it?"

I nodded and gave her a tiny grin.

Melia finished what she considered to be the best pep talk in the history of pep talks before melting back into the crowd. I looked around for Bronwen but I didn't see her.

Too late, it was show time.

I didn't have time to worry. I didn't have time to find Mike and tell him I was sorry before the buzzer sounded, the Trial began, and I had to go.

It's time.

Closing my eyes, I shut out the rest of the world, focusing on the small ball of heat at the base of my spine where I always imagined I kept my magic stored. It helped to visualize it as an actual physical space. Especially considering how my inherent power was cognitive manipulation.

I willed the power to grow and change into a huge fire fueling the magic. With it, I called out the words to the spell set to animate one of the suits of armor from the castle. If this went well, I'd cross the finish line without accessing earth, air, fire, or water magic. If this went poorly—

Yup, *dead*.

Getting the rusty metal to move was one thing. Getting it to walk out of the castle and pick me up and carry me through miles of rough terrain was another thing entirely.

I didn't want to focus on what the other students were doing. They were not my competition. I was. The only person I needed to beat today was myself.

The spell took hold and I waited precious seconds for my awareness to expand. Of course, if I'd been allowed to use my transfiguration, not only would I have made it to the finish line before everyone else, but I would have hands down won without breaking a sweat. Did anyone really think about how quickly a peregrine could fly? And it wouldn't take any kind of magic tied to air or earth. Only to myself.

Yeah, transfiguration was a great idea if I wanted to

expose myself and be thrown out of this land for the rest of my inhumanly long existence.

I held tightly to the connection to the magic, hearing the words in my head: *Etanimae quaea venire mai. Etanimae quaea venire mai.*

Please let this work, please let this work!

It was my own personal chant.

Mike and I had decided on the armor because it was lighter than a statue with better joints for walking. Praying I'd done enough to at least get the armor out here, I repeated the spell. Then I felt cold steel press against my back and I leaned into the contact. Allowing the armor to pick me up and carry me off the field. A blanket of cold air fell over us when we passed through the tree line, the wind biting deep.

I wanted to whoop in excitement despite the chill. The damn old thing was moving! And at a pretty decent speed, too. At this point, I either held onto the temperature spell keeping me comfortable or I could keep this connection alive, but I couldn't do both, and I knew which one mattered.

Teeth chattering, I pushed my strength into holding the spell. Listening to the satisfying clink and clank of metal.

Mike had been right on the money to delve into those old books. The kind of old books people tried to ban because they contained powerful forgotten magic.

I purposely kept my eyes focused straight ahead. I didn't want to see what the others were doing and risk breaking my focus or wondering if there was something I could have done better. The spell I used—Mike as well—was an archaic one and didn't rely on any kind of elemental power to boost it. That would go against the rule of using the elements. No, the spell relied solely on the user's life force and personal will.

Creative? Maybe not the most. Dangerous? *Absolutely*.

It was along the same lines of the first trial, in which one needed to know when to stop or else the magic might take their entire life force to sustain the spell. Except today, if I reached that point and I cut off the spell, I'd lose. I had to hope I could keep the armor going even over the roughest terrain without dropping me or becoming stuck or somehow disabled.

Touch the ground and I'd be out; that was the biggest rule.

I hated the rules. I hated the monsters who made up the rules.

The armor kept moving, kept pushing forward slowly. Its metal toe hit a rock and it stumbled, going down on both knees and I scrambled to hang on and not come in contact with the ground. I gripped the thing's neck to keep from slipping.

Close, too close.

I wasn't sure how much time passed with the late spring wind biting into my skin. There was no snow on the ground, thank goodness, but there were tripping hazards galore. It took everything inside of me to navigate the armor and make sure it didn't run into a tree or break off a leg on a boulder or fallen log. We were alone in the woods.

And I felt my strength begin to dip.

I panicked at the first wavering. The first feeling of being out of control. The sound of rushing water became louder the farther we walked and I knew we'd soon hit the river, the same one winding through the village. How was I supposed to navigate the thing across a freakin' river?

The armor slowed in response to my doubt and its arms began to lower. With a panicked yelp I clung on tighter. *No, not now!* Not when I still heard the faint roaring of the crowd near the palace. It might be my imagination but I knew we hadn't gone far enough. Not nearly far enough.

My magic began to sputter and I dredged up every smidgen of energy and power within me until sheer exhaustion won out. The armor stopped at the edge of the river and the sound of rushing water filled my ears. I didn't have any magical juice left to get across the water. I wasn't going to make it. No way.

Emotion nearly overcame me and I let out a sound suspiciously like a sob. *I'm not good enough.*

Forget making it through the Elite Academy. That was only the here and now. The truth was I'd never been good enough. Always half this and half that, never fully one thing or the other. Divided. Weak. Not good enough. Raised as pack but having to keep my Fae nature hidden...what good did it do? All those times I'd followed the rules and did as I was told, all the people who had died around me, all the shit I'd been through. All of it was so I could get here to this point—and I didn't have the mettle to make it through.

Raw fury exploded inside of me. I wanted to rip the armor apart piece by piece, imagining the king's head in the empty helmet. I screamed out every bit of frustration and injustice until my energy level dropped dangerously low and I knew if I didn't do something I would die. The spell would take the last bits of my power and use them up, leaving nothing left for me.

What did I have to lose anymore? I'd already had everything tossed at me without end. People who didn't even know me hated me. Even though I'd never shown my true power people feared me. People underestimated me because I'd needed a tutor's help.

Magic radiated from me, fueled by the fury I'd been masking under a guise of pity. The ground beneath the armor began to shake and shudder.

I shouldn't let myself get worked up because it wouldn't do any good. I should put those feelings away and focus on pushing through and dealing with it later.

It was always later, though, wasn't it?

But something twisted inside of me and the magic filled every cell, every pore, threatening to ricochet out and spill onto everything around me.

This time, I thought, I didn't want to pull the magic back. I didn't want my anger and my pain to collapse in on itself when I stuffed it away.

And despite the pain, I pushed through. I laid my hand on the armor's hollow shoulder to urge it forward. One step at a time, it crossed the river without issue and the tenuous cord binding me to this spell began to grow. To surge. To strengthen to the point where I knew no matter what I did today, it wouldn't stop until I wanted it to.

I held my magic to me, imagining it like the sun. A swirling circle of endless energy with no beginning and no end. It was my birthright.

I remembered the day Juno set me on that practice trial, her words to me. I remembered the tiny flicker I'd managed and the way my strength flagged no matter how hard I'd tried.

It's your internal fortitude. You're doubting yourself and it's not allowing your magic to manifest to its fullest potential.

How many times had I held myself back because of doubt? Because I didn't feel safe being myself?

With the sun spell, I'd needed the connection to the earth. I'd thought if I drew what I could from the land itself, it would be enough. I didn't realize *I* was the source. *I* was the connection to the land through my blood and where I'd come from.

I refuse to let you use your halfling status as an excuse anymore. I've felt the level of power inside of you, Tavi. This is not the time for excuses nor is it the time to doubt yourself. You have as much power as any of the students you go to school with, no matter what you think. Now focus.

She'd instructed me to call down the sun and hold it for as long as possible. What I hadn't understood at the time was that it wasn't the power of the sun—it was the power of *me*. My power. My magic. And now I must find the same kind of mental and physical endurance.

Juno was right. That was my first thought when I pulled myself up by the bootstraps and conquered that plateau, pushed through the boundary. And it was as if a dam keeping the majority of my magic in check had burst. She'd been right about more lurking beneath the surface. More power than I knew what to do with, and I'd been afraid of it my whole life.

No more flickering light. No more doubting my energy and trying to bear down to force something to happen. Now it came to me easily.

And not long after, I crossed the finish line. I could finally tune in to the cheers and howls and applause. Not just a finisher. One of the top few.

"Tavi! Oh my God! Oh my God, *you did it!*"

Melia's voice reached me and at last the suit of armor halted and lowered its arms, allowing me to slip from its grasp. I wasn't feeling the cold when my friend grabbed me and tugged me into a lung-squashing hug.

From over Melia's shoulder I saw another figure coming through the woods. A second suit of armor. This one carried the golden-haired prince on its shoulders.

No matter how we'd ended things between us the other day, nothing could stop me from holding out my hand to him. And amidst the screaming crowd chanting his name, Mike came to me, hugging both Melia and me at the same time.

"You guys!" she was saying. "You're in the top finishers. You're in the *top*!" Her voice ended in a screech and I allowed myself a moment of rare and surprising joy. I howled with her. I jumped up and down surrounded by two of my best friends in the world. I sank myself into the moment because the small voice in the back of my head told me to savor it while I could.

"Well done, you two." A familiar voice chuckled dryly near us and when I glanced over I saw Headmaster Cyrus staring at us with a small smile. His one milky blue eye still freaked me out, but I returned the smile. "Very well done," he said. "You can take your places with the rest of the top winners."

"It's fine. I'll catch up with you later. You can tell me everything." Melia rubbed a circle on my back and bid goodbye to Mike.

There were only five other students who'd managed to cross the finish line so far. Mike grabbed my hand and we joined the others, Arlyss among them. It was the best mood I'd been in for days. Must be, because I wasn't even annoyed to see Arlyss's smug face.

"Well done," Arlyss said. Mostly to Mike. But I caught the way his gaze flicked to me. "What sort of magic did you work?"

We circled up and compared notes. Mike still held my hand. I didn't know much about being happy these days, but I figured it must look like this. It had to.

Minutes passed until Headmaster Cyrus stepped into the middle of the clearing, clapping his weathered brown hands for attention. "Students! Your ears to me, please. Attention, everyone!"

It took precious seconds to get our excitement to quiet long enough to hear him.

"Everyone please return to your homes immediately."

Mike's fingers tightened around mine.

"What's going on?" I whispered to him as I craned my head to see above the crowd.

"I'm not sure."

"Quickly now," Cyrus barked out. "We're opening a portal to transport you all back to the courtyard of the academy. Everyone, please. Let's go. Now."

It didn't take long for the news—not a rumor—to reach us: Another student was dead.

Oh no!

I slid my arm around Mike's waist. At least he was safe.

"Come on, stay close to me. It's going to be fine."

He kept his gaze trained ahead as we all made our way slowly toward the hastily opened portal. The familiar clench of magic pinched against my skin as we passed through.

Much to my surprise, Melia hadn't left yet, and she followed us through the portal, her expression of worry no doubt mirroring my own.

"Did you hear?" She stepped closer to my other side opposite Mike.

"Yeah, we did." I swallowed over a lump in my throat. "What happened?"

She shook her head. "I'm not sure but I'm going to stay with you two for a little bit. I hope no one will mind."

"I surely won't mind. Stay as long as you like. Just know you'll be dealing with some really obnoxious people," I warned.

"Oh, it's okay. I've gotten used to Mike."

"Hey now!" He pretended outrage, but I could tell he was equally happy to have Melia around.

A little later we were all asked to gather in the public dining hall of Elite together. Soon a handful of other students poured in from the portal, some who had made it through the Trial though not in the top times, and others who had failed or been officially cut short by the newest development. Someone had the bright idea to break out refreshments to celebrate. Among the faculty I saw Miss Wicks pouring glasses of champagne for us.

I also saw Coral. Guess she'd made it through too. Like I had any doubt about her ability to win. I secretly—and a bit juvenilely, I admit—stuck my tongue out at her behind her back before happily accepting a glass of bubbly from Melia.

"Cheers to your win!" she called out before tipping her glass for a long sip.

Suddenly, despite the latest tragedy, things didn't seem so bad after all. Mike had his arm around me, Melia was smiling, there were glasses clinking together, and everyone was happy. Chatting and excited despite the bad news.

Somewhere along the line word caught us about the student who'd died. A quiet girl, one of the bookish sort I might have been friends with if I'd been at the top of the class at Elite with her.

"It's happening again," Melia moaned, shaking her head so hard golden-brown curls fell over her face. She took another drink. "The same damn thing trailed us here from the mortal world."

"Aw, come on," Mike said. He kept his arm around my waist and heat spread from where he touched me. "Surely it's not as bad as you think. It's not like we have another serial killer in our midst."

Except Mike didn't know what I knew.

Maybe I really was too good at keeping secrets.

"I'm sure your father has all of his people on the case." Melia took a step closer and lowered her voice. "I mean, it's not like what happened at the halfling school. This was a full-blood Fae. The king is probably sparing no expense to make sure this is stopped in its tracks."

"Yet it keeps happening," I said. I hadn't told Melia everything. Funny how I would keep the Claw & Fang from her even though she knew about my secret halfling status.

Great idea, Tavi. Stir the pot a little more, why don't you.

"I don't want either one of you to worry," Mike said. "We have people on it. Not only my father and the guards, but the Faerie Bureau of Investigation." He jostled me. "Tavi is well acquainted with their bulldog ways. Right?"

I rolled my eyes. "Sadly, yeah. They are focused on finding the killer. Or finding a guilty party, at least. Someone to pin it on and restore order."

Hopefully with this latest body, they would find the real killer, because this witch hunt needed to stop.

"Hello, Tavi."

I jerked at the familiar voice. I spun around to find Selene staring at me, her black hair gleaming under the light of the chandeliers.

"Have some time to talk to little ol' me?"

"Isn't that the reporter who bothered you during the Spring Games?" Mike asked under his breath.

I patted his arm. "It's fine," I assured him. "I'll only be a minute. She probably just wants to talk about the Trials, I'm sure."

I knew she didn't. I'd seen that look in her eyes too many times during our meetings. My skin prickled as dread settled beneath my sternum.

"What's wrong?" Selene and I kept our footsteps purposely slow and normal on our way out of the dining hall. "What's happened? Is it about the latest student victim?"

She waited until we were alone to answer. "It's not about the student. I'm sorry to pull you away from the celebration—"

"It's fine," I interrupted with a wave of my hand. But she hesitated. What didn't she want to tell me?

She was clearly nervous, her normally flawless makeup smeared in places, and lines where there had never been any lines before.

Her next words chilled me to the bone. "It's Bronwen. She's been attacked."

25

Selene took hold of my hand and the moment we were sure we didn't have an audience, we took off.

What had happened to Bronwen? When?

Was that why she didn't show up to cheer me on for the Trial?

Worry gnawed at my gut as we transformed and flew over the treetops. I followed Selene's lead, waning afternoon light glinting off of her midnight-dark wings. She flew faster than I did. Panic pushed us both and I struggled to keep up, following Selene's swooping motion in her owl form down through the trees, away from the city center of Eahsea.

We landed with Selene already talking, striding forward on killer high heels sinking deep into the forest floor, morphing from owl to normal form seamlessly. "This is a safe space," she told me. "It functions as a half-shifter hospital for those of us who need to remain under the radar."

"I don't see anything."

"Of course you don't. It's hidden from the eyes." Selene waved a hand and a burst of magic revealed a doorway with a gleaming brass knob in the middle of a tree. "It's not safe for those like us to use Fae hospitals or health centers, in case they want to do any in-depth testing." Her hand twisted the doorknob and she pushed it open. "It might reveal our true nature."

"I understand."

My hands trembled and the rest of me was ready to burst. I knew the feeling wouldn't go away anytime soon, at least until I knew Bronwen's condition.

Selene held the door aside for me, waiting until I'd stepped through before closing it smartly behind us. Magic pulsed once before the doorway disappear. The inside of the shifter hospital opened up into a large room more than likely connected to a separate pocket of space because no way would all this fit inside the tree itself.

Whatever magic anchored the room to Faerie must have been heavy-duty powerful, I thought as I stared. The ceiling soared up into an intricate knot of what looked to be intertwined tree branches. Lines of hospital beds were pressed against the left and right exterior walls, some of them filled but most of them empty. I spotted a familiar face three beds down and rushed forward without thinking.

"Oh God. Bronwen!"

My own aches and pains disappeared the longer I looked at her. A small part of me thought: *This is my fault. This has happened to her because of me.*

"I knew you would want to come as soon as possible," Selene said, stepping closer. "It was a close call."

She'd lost too much blood was my second thought. Though she was awake, staring at me with wide dark eyes, her skin was pale as snow. "Tavi?" she said softly.

"I'm here." I knelt down at the side of the bed, still wearing my clothes from the Trial, and grabbed her hand as gently as I could. "Are you okay?"

She tried to shake her head and winced. "I thought I could do it alone. I thought...I don't know what I thought."

"Don't talk. I'm here. Save your energy to get better."

Her eyes filled with tears. "You fought him and you were fine. Why couldn't I do the same?"

I glanced at Selene. "What happened?"

Why was no one giving me the details?

"We've got to stop him, Tavi," Bronwen muttered. "He's nuts. And he's strong. I was only able to stop him from killing me by shifting to wolf and fighting dirty. I don't know if he's going to stop killing, now that he's started. He's...he's a monster. He's mad."

The half-shifter who'd attacked Juno... Now it made sense. Sort of. Bronwen had tried to take down the killer by herself, but had gotten too deep into the fight with the half-shifter and instead of coming out on top, she'd barely escaped with her life and limbs intact. I knew how she felt, though. I understood the combination of fear and anger in her eyes. Angry at herself not just for putting herself in that position but also for losing, for being beaten. Fearful of another encounter.

"We're going to get him. I promise."

"You need to rest, Bronwen," Selene said through the low hum of healing magic pulsing through the space. She laid a hand on my shoulder. "Enough for now."

"Yes. I'll come back as soon as I can," I told Bronwen while keeping hold of her hand. I gave it one last squeeze before rising, but Bronwen didn't let go. She pulled me closer.

When Bronwen spoke again, she did so through her teeth, swallowing over a wave of pain despite the magic helping to knit her back together. "I almost had him. One more strike and he might have gone down. I'm sorry, Tavi. He's still out there because I messed up."

I shook my head. "Damn it. I don't want to hear you apologize."

Her fingers clenched around mine. "I'm a shapeshifter. I should have been able to help him."

"Why did you go at it alone?"

"Because you did. And I...I thought I could, too."

So. It *was* my fault after all.

Bronwen closed her eyes then and soon her breathing evened out and her grip on my hand loosened. I tucked her hand back at her side before turning to Selene.

She gestured for me to walk away from the bed and I followed her. Selene pointed to a group of chairs near the rear of the room. I didn't see anyone else around. The healers must be out of sight. We took two seats and faced each other. Even Selene looked pale, a difficult thing with her bronzed skin.

"Bronwen was patrolling last night and came across a woman walking alone," Selene informed me softly. "Something must have struck her as suspect because she began to follow the woman through the village. Maybe she had red hair, I didn't get all the details. All I know is the shifter suddenly appeared and jumped them. From what I understand, the woman got away unharmed but Bronwen was savagely attacked instead."

"Why didn't she call out for someone?" She shouldn't have been there alone. The thought plagued me because I was supposed to be patrolling with her. And I'd backed out.

Now she was hurt.

"At least she was able to get away alive, and her injuries, though serious, will heal." Selene kept her tone soft as her hand fell on my shoulder. "I know what you're thinking."

I let out a little laugh, more an effect of how my whole body trembled. "I know. I'm pretty transparent."

"It's not your fault. Okay? You have a lot going on and

blaming yourself isn't going to heal her and it isn't going to help us catch the killer. Bronwen decided to go alone. That was her choice. It was her choice to intervene when it would have been safer not to. Still, she did us proud."

"And look where it got her. I'm so sorry." I knew it wouldn't make a difference what I said but I had to say it anyway. "*I'm so sorry*."

"You can tell her that when she wakes up. But I know she doesn't blame you. Not even a little bit," Selene said.

"She *should* blame me."

"No, she shouldn't. All those in the Claw & Fang share equal responsibility for keeping our kind safe. Bronwen did her part, and from what you've both told me about the attack on your mentor, you would have done the same thing. You *did* do the same thing. You jumped right into the fray to protect someone in need." She patted my knee. "So buck up, kiddo. We're going to stop this guy."

"I don't know how," I said wearily. Suddenly the chill was too much and every inch of me began to shake, from my knees to my teeth.

"We'll think of something," she told me with certainty. She did everything with a calm assurance I'd never be able to match. "The others and I are looking into a way to neutralize the shifter's ability to maintain his halfling form. If we can expose him, we can find a way to stop him."

"How? I didn't think that was possible." Knowing her, she'd already have a plan in place but so far she hadn't revealed it to me. If I had things my way, I'd be out there right now trying to find the guy who did this, the guy who might even be injured enough from Bronwen's attack to be at a weak point. It was a good time to hit him, but the chances of finding him, even with the combined power of the Claw & Fang, were slim.

Besides us, there were others out there looking for him

too. The bureau, for one, and the king's guards for another. How were we supposed to catch a killer when even the king himself was convinced I was somehow involved?

Selene sighed and fixed me with a stare. Her eyes were devoid of their usual sharp humor. "Neither did I. And it may not work. We won't give up, though. And whatever happens, know that we are going to take the best care of Bronwen that we can. We aren't going to let anything else happen to her. So stop beating yourself up."

"I can't help it," I moaned, dropping my head into my hands. "If I'd been there—"

"No more," she interrupted. "Stay with her for a little bit tonight. Then tomorrow we'll start fresh. We'll have a plan of attack by then. Understood?"

I didn't have a choice. With a grimace, I agreed. "Understood."

~

On Monday Headmaster Cyrus called an academy-wide assembly to discuss the information for the third Trial. This one would test Bravery and had something to do with a tournament of magic where only the best would make it through. Another damn tournament pitting us against each other to see how we would perform, like show ponies.

There would be potions to brew, spells to cast, obstacles to overcome, and danger at every turn. And for what? To entertain a bunch of privileged voyeurs?

It didn't seem fair to me, but with my attention fractured, I might have missed something important, some reason why we were forced to compete. Nothing I'd heard up to then seemed a good enough reason.

I managed to make it through the assembly with my

knees bobbing and my fingers tapping on the armrests, just waiting until it was over. Sure, I worried about making it through the next Trial. But there were other, more important issues that needed my attention. Like finding Bronwen's attacker, for instance.

I didn't want to get Mike involved in what I had planned. Especially not when my secret had a huge potential to be exposed because of this. After the assembly, I made an excuse to him and hurried to send a call out for Melia and Onyx to meet me. They were the two people I knew I could trust.

We met at the same small café where Melia had first ambushed me with the proposition of meeting with another half-shifter, someone who could teach me more about my transfiguration power. The same someone who ironically turned out to be my fated mate's son.

A guy who also happened to have a crush on me. Could my life get any *more* complicated?

I pushed those thoughts aside and cleared my throat as I stared at the two of them. Onyx looked like he'd rather be chewing rocks than sitting down with me. He grabbed his chair, turned it around to straddle and brace his arms on the back, and looked at me.

I looked back at him. "It's time for me to put everything out on the table," I said, gesturing with my hands.

Onyx rolled his eyes. "Sounds like a dangerous proposition."

"Are we ordering food?" Melia asked. She glanced around the rest of the diner. "And where's Bronwen? Shouldn't she be here?"

"She's part of the reason why I wanted to talk to you guys. Yes, we can order food, get whatever you want." I pressed my palm against my stomach. I was way too nervous to eat anything. I hadn't been able to stomach even the thought of food since visiting my friend the night before.

Slowly, I sketched out the recent events for the two of them, describing the attack on Bronwen.

"Oh no! Is she okay?" Onyx asked.

"She will be. She's strong."

I knew what they were thinking—shapeshifters were notoriously hard to track and kill, and it was a good thing Bronwen shared the same DNA otherwise there was a chance of the shifter's blood infecting her. The transformation had been known to kill humans in the past. At least there was no chance of her being adversely affected in that way.

"Here's what we know." I spelled out everything, from the attacks on the full-blood Fae women to what I'd found during the first Trial. Through my explanation food was delivered and Melia dug into the appetizers. She never took her focus from me, and although she interrupted a few times with questions, she never offered anything but full support for whatever I had planned.

Onyx, on the other hand, was quiet through it all. Watching and storing away the information to process in his own manner no doubt.

"Whoever the shifter is," I told them, "he attacked at both of the first two Trials. It stands to reason he'll try something for the third one too. Don't you think?"

Melia nodded. "So we have to figure out who is the most likely candidate to be attacked next and work on finding a way to protect them," she offered.

"Not to mention getting you through the Trial without bodily harm," Onyx added. "We have to keep in mind they are designed to test your will and your magic. You can't divide your attention to the point where you put yourself in harm's way."

"I'm going to be fine," I insisted with much more confidence than I felt. Onyx snorted. "I know Mike and I will come up with a workable plan. He's probably researching right now even as we speak. But I refuse to let anyone else be hurt. I'm determined that nobody else will have to die."

Melia grabbed another fried zucchini blossom, stuffing it into her mouth and talking around it. "You've never been able to stay on the sidelines for this kind of thing. You are too much of a humanitarian."

Ha, as if.

"Let's start with the basics," Onyx said and began ticking items off on his fingers. "First, the type of look this maniac is targeting. Specifically, girls who look a lot like Tavi. Which is weird."

"You're telling me. The victims do seem to have the same aesthetic, with light eyes and red hair. All except for Juno Ians."

"Yes, but she's your mentor," Melia said. "There's the connection to you."

"And now targeting students in the Trials instead of random Fae in the streets. It's like he's narrowing his focus," Onyx offered.

I shivered. I didn't like to be reminded of their similarity to me, or how I'd already noticed a pattern. Like a circle getting smaller and smaller until it tightened, noose-like, around my neck.

"So like I said before, we need to figure out the most likely candidate for the next attack and find a way to protect them." Melia finished off the plate of appetizers and stared down at it, as if unsure how the delicacies had disappeared so quickly.

"Yes," I agreed. "That makes the most sense."

"Since we don't go to school with you, you're going to have to take us through the girls who will be competing.

The ones with looks similar to yours, at least. Give us the details and then we can begin to narrow it down."

"And the Trial?" Onyx asked.

"One thing at a time, friend. One thing at a time." Melia patted him on the leg and Onyx looked like he wanted to bolt.

But he didn't. Onyx showed no signs of backing down, which I appreciated about him. He was always there to help if I needed it, even after the terrible argument we'd had. I shot him a smile to show my gratitude. For meeting me. For staying. For being reasonable.

He leaned forward in his chair. "Show us what you've got, Tavi."

I brought up a list of names I'd already thought about, along with pictures taken from the student roster. That was one thing I could say about the technology of Faerie—the magic made it much easier to access things. With my cell in hand, I swiped through the electronic roster.

There were very few halflings at Elite. In fact, there were only a handful I knew about, and none of them were half human, let alone half wolf. It simply wasn't done. Part of the reason why I was so unpopular.

We quickly disregarded the boys, then skipped over girls with dark skin, light hair, etc. Going through and narrowing the focus until there was only one name left on the list. One photo that had my gut twisting all over again.

I sat back in the chair and had to work hard to keep from groaning.

"I take it you know her?" Onyx asked, his finger pointing at the picture on my phone screen.

"In a manner of speaking," I hedged. *Ugh. No, please. Let us be wrong this time.*

Melia laughed. "I can tell from the look on your face you aren't a big fan."

"I mean...well, no, actually, *not* a big fan." The confession drew a similar smile on both of their faces. I didn't feel like smiling. Not when I knew intuitively they were right and we'd found the next mark. Especially knowing she was going to make this *very* hard.

Onyx tilted his head, staring at the picture. "She's cute. In a snobbish sort of way. And I can definitely see a resemblance."

"If Tavi were a stone-cold bitch who wore too much makeup, then maybe," Melia argued. Good, she had my back. "I'm not convinced."

"We don't need you to be convinced, just to accept the probability that this is the best lead we have in catching this killer," Onyx insisted. "Are you on board or not? This is for the good of the realm, and for Tavi. We need to stop this killer before he gets too close to his real goal." His gaze shifted to me.

"Duh." Melia shot me a small smile. "You know I'll do whatever it takes to keep my girl safe."

While that made my heart feel warm, looking at the photo on my cell phone chilled it again. We'd narrowed it to one person.

Coral Ferenze.

And I knew she wasn't going to make this easy.

26

The day of the third Trial came before I could blink, and I stood with Mike, keeping a discreet eye on Coral. Mike didn't understand my sudden fascination with her. I did my best not to make it obvious, but he always knew when something fishy was going on. Today was no exception.

"I'd rather you look at me like that," he leaned close to whisper.

I shook my head. "I look at you enough."

He seemed surprised. "You do?"

"Seriously?" I grinned and reached out to pinch him lightly. He looked adorable today, in a green tunic to match his eyes and a pair of tight jeans. I wasn't sure why he wanted to wear jeans instead of the workout gear the rest of us had chosen...but I appreciated the view. "I look at you all the time. And I'm not the only one. You'd be surprised how many people find it hard to keep their eyes off of you."

His eyes twinkled with mischief. "I don't care about them, though. I only care about you."

And that admission made everything inside of me go warm.

Not the time. Focus!

From the corner of my eye I saw Coral's attention shift in our direction. But when I glanced over at her, she resumed her warm-up routine of pointedly ignoring me while stretching out her arms and legs in exaggerated yoga moves. She had her face painted for the balcony—full complement of foundation, eye shadow, eye liner, mascara, blush, and lipstick, all applied with an obviously heavy hand—and her outfit probably cost more than my entire wardrobe back at Uncle Will's combined. And I didn't exactly come from nothing.

Honestly, who wore diamonds to a magic tournament?

"She's taking things a little far, don't you think? I'm not sure the workout routine is really necessary," I said, trying to divert his focus off of my focus so he wouldn't be suspicious. Because Mike needed to keep his distance during this Trial. Otherwise my cover would be blown. I also didn't want to risk him getting hurt if the half-shifter showed up for Coral.

"You know how Coral is, though. She doesn't do anything halfway." Mike's expression soured and he narrowed his eyes, partly against the glare of the spring sun and partly because...well, Coral. "She's always over the top."

I smirked. "*Over the top* is putting it nicely."

Although I was nervous for the start of the Trial, I was more nervous for what I'd be facing. Through the last few months of classes, Mike seemed to have really come around with his behavior toward the other students. He no longer adopted that cold persona when it came to people like Lane or Coral. In fact, whenever Coral was around, Mike took great care to keep the conversation short and leave the room as soon as possible.

While I was happy enough to take credit for Mike's turn-around, I didn't have time to gloat.

Coral continued stretching those long, long legs, her red

239

hair in an intricate series of braids at the top of her head. Mine hung in two low ponytails, looking like I hadn't showered this morning. She was the golden girl, the perfect one, put together even on her worst days.

The rest of the students participating in today's Trial gathered close to Coral. Moths to a fake flame who didn't know enough to question it. No matter how awful I found her, no matter how much of a bitch she'd been to me, she still didn't deserve to die.

And I was going to make sure of it. I hardened my resolve.

"You have everything you need?" Mike gestured to my backpack. "You didn't have to bring the kitchen sink with you. The whole point of the first sprint today was to find the mineral we need to fashion a weapon."

I shrugged against the weight of the bag, filled to the brim with spell supplies I might need or whatever. "It's better to be prepared for anything," I replied. "We can't all be the prince with his amazing magical stamina."

We looked at each other for a long moment, both smiling, because I knew. And Mike knew. He had the *Augundae Totalis* helping him with his powers.

"You're teasing me." He tweaked my nose. "We'll see what kind of mood you're in when this ends today."

"Oh yeah?"

"I thought maybe you and I could have our own celebration party. Maybe we could hang out and watch a movie."

My cheeks heated and my grin widened. "You're on."

I suddenly snapped to attention when I realized I didn't see Coral anymore. I jerked around, sweeping the crowd until I spotted her sidling up to Arlyss and flirting as if she wasn't facing a dangerous task.

Arlyss lapped up the attention, with Lane standing at his side looking like a third wheel. An embarrassed third wheel.

"Students! Students, please quiet down." Headmaster Cyrus and the rest of the school officials judging this trial called for our attention with a clap and a boom of magic.

At once the crowd hushed. Mike and I moved closer to hear what he had to say. To prepare ourselves for what we would face today. My focus narrowed on Coral. I adjusted the weight of my backpack again.

"Your first step today will be an easy one, for those of you proficient in conjuring. Simply remember what Professor Ninea told you during charms class. Keep your focus strong, your heart light, and your intentions pure. Then the work begins."

I barely heard the rest of his speech or the starting buzzer, and might have stayed in place watching Coral until my eyes blurred if Mike hadn't pushed me into action. "Go on," he called as he jogged in the opposite direction. "I'll meet up with you at the end of the day. Try not to die."

Was that going to be our new goodbye slogan? *Try not to die?* I wasn't sure I liked it.

We were not supposed to work together for this one. The handful of students participating today headed off in different directions, searching for an element only found in Faerie, knowing once we found it, the true test part of the Trial would begin in earnest.

We were tasked with fashioning a weapon of choice, and once we did, it was on to the tournament. Headmaster Cyrus had given no details about the tasks ahead outside of saying we'd be forced to use every bit of knowledge we'd acquired at school. His words were no help. I felt less and less prepared with each announcement.

I trailed behind Coral at a respectable distance. Her attention was so focused on the goal, I had a feeling she wouldn't have acknowledged me even if I rode her piggy-back-style.

The moment I was relatively sure there was no one around to see it, I transformed. There were no judges here to put a magnifying glass over me, no camera orbs overhead, at least for the moment. I transfigured into something small and unnoticeable but fast.

A fox.

There were plenty of foxes in the forest. I'd seen them from my bedroom window in the castle. I could use the stealth, the eyesight, the senses of the fox body.

The black vixen knew her way around the underbrush. Although Coral was speedy, running faster than the average Fae, I was able to keep up with her. I was the spectator here, not the competition. I was the one waiting and watching and wondering.

The vixen would definitely be able to sense the shifter before he came into view. Although my nerves were on edge, I knew what I had to do, and I kept it in mind.

Save Coral.

She got into plenty of scrapes along the way, I was pleased to note. At one point, she ran too fast and tripped over an exposed tree root, flying forward and landing on her hands and knees. She tripped, she fell, she cursed. I'd say she was just like a regular person but she'd made too much of a point of being pure-blood for the comment to mean anything.

It took her a long time to find the element we'd been tasked with retrieving. Most of the spells she used to locate the material didn't work, and more often than not Coral was fuming and pulling at her braids as though she wanted to rip out her hair.

Inside the body of the fox, my subconscious gloated. A little. It made me feel a little better seeing her struggle. Not everything came easily to her. *Almost* everything, but not all.

The more I watched, the stronger my conviction

became. Bitch or not, Coral was skilled, totally adept at magic. She wielded it easily and naturally and with a confidence I wasn't sure I would ever match. To her it was as easy as breathing. She didn't worry whether or not she'd pass the Trial. She *knew*.

My gloating subsided.

The element Cyrus and the judges wanted us to find turned out to be a gemstone with a metallic glint on its surface. Coral finally used the right spell and after several hours of searching I watched the small stone jettison out of the earth's surface and into her open palm.

Oh, wow.

She clutched the stone to her chest, raising her face to the sky with a slight whoop of excitement. Then, she looked much younger than her years. There was a lightheartedness to her I'd never seen before.

It was hard not to admire her right then. I hated admitting it, especially when her smile turned smug as she stared at the stone, but Coral had the skills to back up her claims of being the best. Despite falling on her face and nearly breaking her arm at one point, she'd done it, and quickly. A few hours seemed like nothing now that she'd found the stone.

She tucked it into the pocket of her leggings, and then took a moment to stretch her arms overhead and do a little celebratory dance, her excitement clear. I glanced down at the moss-covered area where she'd called up the mineral. Did I have time to try a spell and grab a piece for myself, too?

I'd better, or else I'd have no hope of making it through today.

I lost sight of Coral for two minutes. Two minutes after she left the clearing while I transformed and called up my magic. Another minute trying to get the spell to work and faltering when it didn't produce immediate results.

Yeah, this was why everyone else made fun of me. As a halfling, they already thought me less-than, and when I began to fail my classes, it only cemented their view of me.

I struggled to block out those negative thoughts, closing my eyes and centering myself as I tried the spell again.

No time to waste.

The spell worked the second time around. A second stone flew out of the ground and smacked me on the cheek.

"Ouch!"

I blinked against the sting. It was much smaller than the stone Coral managed to gather. With luck, I'd be able to fashion a small dagger at best. What kind of damage could I hope to do with a little needle?

Hopefully it would be enough.

I bagged the stone, tucking it into my backpack before shifting into fox form again. The magical toll it took was much smaller than the first few times I'd tried to transform. Living, breathing organisms were much easier to hold and maintain than wood or stone or steel. Then again, I'd been trying to become one with the walls of a castle. Turns out I should have died.

At least, according to Onyx I should have died.

It made becoming the fox a small win for me. I trotted off after Coral with a yip, ignoring everything else in my surroundings to focus on her.

That's when I sensed something off in the air.

That's when she began to scream.

27

I couldn't risk Coral seeing me transform. It was time to be smart.

Taking a moment to breathe, I called my magic, forcing my body back into normal form and bolting through the forest after her. Listening to the screams get louder and louder.

I slammed my body into the boy trying to drag the stone from her pocket and sent him sprawling. He hit hard on his tailbone, wincing, then scrambled up to face me. He stared at me angrily with his hands curled into fists at his sides.

"Tavi!" Coral didn't sound grateful. "What the hell are you doing here?"

I growled at the boy and his eyes went wide before he took off in the opposite direction. A first-year. One I hadn't seen much before but I recognized his face. I turned to Coral and saw her hands on her hips. Oh yeah, she definitely didn't appreciate my intervention.

"What? I'll take a thank you," I told her. "He was trying to steal from you instead of doing the work himself."

Good job playing it off.

Except the longer she stared at me, the more my gut began to squirm.

"And you're the one following me." Coral pointed a red-painted fingernail in my direction. "Why are you here? Tell me. Are you trying to copy me and get credit for passing this Trial?" She clucked her tongue. "Off of my hard work. It figures."

I had no good excuse to offer her and frankly I doubted Coral would accept anything less than the truth.

Sighing, I adjusted my backpack. "Well, it's a funny story. Why I'm here, I mean."

She shook her head, her eyes squinting and her lips pinched, finding me absolutely ridiculous. "Well, hurry up and tell me. I'm a little busy here. Actually, you know what? Whatever. It doesn't matter what you're doing because *you* don't matter. Getting to the finish line matters," she said.

"Wait!" I reached out to grab her arm to keep her from running off. Might as well tell her. "You're in danger."

She stared down at my hand until I practically felt the burn and released her. "In danger of being seen associating with you."

And there was the snooty tone. The one she always reserved for me or anyone else she saw as beneath her.

I wanted to really let her have it then. I wanted to tell her everything I'd kept inside about how hard I'd tried and none of it mattered to people like her.

Just like I knew anything I said wouldn't matter now.

When I spoke again, it was harsh, matter of fact, and through my gritted teeth. "Listen. I'm sure you've heard by now about the student found during the last Trial. The one ripped apart by a shifter? Or so the authorities are saying."

It wasn't enough to keep her still. Coral began to walk away from me. "Get real, Tavi. I know you're trying to distract me. What, are you trying to steal the piece of

Magnasterium from me, too? If you weren't so far up the prince's behind, then maybe you'd be able to conjure enough magic to find a piece for yourself."

"It's not about the Magnasterium. And besides, I already have my piece, thank you very much. You're in danger because the shifter has been attacking redheads." I jogged after her and tugged at the nearest braid, listening to her outraged yelp. "Redheads like us. In fact, every single Fae girl who's died has looked weirdly like us. Do you understand what I'm trying to tell you?"

Coral waited for me to get to the point.

"You're in danger, Coral. You might be the next to die."

"I'm sure if anyone is going to die, Tavi, it will be you. I don't trust you to tie your shoes, let alone escape a madman."

At least she wasn't doubting the existence of said madman.

"Yes, and I'm sure I'm on his list as well," I replied.

"Then why don't you stay away from me? That way, I'll be safe, and you can do..." She paused. "Whatever it is you do. I'm sure I don't want to know."

"Coral, stop being yourself for a second and listen. One way or another, you're going to get hurt. The shifter won't stop. It's the only reason I'm here right now. Otherwise I'm sure you know I wouldn't be."

Part of me was positive she'd ignore the warning. But something I said must have gotten through to her. Or maybe it was the look on my face. The way she could see, clearly, that I wasn't lying to her.

"Yeah," I said when she began to shake. "Exactly. I'm here to make sure nothing happens to you today, because the person behind the attacks seems to be using the Trials to make his move. And I..." I swallowed. "I don't want anything to happen to you."

Coral was trembling, shaking her head and refusing to look at me. "No. No, you're wrong."

"I'm here to keep you safe."

"It's ridiculous," she argued, twin blossoms of red on her cheeks now. "Why would someone want to hurt *me*?"

Did she need me to count the reasons? I rolled my eyes. "I can't speak for motives, obviously. I'm not inside his head. All I know is that this guy is dangerous and it's likely he'll try to come after you today. It's the only reason I'm with you right now."

"That's it." Coral threw her hands in the air. "I'm dropping out of this Trial. I'm going back to the school and then I'm going home. At least there I'll be safe from the riffraff."

By which she clearly meant me.

"Hey, hold on. It's okay."

She pressed a hand to her chest. "Do I look like a victim, Tavi? Do I look like the kind of girl murderers hunt for sport? Absolutely not. I'm taking myself out of the equation. He'd have to be insane to come into my house. Ergo, if I'm in my house, then I'm safe and away from the crazies."

The way she said it, I knew she was lumping me into the *crazies* part as well.

"No," I repeated. "You and I are going to get through this Trial. We're going to finish what we started and we're going to win. Together. I won't let anything happen to you." If she thought her bad attitude would keep me from sticking by her side, then she'd better think again. The bad attitude would make it difficult but I always saw things through to the end. Period.

Coral scoffed. "What the hell can *you* do about it, half-breed? You barely managed to get through the Summer Games. It's a wonder you've made it this far into the Trials without having to rely on Michael to pull you through. It's bad enough the school had to assign you a tutor just to pass your classes."

It took everything inside of me to rein in my temper. Bristling, I faced her head on. "Look," I said through gritted teeth, "we're wasting time. Right now, we both have the pieces we need to make a weapon. Let's get a move on because we are wasting time."

She heard what I didn't say. *I'm not going anywhere. You're stuck with me.*

Coral had her hands on her hips again, staring at me, willing me to back down until she had her way. "Tavi—"

"If you say my name like that one more time, I'm going to leave you alone and let this guy have you," I warned. "Trust me when I say I want to keep you safe."

"I don't understand why you care."

"Neither do I. But through it all, you're really...you're really not a bad person." I died a little inside saying it. "You don't deserve to be murdered. I've seen what the killer has done to his other victims. It's not pretty." Yes, I'd seen first-hand what he was capable of doing.

Her finger was back in the air and waving around like a wand. "Just stay out of my way," she insisted.

I wrestled with my conscience for a moment. Maybe she was right and I should leave her alone. It would be much easier going forward. Easier on my mind, my head, the outcome of this Trial...

No. That felt wrong.

"Gladly," I answered her, and my voice had lost all of its charm.

As Mike had done for me, and I got a lot of personal satisfaction out of it, I pushed Coral to keep her going. She huffed angrily and sped up her steps to keep a full six feet ahead of me.

We'd never been advised where to go for the next step of

the Trial. I only assumed we would face obstacles along the way. We walked along the sunlit path, new leaves on the trees and purple crocuses sprouting out of the ground.

"I'm not sure why you're even bothering with me." Coral twisted her neck to look back over her shoulder at me.

"Yeah, I'm not sure either."

"Why don't you let the authorities handle this murderer? I mean, if he's as dangerous as you say, then what can *you* do?"

I kept silent, listening to the sound of our footsteps.

I didn't need her to tell me how she felt about me. She might as well have had a sign above her head: TAVI IS USELESS.

She swept along the path like the queen herself. I took a moment of pleasure seeing her jump when the harpy bolted down through the trees and blocked the path with a screech.

Then I realized we were facing down a freakin' *harpy*.

This one made the ones I'd seen in the stands during the commencement ceremony look like parakeets.

Large brown wings expanded to the point where the feathers touched the trees on either side of the path. Wicked sharp talons curved from eagle feet and dug into the earth leaving trenches behind them. In her eyes I saw nothing but fury.

"Tavi!"

I definitely didn't expect the first word out of Coral's mouth to be my name. And we didn't have enough time to fashion a weapon from the Magnasterium. I dropped my backpack and drew a vial from its depths.

The *Eius Repellere*, a one-use concoction to repel anyone or anything from you without harm and can be used on upwards of twenty enemies at a time. Back at the Fae Academy for Halflings, the last step of our final exams to get into year two involved making the concoction using our wits to fill in missing pieces of the recipe.

I'd won.

It was just one harpy, but I wasn't taking any chances. I tossed the vial at her and watched it explode in a cloud of sparkling green. The harpy jettisoned up and out of sight before she had a chance to attack, pulled away by the force of the spell.

Safe. Still, my heart refused to slow.

Coral turned around slowly to stare at me. Not with appreciation, no. With disgust. "I was saying your name to get you to step back and let me handle it."

I suppressed a shudder. "You're welcome!" I huffed with as much sarcasm as I could muster.

"I told you to stay out of my way. Seems you really do have a problem following the simplest of orders."

If her words were claws, they'd be pressed right to my throat. I swallowed everything terrible I wanted to say and let her walk away, keeping my distance once again as I shouldered my backpack. *Don't engage*, I told myself. Let her say whatever she wanted to about me. I knew what just happened.

I'd saved her life when she didn't expect it, and it unbalanced the normal dynamic between us. She didn't like that. Neither did I.

There were no more harpies on our walk back to the green meadow behind the palace. There were, however, spells hidden in the forest surrounding us. We traveled together and made it through whatever we faced.

There was a spell that switched our faces and we had to try and get them back to normal. There was a spell causing us to lose our hair. There was a spell turning the earth into slime and we had to reverse the process to move out of it.

There were monsters and there was fire. Coral and I met

them all, and with the sun going down at our backs I turned to face her, watching her bare her teeth. Seeing the predatory light flaring in her eyes as she chuckled and unwound the tangled layers of spells keeping us in place.

The effect was chilling.

By the time midnight rolled around we'd been working together for twelve straight hours—tired, worn out, and still hating each other—with no food outside of the snacks I'd thought to bring in my backpack.

I conjured a fire for us when we both felt chilled. Then stared at Coral from across the flames.

"We should try to get some sleep. This is really a test of endurance, I think." I rubbed my hands together near the flames.

She scoffed. "I don't feel safe falling asleep with you."

"After everything we've been through today," I muttered.

"It's not enough to make me trust you."

"My line."

I understood how she felt, though. Working through the obstacles of the tournament had me bone-tired and at the end of what I could tolerate magically and personally.

Which was the whole point, my exhausted mind argued. The point of the Trials was to test our endurance and, in this case, our bravery.

And although it pained me to admit it, I knew things would have gone much less smoothly if Coral were not here with me. Damn her.

But I watched the way her eyes fluttered. "Rest," I said. "I'll take the first shift and wake you up in a few hours."

She sighed. "Whatever."

That's when the wolf shifter showed up.

28

Worse than the harpy, I knew at once, bolting to my feet at the commotion to my left. The lumbering halfling form crashed through the trees and sent one of the smaller oaks tumbling to the ground. I had to give Coral credit. She didn't scream, didn't panic. She stood to attention with her spine straight and her focus on the warrior form.

Why did he suddenly look larger to me?

Huge paws were clenched at his sides and darkness surrounded him. Muscles bulged, more than I remembered, and he looked mad enough to tear a body into pieces.

In fact he already had.

The shifter saw both of us and raised his head, opening his jaws and roaring. The sound shook the tree limbs.

Coral and I didn't move. We stood there until he cut off, the echoes of the roar reverberating around us. She stared at him, her cheeks white with shock. She didn't have a chance to speak before the shifter was in motion.

I didn't pause. I didn't stop to think about what to do.

The shifter burst through the fire on a growl, his fur lit

by the embers, and the force of his magic, his scent, tore at me like a tornado. Wild and furious.

I screamed and Coral echoed it, finally releasing the fear she'd held inside. With all of my strength I grabbed her at the last instant and jerked her out of the way. A second too late, the shifter slammed his paw down where she'd just been sitting.

Then I launched myself at his throat.

He swatted me aside, landing a hit to my ribs hard enough to shatter them, and howled again, his enormous jaw unhinging until all I saw were his fangs.

He'd gone mad.

The shifter's eyes glowed when he looked at me, the gold overtaken by white and I saw nothing in them outside of pure rage. He burst into motion, a raging tempest of fury, doubling his effort to reach me. I dodged out of the way and grabbed his fur on his way past, jerking him off his feet with everything in me.

Don't let him get to Coral.

That was the point of this, wasn't it?

"You are not going to take me down," I ground out, keeping hold of him. "Sorry."

"What do we do?" I heard Coral's screech somewhere in the distance and when I glanced over, the desperation on her face nearly broke me. She'd been ready to do battle with the harpy, but a shifter was a different story. This wasn't her world. None of this should be happening to her.

Except it was. Because of me.

"I'll call for help!" she continued.

I didn't have a chance to see her work. The whole of my attention focused on keeping the shifter away from her. Keeping him distracted so he wouldn't attack her.

"It's not working. The spell isn't working!" The one the judges had agreed on for when students got into trouble.

We'd seen the signal flares multiple times during the day and I'd had to listen to Coral laugh about the weaklings who couldn't hack their way through the third Trial. I wondered how she felt about being the one to use it now. Or, well, *not* use it.

"He must have blocked us using a spell of his own," I told her.

The shifter crouched on all fours next to me, those wicked eyes boring into mine. If I couldn't keep him distracted, then I'd need her to—

"Run! Coral, run and get help."

Magic swirled around me as I tried to keep the shifter contained and give Coral the chance to escape. She leaped up and dashed into the dark woods like her life depended on her speed.

It did.

The shifter took off after her, his body twisting and jerking. I took off after him.

Hell no. I wouldn't let him hurt her.

I pumped my arms and legs and saw Coral several feet ahead of the lumbering shifter. A blast of magic sent him stumbling. Every inch of me hurt from too much magic spent in one blast, too quickly.

Another burst of speed brought me around in front of him and I quickly reversed and charged. Blocking him as the world around us ground to a halt. I heard myself breathe, once, before he crashed into me. It took three seconds for us to slam to the ground, as if in slow motion. His claws swung past me and I ducked. Rolled. Felt the force of his next attack.

A fist slammed down into my shoulder and I yelped.

"Get off of her!"

I didn't expect to see Coral leap on the creature's back with her hands at his throat. A pulse of power crashed into him from her palms and lit the woods around us in a glow of orange.

Coral versus a seven-foot-tall shifter? I never thought I'd see the day.

The magic, however, bounced off of him and did nothing. His rage-filled roar left my ears ringing. He shrugged her off and before he had a chance to move, I hit him with a whirlwind of punches. My fists flew faster than even my eyes could follow but I needed him to focus on me.

On me, damn you!

If I kept him busy, Coral would have no trouble getting out from the barrier of his spell and contacting the committee.

Over his shoulder I saw Coral dashing back the way we came. Magic pulsed behind her. A containment spell. She wanted to keep the shifter trapped, with me.

I might have been upset about that if I hadn't told her to run and save herself.

The shifter kept pushing me back toward the edge of the spell Coral worked. I ducked and dodged his attempts at an attack but he kept barreling toward me. An unstoppable mass of muscle.

There wasn't any room left for fear. Though my chest heaved and my arms ached like they were going to fall right off, I maintained my defensive position. Legs spread for balance, I braced for his next attack.

"Tavi, here!"

I turned in time to see Coral send something in my direction and the shifter chose that moment to make a move. The tree limb he'd broken off stabbed at my left side and I yelled, dropping down to one knee in agony. The area where he'd hit throbbed like someone threw acid on me.

Snarling, I rolled over on the ground. *Wrong way.* I avoided his next strike by rolling to the opposite direction, the rocks protruding from the ground hitting right where he'd wounded me.

There in the bushes I saw what Coral had been trying to send me.

The two pieces of Magnasterium glowed blue in the darkness. My smaller piece, and Coral's larger one—she'd found them both.

I scrambled to grab them before the shifter realized what she'd done.

He cut me off, stepping on my hand before my fingertips touched the stones. Out of options and with pain shooting through me, I kicked up at him, using the same kind of magic Juno demanded of me when calling down the sun. Flame shot out from my leg. I turned and watched it sink into the fur of the shifter's right arm, a tiny streak of smoke rising. Then the smoke disintegrated into nothing.

This guy... Nothing seemed to faze him.

He pressed down on my hand harder until I screamed from the force.

"I swear, I shouldn't have to do anything if you're the one trying to save *me*." Coral's voice reached me, and behind us mist churned just above the ground. She was a shadow stepping through her own protective circle. Sending a surging blast of power at the two of us, locked inside of the ward. "You really are useless," she continued.

She was enough of a distraction to get the shifter to ease up on the pressure. I pulled my hand back with a hiss and I used the other one to grab the stones. Sending the rest of my power into melding them together. The spell took precious seconds to complete but finally the two pieces had merged into a long slender blade. One I intended to use.

Except when I managed to stand, I saw Coral's protective spell fading. The shifter dived at her and I was a moment too late.

"*No!*"

He made contact, his large paw connecting with her skull. The hit sent her flying backward into me until we both crashed to the ground.

I saw stars. My head spun in circles and the rest of me was nothing but a mass of pain.

Coral wasn't moving.

"Come on, you need to run." I managed to cover her prone body with my own, using every bit of fortitude left in me to stab up at the shifter with the makeshift dagger. No matter where I tried to hit, the blade never found its mark. "Run, Coral!"

She didn't move for the longest time. When she finally stirred, staring at me with unfocused eyes, oddly the one thing that stood out to me was her hair. It had come loose of the fancy braids she'd kept in perfect place all day. Strands hung in her face, stained with a combination of sweat and mud from her fall.

"Get up and run for help!" I told her again.

She shook her head and a little bit of the fog cleared from her eyes. I clenched my teeth when she bolted around the other side of the fire. The shifter tried to run after her but I herded him closer to the heat, watching the flames lick at his fur.

He screamed. That was when I jumped him, hanging on with everything I had. Every ounce of anger I had at the situation, at the circumstances of my life, every bit of guilt at watching Bronwen lying in the hospital bed because I'd backed out on her, I dropped on him. I sank all of it into my hold on him and sent my magic straight down.

The air stank of burning fur and the shifter flailed against me trying to shake me loose.

"Does it hurt? I hope it does!"

Heat and pain were my world too. I squeezed my eyes

shut against it. Tears swelled and the flames burned at me. Still I clung.

Trying to give Coral time to get away.

She didn't make it far, I realized. She'd doubled back around and now magic in ribbons of blue swirled around her.

"Duck!" she called out to me.

I had a moment to register what she was doing before she let the spell explode out from her. I dropped to the ground, kneecaps slamming hard into the dirt, and felt the wind around me as the spell knocked the shifter off of his feet. He sailed past, slicing against me.

What happened next turned me inside out.

With his fur still smoldering, the shifter used the momentum of the spell to his advantage. He landed against the nearest tree and then catapulted himself forward, straight into Coral. She howled when he hit her, slamming her into the ground with the remnants of her spell redirected toward herself. Light exploded in the clearing and ripped through the three of us.

Pain crushed me, clamping around my skull until my thoughts fragmented. I finally managed to open my eyes. Then lost the rest of the air in my lungs.

The halfling stood over Coral, his chest heaving, dark crimson rivulets winding through his fur. Coral's eyes were open but glazed, her arms and legs at unnatural angles, and she was bleeding from multiple wounds.

For a moment, the world went still. It felt like someone had punched me right in the solar plexus. I stared at Coral, feeling my failure keenly.

She was dead.

29

The shifter's blood dripped down on her, smearing together with the blood from her own wounds, her magic leaking everywhere. I felt it in the air, like someone had burst a balloon and let the pure power fall down, evaporating into nothing.

He didn't give me much of a chance to feel guilty because he immediately turned to me and snarled, his lip curling up over those ferocious white teeth in a definite challenge. A challenge to deny his superiority.

"What have you done?" Screaming with rage, I launched myself at the shifter, my breath cut off when he easily dodged my attack and his claws ripped at my midsection, right above my fresh wound.

Sloppy. I couldn't afford to be sloppy. Not now.

Shaking my head and pushing the pain into a smaller and smaller corner of my mind, I threw a spell at him designed to trip him where he stood and take away his balance. Not surprisingly it had no effect against the rampaging halfling form. Nothing I'd attempted had had any real effect.

But that didn't stop me.

"*You will not take me down,*" I managed to get out.

My arm holding the dagger hung limp at my side and I raised it now, slashing at whatever part of him I could reach. Although the dagger seemed to glance off of him, I kept trying, kept pushing to gain whatever ground I could.

He twisted and dodged my blows, trying to find an opening but I slashed on furiously. It was draining me physically and I couldn't help but worry that I wouldn't be able to keep it up long enough to finish the fight.

Desperation broke inside of me. I clawed at the well of strength I'd recently tapped into. Pulling every drop I could reach to me just to keep myself upright. Still the shifter kept coming.

The dagger was no help. I wasn't strong enough. *I can't beat this guy.*

He wasn't going to go down; he was too strong. How had I managed to fight him off the last time? Although I'd gotten the upper hand the last time we fought, I hadn't been able to take him down permanently. I knew I would have a hard time beating him even in wolf form.

Do you want to be fair? Or do you want to win?

Because the difference might be life or death.

Uncle Will's words echoed in my head. Did I want to be fair? Did I want to do the best I could and still maintain my integrity? Or did I want to make this guy pay for hurting innocent women?

He crouched in the middle of the forest, his dense fur flickering, flaring with his anger. Feral, animal. No trace of anything human remained.

I was staring at a nightmare. A dangerous, violent nightmare with long limbs and a supremely muscled body. Capable of killing me and everyone else around.

The half-shifter crashed into me the moment I called a protection spell. Magic boomed and reverberated outward but it was too little too late. Before I had time to gather myself for a second spell, he hit again, and the impact of his body sent me flying. I should be used to it by now. The last thing I saw before I smashed into the ground was the white blaze of his eyes.

Shock filled me as he rammed me again, roaring, his expression ferocious.

Something snapped to the forefront of my conscious-ness. He might be a half-shifter, but so was I, and I hadn't survived this many games and tests and trials for no reason.

I didn't know how to get to my own halfling form. But I'd grown up wolf. I'd grown up training to fight like a wolf and to use my shifter senses. I knew *how* to be a wolf. I centered my power on my core and grew the kernel there, merging with and releasing the female alpha inside of me.

Show me what to do, I begged her. *Show me how to beat him.*

And I had a faint awareness of her satisfaction as black fur burst from my skin.

The shifter leaped at me again, this time accompanied with a guttural growl. I snarled and dodged to the left as my body completed the transformation. Sliced at him with my claws as I went. He bounced off of the nearest tree and twisted his body, lunging forward again. His claws gripped my shoulders and I sagged under the pressure when he began to squeeze.

Those moves...

It was like he somehow anticipated my next move or how I would react.

I needed more power. I needed to be better, stronger.

I pushed through the barriers I'd put in place, one in the mortal realm to hide my Fae half, and one for Faerie to hide my wolf shifter half. Along with deception barriers for protection, there were physical restraints with any form. I didn't want them anymore, any of them. I wanted to match this guy move for move, muscle for muscle. What did I need to do to improve?

His rear leg knocked into my midsection and sent me down again. Crashing back into a boulder, pain exploding through my spine and ribs. I coughed, muscles seizing. I finally managed to get up when the shifter brought his elbow down a split second later on the same spot where I'd landed.

I rolled into a crouch just in time to avoid the next bone-crushing blow and tried to swipe his legs out from under him. He jumped, striking down twice. Lashing at me with those impossibly long claws.

Nothing I seemed to do damaged him enough to matter.

I need more. My tongue lolled out as I lost my breath. Panting. Why could I not summon the halfling form? And why did it always seem like I never had enough power?

Blood dripped from a multitude of wounds and poured from his mouth, but he kept coming. His pounding steps toward me seemed to shake the earth and his next kick took me below the ribs, driving me back. I hadn't had the strength to even attempt to dodge. A few more of those and I'd be done for...

Enough!

Except I didn't say the word out loud. It reverberated in my head and a magical torrent burst forth from me, tearing at him with a million claws of fierce magic. He stumbled once and shook himself, like a dog shaking off water. The last of my desperation surged even as I questioned everything about my life, about my heritage, about my innate power and magic and why it wasn't enough. I had just one last chance, and if there was ever a moment...

I took the magic I'd been sending at the shifter—and

turned it on myself instead. Everything I'd planned to hit him with in wolf form, I now channeled inward.

And felt my body growing. Shifting. Larger, leaner. My fur grew longer and the bones along my spine protruded.

I writhed under the force, one I was not used to. The halfling took another step forward and my in-between form clawed at the air in front of his face.

He stopped just short, as if shocked at the sight of my claws growing longer, my muscles thickening.

More magic, I told myself, even when the logical part of me howled to stop before I self-destructed. But I didn't want to stop. I *couldn't* stop. Not when the power building up in me felt as if, for once, I might get the upper hand in this situation.

The down side? There just might not be any Tavi left when I was done.

A small price to pay if it meant taking this monster down at last. I let my inner nature take over completely. For Coral, for Bronwen, for all the women he'd hurt.

When I looked down, I no longer saw the usual wolf paws of my normal shifter form. I saw a nightmarish conglomeration of fairy and wolf together. Because it had finally dawned on me that I wasn't a garden-variety halfling, half human and half wolf. Rather I was half wolf and half Fae. With innate powers of both. It just took an extraordinary event to make me aware at last that I was not tapping, in fact had never tapped, my full potential of each at the same time.

A lifetime of hiding my *true* nature no longer mattered. Even if I risked being exposed for what I really was— assuming I survived this encounter—I no longer had a choice.

I spotted the elemental dagger Coral had created from the mineral shards we'd collected in this Trial. Snarling, keeping eye contact with my opponent, I circled around until I could reach down to grab the dagger. It looked like a twig now compared to the size of my paw.

I attacked again and again. Ramming into him with my now-powerful body, slashing with claws and fangs, stabbing with the dagger anywhere I could reach. I grabbed the fur near his left ear and slammed him down into the ground with all my might, forcing his muzzle into the dirt, hoping to stun him long enough so I could get a few more slashes in with the dagger.

My fangs tore into the tendons at the back of his neck and I tasted his blood. The shifter let out a scream. Crimson pooled around him as I stepped back, panting, waiting to see what he would do next. He remained on the ground, barely moving, in obvious pain.

I should finish him now, I thought. Sinking the dagger into his chest should do the trick.

I wasn't entirely surprised to see the fur on his arms begin to shrink, to withdraw back into his skin. His snout went next, shifting back into human form. Black fur turned to white hair.

My stomach dropped and roiled in a way that had nothing to do with the blood and gore. Fresh adrenaline shot through me, and I barely acknowledged it as my own body returned to normal form. I was in shock at the sight I was seeing before me.

"*No*." The word sounded more like a moan to my ears. *No, it can't be.*

Within seconds the half-shifter had returned to human, incapacitated in his agony. I knew this person. I knew him well.

Onyx.

His hands moved to his head, testing the back of his neck where I'd so viciously bitten him. Blood continued to gush from the wound and it looked even worse now. And suddenly a rush of regret filled me as I hoped I hadn't dealt him a fatal blow.

"T...Tavi?"

Oddly, I didn't hesitate. I knelt beside him, my friend.

A killer. A *murderer*.

"I'm here, Onyx." My voice shook and the rest of me wasn't far from complete breakdown.

Onyx tried to move but his body didn't want to cooperate. He stared at his hands and the blood staining them. A horrible sound erupted from his mouth. "What's happening? Where am I?"

How could he not know? I didn't know what to tell him, or what kind of an answer he expected.

"Shh, don't try to talk," I said gently. I took his hands and found them trembling. "Everything is going to be fine."

His eyes met mine, wide and terrified, his pupils pure black. "I don't understand. Where am I? I can't remember. Oh God! This is the fifth or sixth time this has happened to me. Am I going crazy? I'm going crazy, aren't I?"

And I wanted to cry.

His words clamped around me and made it hard to breathe, hard to do anything around the press of panic crushing my chest.

"Please, Tavi. Tell me what's happening. Why can't I move my head? My neck..."

I shuddered, pressing closer to him, listening to his hoarse groans as he tried to breathe through the pain.

"I'm really sorry," I whispered. Calling my magic, I focused it on Onyx. I closed my eyes and said, "I need to bind you. Something—or someone—is controlling you with magic." I knew it in my gut. "I need to make sure you won't put up a fight for this next part."

Onyx said nothing as the spell reached out, encompassing his body, his arms and legs and spine, and at the same time keeping his own magic contained. The same kind of spell the king had used on me, like his version of house arrest. If Onyx tried any kind of spell, I would know, and it would return to him times three.

When Onyx looked up at me, I didn't see the beast who'd murdered all those Fae. I saw my friend, looking at me with terror in his dark eyes, covered in blood.

"It hurts," he moaned.

"I know. I'm sorry." There was nothing I could do about the pain, at least not here. "We'll get you fixed. I promise."

I pressed my hand to his cheek once before sending out the call. I couldn't do this, not alone; I needed reinforcements. Selene would be here in a matter of moments, if I'd sent the spell correctly.

Now to check on Coral.

When I stood and approached her, I feared she was dead. Coral was a twisted mess of limbs. Her wounds were severe enough to kill, blood pooled beneath her, and her skin had taken on a sheen I wasn't sure was sweat or something magical.

I searched for a pulse, swallowing over a lump in my throat as I tested first her wrist then her throat. I sagged with relief. Oh thank God. Weak, but there.

"Hang on," I begged her, pressing my hands to the worst of her wounds and calling on the strongest healing magic I knew.

How could she be alive? She was mangled beyond repair. She might not have much longer. Using the last of my strength before collapsing, begging Coral to stay with me, I sent out another call for help.

Praying it would arrive in time.

30

———

They cancelled the rest of the Trials. It was the first time in over five hundred years where the final two rounds would not be completed due to extenuating circumstances.

Headmaster Cyrus wanted to honor the memory of the student who'd died at Onyx's hands, as well as the other unfortunate female victims. Coral was on the mend, since help had arrived in the nick of time. Selene, with the rest of the cavalry and Bronwen in tow, had quickly taken charge of everything, including securing my hostage.

My hostage, they'd called him. Like I'd somehow done something wonderful in crippling my friend and mentor. I felt terrible about it.

Onyx was not a bad guy, unlike his father. He wasn't the kind of man or wolf to hurt innocent people for no reason. There had to be another explanation for why he'd attacked those women. He'd said he was having black-outs, couldn't remember. Hadn't the same thing happened to me?

Except he wasn't taking the brain boost powder, as far as I knew.

Which meant someone else was controlling him.

Who?

I gritted my teeth, enduring the capture process and the questioning that followed, trying my best not to look at Selene though she stood close to me. To keep up the deception, she wasn't there as a leader of the Claw & Fang. She was there as a reporter, and on her heels came the very familiar faces of the Faerie Bureau of Investigation, including Rooker, to take Onyx into custody.

He was still in custody, with Coral in critical condition but stable at the healing center. I'd somehow managed to slip away before anyone forced me to go to the center. Selene found me, under the guise of wanting an interview, and calmly escorted me out of the area.

I walked on numb legs with Selene at my side keeping me upright. Everything hurt. "Just a few more steps and then we'll be there." Urgency filled her voice.

"Fine." At least, I thought I spoke. I still wasn't sure. My eyes were closed and when I opened them a crack, I glimpsed the bright bronze knob of the tree door.

I hadn't been able to fly on my own either. Selene had to force me to change form into a mouse and she carried me in her talons toward the half-shifter hospital.

There were broken ribs to mend, a dislocated shoulder and some torn muscles in my hip and left thigh. Onyx had really done some damage. But I was alive. He was alive.

"Try not to move. The healers are going to do what they can but you might have a scar on your side from Onyx's attack."

My eyes snapped open at the name and I instantly wanted to defend him. He hadn't meant to hurt me, or kill those women. I didn't know what had happened to him, but part of me almost wished he hadn't made it through our final fight, because the consequences he faced now might be worse than death.

I worried about him. Whatever had happened to make him kill hadn't been his fault, I was sure of it.

I sat up on the cot and the dark bloody stain on the sheet beneath me had my vision blurring.

"Tavi!" Selene hissed. "Don't move. How come you never listen?"

Sighing, I allowed her to press me back into the mattress, waiting for the healers to arrive. Why didn't I listen? Because I obviously had a severe death wish. Now it extended to those around me.

Of all the magic I had, all the power of my messed-up bloodline, all of it was useless when it came to keeping the people I cared about safe. Sure, Coral was alive, barely. But what had happened to Onyx to push him to such extremes?

Did his father have anything to do with whoever or whatever was controlling him in halfling form? I felt like things were slipping farther and farther out of my control with each passing second, and I wondered if I'd ever know the whole story.

I spent the night with the healers hovering over me to speed the process. Knitting me back together until Selene came to escort me home when the sun rose, her hand on my shoulder.

"I want to let you know," she began with her voice soft, "to be prepared."

I sighed and leaned heavily against her. I hadn't gotten any sleep. "Prepared for what?"

"We all must brace ourselves for the fallout. It will soon go public that Onyx Grimaldi is a half-shifter." Selene paused. "There is no way around it. There is no way to spin his bloodline after what he's done."

"It wasn't his fault. It was mine."

"No," she was quick to say, clenching her hand on my

270

shoulder. Pain exploded from the area but I didn't cry out. "You did what you had to do. You stopped a murderer."

"He's not a *murderer*," I insisted. "He's a good man. He's nothing but kind. Someone did this to him."

"He might be all those things, but he is also guilty. There is blood on his hands and no way for us to keep the authorities from doing their jobs." The door to the healing center closed behind us and melted seamlessly back into tree bark. "Not once this case became high profile. With the bureau involved, it will soon be public knowledge. Speaking of which, you have a meeting tomorrow with Rooker to discuss the events of the last Trial."

I didn't have the energy to be upset about the meeting. I'd known it was coming once I sent out the call for help. Even so, the world broke into a thousand tiny pieces. "Fine. It's not like he and I haven't had our one on one time before," I said. "It will be like talking to an old friend."

"You're lucky."

"How so?" My eyes grew hot.

"Well, your little girlfriend is awake, for one."

That got my neurons firing again. "Coral?"

Selene was nodding as we walked. And luckily not trying to push me away when I clung to her. "Yes."

"How is she? Is she—" I broke off. Oh God, what if she was jabbering on about seeing two wolves fighting?

"She's awake and talking. Not about you and your little, you know, *secret*, but apparently she remembers everything about the attack. At least you should not become some kind of halfling scapegoat." Her gaze cast down on me. "Well, not this time."

"I'll take what I can get."

Selene stopped, forcing me to slow with her. "She's defending your honor, Tavi."

I almost scoffed, but I was still too exhausted so it only

271

came out as a sort of grimace. "That would be a first for her."

"I need you to be up and running so you can hold your head high and protect yourself. Keep the people from panicking. You're off the hook as the culprit, and hopefully this will take the focus off of you for the murder of Madam Muerte too."

I cocked my head to the side. "You think?"

"If we can spin it properly, yes. I'll do what I can to get the story out in a way I can control but the other news stations and reporters may not be as eager to pick it up the way we want. We'll have to wait and see what happens."

"I'm not going anywhere. I'll do what I have to do."

"I know it's too much for me to ask you to stay out of trouble."

"Trouble?" I let out a short barking laugh. "You don't think I try?"

"You try, yes. Try *harder*. Any more of this and we're going to be digging a hole in the ground for you."

I thought about her words later, sitting on the edge of my bed with each new breath a fresh agony. Dawn came and went hours ago but I knew there would be no sleep for me. Not today. Part of me wondered if Onyx hadn't attacked, would Coral and I still be trying to fight our way through the tournament in the third Trial?

I wasn't sure I wanted to know.

A knock sounded at my door. "Come on in," I called out.

A familiar blond head peeked inside. The fire inside of me burst into life at the sight of him. I should have known he'd come.

"Are you decent?" Mike asked.

I was too exhausted even to attempt humor so I just nodded.

He closed the door behind him before fixing me with a

serious look. Then he dropped my backpack to the floor and stood in front of me. "You're home."

"I am," I said with a small smile.

"What happened to you?"

"My mentor found a private healer for me. My wounds were...extensive," I told him, parroting the statement Selene had given to me. Short, believable. Private healers for hire were legal in Faerie, allowed to work outside the confines of the healing center for more extensive needs. Specialized needs, like mine. "I needed more than the healing center could provide."

Mike nodded. Did he accept the explanation?

"You should have let me know where you were. I was worried about you. I heard the half-shifter attacked you trying to get to Coral. What were the two of you even doing together out there?"

I wanted to throw myself at him for a big hug and a good long cry—the cry because I knew I would never be able to tell him the truth. And that sucked.

"We randomly crossed paths out there during the Trial. Then the beast had us cornered. I'm sorry I didn't let you know we were okay. Did you have to hear about it from the news?"

Mike nodded again. "I didn't know what was going on. I went to visit Coral at the healing center. She didn't know where you were, either."

"I'm sorry," I repeated. "I hate that I made you worry. It took all of my magic to get through the attack and call for help once I had him down."

"You're going to have to tell me the story sometime."

I could tell there was more he wanted to say. "Of course. You know I will. Maybe after I get a little sleep."

"At least you won't have to go through the rest of the

273

Trials." Mike fidgeted but he didn't come any closer. "I know you really wanted to sit them out altogether."

"Look where it got me." I offered him a grim smile.

"I brought this." He indicated the backpack on the floor. The bag was covered in blood. Probably a mixture of mine and Onyx's and Coral's. A melting pot of blood. "After the Trial ended, I went to look for you. I found your bag instead."

"Thank you."

Mike reached into his pocket and pulled something out. Keeping eye contact, he laid it gently on the nightstand beside me. "I found this, too."

My skin turned to ice. It was my wolf amulet.

The red-hot shaft of fear tearing through me made the rest of my wounds seem like nothing. I went hot and cold at the same time, clenching the bed covering beneath me. "Where did you get that?"

Mike leveled a serious gaze on me. "This is your necklace, isn't it?" he said softly. "I recognize the chain. I've seen you wearing it a few times and didn't think anything of it until I found it with the rest of your things last night."

Did I bother denying what he already apparently knew? Was it worth a try?

Before I could say anything, he said, "And I know it's the symbol of the Claw & Fang, a secret society made up of shifters that isn't supposed to exist but does."

I couldn't breathe.

Mike knew.

"Is there something you want to tell me, Tavi?" he went on. "About why you have this? What...what you are?"

But I didn't have the answers he clearly wanted. I shivered, the cold seeping through my skin all the way down to the bone. I thought I'd known fear before? Nothing compared to seeing the betrayal on Mike's face. The betrayal, and worse—the sheer fear of what answer I'd give him.

"*What are you?*" he repeated.

I swallowed and felt sick. My secret was out.

THE END

ABOUT THE AUTHOR

BREA VIRAGH is a USA Today bestselling romance author based in the Blue Ridge Mountains. She is a proud Gryffindor, a graduate of Brakebills, and a member of Fairy Tail. When she isn't writing and daydreaming about her newest project, her hobbies include binge-watching HGTV, scouring thrift shops for goodies, and maintaining her alpha status among her puppy and three cats.

Read More from BREA VIRAGH
www.breaviragh.com

Printed in Great Britain
by Amazon

38798900R00159